ARTICLES OF FAITH

ARTICLES OF FAITH

ROBERT L. RODIN

ST. MARTIN'S PRESS

NEW YORK

A THOMAS DUNNE BOOK.

An imprint of St. Martin's Press.

ARTICLES OF FAITH. Copyright © 1998 by Robert L. Rodin. All rights reserved. Printed in the United States of America. No part of this book may be used or reproduced in any manner whatsoever without written permission except in the case of brief quotations embodied in critical articles or reviews. For information, address St. Martin's Press, 175 Fifth Avenue, New York, N.Y. 10010.

Design by Ellen R. Sasahara

Library of Congress Cataloging-in-Publication Data

Rodin, Robert L.
    Articles of faith   / by Robert L. Rodin.
        p.   cm.
    "A Thomas Dunne book."
    ISBN 0-312-18532-4
    I. Title.
    PS3568.034855A89   1998
    813'.54—dc21   98-5521
                              CIP

First Edition: July 1998

10 9 8 7 6 5 4 3 2 1

To Walter G. Rodin: Father, grandfather, son.
May this small token help you finally find peace, wherever you are.
All is forgiven, nothing forgotten. We miss you.
Love is stronger than time.

ACKNOWLEDGMENTS

WITHOUT THE LOVE and support of my incredible wife and children, this book could never have been written. They always (well, almost always) gave me the space and time I needed—nights, weekends, and days off. If I wasn't writing, I was reading. If I wasn't reading, I was thinking or stewing. Whatever sacrifices I may have made penning this story pale in comparison to theirs. And they did it all with a quiet generosity I still find amazing.

I also wish to thank my many friends, some of whom knew my father well. They accepted my caveat of "honesty without cruelty" when reading and commenting on the manuscript, and all of them added something to the process. I won't mention their names—they know who they are. Thanks, guys.

And a special thanks to my editor at St. Martin's, Melissa Jacobs. I was told that "real" editors were a thing of the past. They aren't. Melissa is the proof. She took a breathless leap of faith by signing an unknown, unagented, and unpublished author with an unfinished manuscript because of her uncanny vision. Through it all she was my advocate, critic, and friend—even when I got crazed and cranky. What writer could ask for more?

ARTICLES OF FAITH

1

THE PHONE RANG once, then stopped. I had my coat on, was halfway out the door. If I pushed, I could still make the 6:02 and be home in time for dessert with the kids. I was about to hit the light switch when it started ringing again. I paused. Probably my crazy client Safter with another cockamamy idea for his bathroom, or his closet, or, worse still, his wife's closet. But it was Friday and the week had been full of Safter and his suggestions, demands, and rantings. Enough was enough; I killed the lights. The phone kept ringing.

On the other hand, it could be my wife. Or one of the kids. I trotted back to my desk in the darkened office and pulled the receiver quickly from the hook.

"Hello."

The mad symphony of midtown Manhattan at rush hour filled the earpiece. There were horns, squeaks, squeals, and shouts but no one spoke. I said hello again, angry this time, Safter be damned. I was about to slam the phone into the cradle when the caller finally spoke.

"Danny?"

Blood drained from my head. I became dizzy. I reached for the edge of the desk to keep from falling.

"Are you there, Danny Boy?" the voice asked again. "It's me."

I knew who it was. I hadn't heard the voice for almost thirty years, but it was as unforgettable as the man to whom it belonged—the man who'd disappeared from my life during my senior year of high school, a lifetime ago.

The room stopped spinning as I started to breathe again. "Dad?"

"None other." His voice was cheerful, as if vanishing for over a quarter century and suddenly reappearing were normal father-son relations.

"There's a McCann's on the south side of Thirty-third, just west of Seventh," he said clearly. "I'll be waiting."

The line went dead.

WE WERE SITTING in a dim corner of the crowded, smoke-filled saloon at a table for two. Like Billy the Kid, he had his back to the wall and was eyeing everyone in the bar. Flipping open a worn Zippo, he fired up a short cigar with the same magnificent hands I remembered. When I was a kid, he used to amaze me by popping the tops off the little green Coke bottles with his thumbs. This was in the late 1950s; way before twist-off caps, so the feat wasn't a trick, it was a demonstration of silent, concentrated, unimaginable force. They were also the hands I remembered stroking my fevered brow as softly as a thousand butterflies' wings, or firmly and precisely chiseling away at a chunk of marble or dense hardwood in the north light of his studio, white dust or wood shavings covering his eyebrows and shoulders.

When I'd first entered, before my eyes had adjusted to the perpetually gloomy McCann's, a place as dark and dank as a catacomb, a firm grip took my elbow and started to guide me toward the back. I hesitated. The grip became tighter, propelling me forward. Turning my head just a fraction, I saw his profile even with mine and my heart skittered. It was him.

We sat looking each other over. I'd fantasized and dreamed about this encounter a thousand times. After the police investigation, after everyone had given up and presumed him dead, I went on hoping he wasn't. His car had been found parked on a spit of beach in Bridgehampton on a dreary November evening. The gas tank was empty, the door open, the dome light still on. There was no note, no blood, no trace. Divers searched, but his body was never recovered. The investigation revealed no debts, no girl-friends, no compelling reason for my father to vanish. But vanish he did, without a trace.

In the first weeks and months after, my mother would walk trancelike through the house, eyes red and swollen, chin trembling. As gripping as her grief, I could not bring myself to accept that he'd committed suicide by wading into the icy water, the only logical conclusion.

As the years went by, my conviction that he was still out there somewhere would ebb and flow but never disappear. I alternated between fantasies of finding him and killing him for the crime of deserting me when I needed him most, when I was not quite a man, to misty slow-motion technicolor dreams where we would embrace, all forgotten. Being reunited in the back of a smoky dive that stank of beer, greasy corned beef, and stale cigarette smoke had never occurred to me. I was off balance; the room seemed to be tilting. I was lightheaded and nervous. My hands fidgeted on the pocked and dirty tabletop.

"At least you don't bite your nails anymore," he said with a trace of satisfaction.

"I stopped when you left us. It was one of the many deals I made with God to bring you back."

He laughed that easy laugh of his, the one that always used to make me smile. I almost did now, but what I really felt like doing was reaching across the table and strangling him.

"I don't expect you to forgive me, son. It would be too much to ask."

"No shit, Dad." I regretted it immediately.

His eyelids dropped a millimeter. He was disappointed.

"You hate me." It was a statement, not a question.

"I don't know! What the hell. Hate doesn't do it justice." My voice was loud, quivering.

He looked around the room nervously, scanning the faces, seeing if anyone was paying attention to us.

"Keep it down," he said evenly. "We haven't got much time."

"Time!" I was spinning out of control. "Time! It's been twenty-nine fucking years, and we don't have much time?"

His hand moved swiftly across the table and covered mine. Like a python, his grip slowly tightened until I thought my bones would crack. I remembered this too, the times when I wouldn't listen and one of his big-veined hands would find a shoulder or elbow, squeezing until he had my full attention. He'd never struck me, perhaps knowing that his hands were the keys to his soul, the strongest but gentlest part of him. He probably understood that were he ever to hurt me with those hands, I would forever shrink from his touch, something he could not bear to contemplate.

"Just listen, Danny," he said, his gray eyes boring into mine. "This isn't how I wanted it either, but we don't have a choice. It's unfinished business. You're going to have to trust me."

"Trust you!" I'd followed his command and my voice was low, almost a hiss, but I was still rocked to the core. "Why should I?"

"Because you have to. Or Nick and Marie won't have a daddy . . . or a mommy."

I sat back in the chair, pushed as if hit in the solar plexus. When I could inhale again, I looked over at my father. He was deadly serious. I shuddered involuntarily. Of all the things my father was— or might have been—he was never sarcastic, never prone to tasteless jokes or cruel pranks.

"You know about Tuesday and the kids?"

"Everything. About all of you," he said. It was the first time since he'd called that he sounded like the seventy-five-year-old man he was.

"I've never been far away for long," he went on.

"Then you know—"

His shoulders sagged.

"Yes. I was at the funeral, in the gravedigger's truck up on the hill."

"You never saw her again? Like this?"

He nodded once, slowly, and his eyes seemed to mist over. I had never seen him cry or even near tears; it wasn't possible. It was unsettling.

"A few times . . ."

Blood again rushed to my head. "So if you saw her, how come you didn't . . . ?"

"I couldn't, Danny. Couldn't . . ."

I pounded the table with both fists. The ashtray did a perfect flip. "Why the fuck not! Tell me, you son of a bitch! Why her and not me!"

The noises in the bar stopped one by one until it was dead quiet and still.

My father kept his eyes on mine, level, deadly.

After a minute or so, voices could be heard. Then a glass clinking. A loud laugh. Soon McCann's was back to normal.

My father's voice was just above the level of the noise. "Don't pull a stunt like that again. Understand?"

I didn't understand but shut up and glared at him.

My mother died in 1984. After he'd disappeared, she tried to be both mother and father, working, keeping what was left of our family together, mending the cuts and bruises to my adolescent soul, trumpeting my successes. But she'd never been the same since that day, and neither was I. Always prone to deep funks, after my father's disappearance her mood swings became wider and deeper. If she wasn't depressed, she would be remote. I had always felt guilty, thinking I was somehow to blame—not only for my father's disappearance but for her ennui as well. Sitting across from my father, I was beginning to see it was worse than I could have imagined, much worse.

After I had grown and flown the nest to start a life of my own, my mother seemed sadder still. I always thought she'd come to the top of that spiritual hill where she could look forward and back with equal clarity. The past, as rich as it had been, had obviously been dark and crowded with pain. And the road ahead, without him—or me—must have looked desolate, without solace or comfort. And now I knew she also carried a burden of silence heavier than any mortal should bear, the one thing I always wanted to know—where my father was. She fell asleep one night and never woke up. It was written up as congestive heart failure, but I knew her heart was broken badly and simply never healed. She never got to see her grandchildren.

"You think maybe I'm crazy, right? That this is all a very bad dream," he said, his voice a little rough.

"I didn't . . ."

"You don't have to. I can see it in your eyes. You've got her eyes."

He was right, of course. I *did* think he was crazy. And every moment it was getting crazier and crazier. And he was right about the eyes as well; mine were the exact shape, size, and color of my mother's. They crinkled in the same places as hers had when I laughed, sagged identically when I was sad, as hers had so often. Looking across at my father, I saw the rest of me there, the parts that had come from him: the impish Gaelic twist at the corners of my mouth, elfin ears, sandy red hair; the explosive Irish temper. And though softened slightly by genes from my mother, my hands, just a bit smaller, were his as well.

"Danny . . . my Danny." His voice was tender, soothing. "If it was just me it would be okay. I'm almost seventy-six. I've done all I can, given up everything—you included—to protect you. But it's past that now."

He didn't sound crazy, though he might be, after all. Even with the shock of having over half my life condense into these few minutes, I saw the familiar solidity he'd always had, the unconditional love, the feeling—no, knowledge—that he'd always be there, stand by me, right or wrong. The feeling that had kept my faith alive. The faith that he was still out there somewhere, even when the rest of the world had forgotten him. He'd abandoned me, but right now, at this moment, it didn't really matter. He was here, in front of me, flesh and bone, not some dream or apparition.

He started to wrap the scarf around his neck and zip up his dark gray parka, and I felt the same old fear take hold of my soul. He was leaving me, again.

"I'm going to leave now," he said firmly.

"No. Wait. I'll come with you. We can do . . ."

He was standing now, keeping me in my seat with the force of his stare, pulling a pair of very thin black gloves on his oversized hands. He knit his fingers, pushing and smoothing the latex-thin leather. With the gloves, his hands became dangerous, almost sinister.

"No, Danny. I want you to listen carefully, as carefully as you can. Everything depends on it. I'm not leaving you. Not this time. Never again. But you have to follow my instructions. Completely."

He must have seen my panic growing.

"Concentrate. I'll contact you as soon as I can. Don't do anything different—I mean nothing at all. Don't tell Tuesday. Just go to work, shovel the driveway, do everything normally. Can you do that?"

I felt as if I were ten again and that without him I'd be lost.

He leaned closer. His eyes were hard but suddenly older, wearier.

"I wouldn't have come to you if I could have handled it myself," he said. "But I can't. Not anymore. I'm sorry it has to be this way. But there's no one for either of us to trust except each other. Understand?"

I shook my head.

"Good. Either one ring then two, or two raps then one. Meet twenty minutes before, and one block south, two east of what I tell you. Remember?"

I nodded once in understanding. It was our old code. When I was a boy, my father had schooled me in the use of mysterious, obscure procedures. If we were planning to meet, instead of telling me to wait for him on the corner at four in the afternoon, he'd instruct me to walk slowly on the east side of some side street at ten minutes to. His car would silently sidle up to me, and he'd open the door for me to get in quickly. Locations and times were given but had to be encoded with offsets only he or I knew. If he said "Meet me on the southwest corner of Forty-eighth Street and Fifth at three thirty," it really meant I should be waiting on Forty-seventh Street and Park at ten after three. I knew it was his knock if it were two quick raps, silence, then a long tap. I'd know it was him calling if the phone rang once, stopped, then started again. I'd always thought it was an exciting, private game, something he shared with me only, to let me know I was special. Suddenly it became clear that maybe I'd been missing something all along.

I fell into the easy rhythm of our old adventures and responded in our abbreviated codes of instruction, recognition, action.

"Yes. Twenty minutes before, one block south, two east."

He winked in confirmation.

"Give me forty minutes' head start," he said, taking a step backward, eyes hooded and wary. "And remember, not a word. To anyone."

Then he was gone.

2

I RODE THE Long Island Rail Road to Port Washington in a daze. As instructed, I'd waited in McCann's forty minutes, arriving at Penn Station as the doors to the 7:52 opened. Christmas was ten days away and most of the passengers were lugging briefcases and shopping bags full of wrapping paper and gifts. A huge blast of arctic air from Canada had swung down last night, and everyone was wrapped in thick layers of down and wool. The car was overheated. The result was that it felt as if the air had been sucked out of the train, and suffocation was probable. I shouldered my way to a window seat.

I was as detached from the rest of the exhausted, weary commuters as a ghost. Stations passed, people exited and entered, the woman next to me dozed fitfully, her head resting on my shoulder. I was oblivious, invisible, not there.

The multicolored Christmas lights on the row houses of Queens flashed by the window as the express bounced eastward. The sparkling decorations slowly disappeared to be replaced with longer stretches of darkness as we neared the Nassau County line. And once on the old trestle bridge crossing the muddy flats at Little Neck, all light from the outside vanished, turning the window into a darkened mirror, bringing my reflection into focus. I looked carefully at the face, amazed.

While shaving this morning, by coincidence or the hand of fate, I did something I almost never did: I took a long look at my reflection. Turning my face this way and that, what I saw was an unremarkable man solidly into middle age. I had the kind of lines and creases some said gave me character. My hair was still its original reddish brown, but the corners of my forehead now reached to almost above my ears. And the eyes, my mother's soulful eyes, seemed dimmer and more knowing, lacking the joy or surprise of youth.

As the wheels clacked rhythmically on the rails, the face reflected in the train's window was as different from the face this morning as a scream is to a sigh. It wasn't that it looked younger, but there was a manic animation to its features. I now wore the kind of expression of people you saw muttering to themselves on the streets of Manhattan, desperately in need of medication, a priest, or a bathroom.

Thankfully, the mirror became transparent from overhead lights as the train pulled into Port Washington, erasing the disturbing image. The station was the train's last stop, and looking up for the first time since I'd boarded, I saw there were now fewer than a dozen people with me.

The doors slid open. I tightened my scarf and stepped onto the platform, merging with the others as they made their way toward the small depot in the winter night.

My house was a little more than a mile from the station, and I refused to drive or even take a bicycle in the summer. I'd arrogantly announced that when the day came that I could no longer walk the fifteen or twenty minutes from door to train, in any weather, I would simply quit and retire. It was an empty boast and everyone knew it; after all, I was a small-time contractor with two kids and no money. I'd have to work as long as someone was willing to pay me, or I dropped dead, whichever came first.

I walked past waiting cars parked in the forecourt of the train station on Main Street. Engines were idling, voluminous clouds of exhaust floating skyward in the still winter air. Inside each was a solitary wife or husband, staring out or reading the paper under the dome light. Windows were rolled up tight, heaters and radios on. The ritual never changed; come summer the windows would still be rolled up, air conditioners working overtime.

Once on Main Street I was alone. Walking to and from the station was a peculiarity few indulged in. In the paranoid mores and culture of suburbia, walking was somehow suspect, an affront to the automobile.

I walked at a steady pace, passing stores decorated for Christmas that were now closed, feeling the strange elation I always did. The street was lined with small two-story buildings that still thrived with family owned shops, restaurants, and small businesses. Walking Main Street in Port Washington, I could almost imagine I was in Vermont or a small lazy coastal town in Carolina. The fact that superstores, discount shops, and huge malls completely surrounded the struggling town in a death grip could, if only for a moment, be forgotten.

But the shock of my father's appearance loosed a flood of memories that turned the usually comforting tableau into a waking dream. Flashes of strolling this same street hand in hand with him as a child, looking at the Christmas displays, came jagged and unbidden.

Beneath the marquee of the movie theater, which my mother had laughingly dubbed "The Itch" due to persistent rumors of flea infestation, I had a vivid image of the day we'd gone to see *Spartacus* with Kirk Douglas. I was a seven-year-old boy with a crew cut sitting in the darkened theater, watching gladiators with swords and tridents, hearing the thundering hoofbeats of chariots fill the air. And there, mixed in with the smell of buttered popcorn, was the aroma of my father's Bay Rum and my mother's Chanel. Time had not faded the feeling of security and inexpressible joy of that day, secure in the womb of my family, the home I thought would last forever. The feeling of loss became so strong I found myself stopped dead in front of the theater, throat tight.

I shuddered again, as I had in McCann's, like a dog coming in out of the rain, and started off again. But the memory of the day at the movies, something I hadn't thought consciously of since that day, did not fade until I was past the public library, walking down the long curving hill past the tackle shop and delicatessen. The town dock came into view. I was close to splitting apart and now only a few hundred yards from my front door. I realized that if I were to act normally, I'd have to pull myself together, and in a hurry.

I worked for myself and made or unmade my schedule as I wished, having no set time when I left or returned home. Still, I was usually back before seven in the evening, in time for dessert, or at least to help clear the table and wash the dishes. It was now almost eight-thirty, and contrary to usual practice, I had not called in.

Opposite Louie's Restaurant I turned left onto Jefferson Street and began the climb up the steeply sloped, narrow dead-end road. The house sat on a level plateau at the top of the hill, backing up on a narrow wood. It was a small shingled two-story colonial with champagne-yellow clapboards, titanium-white trim, and jet-black shutters.

Light was spilling from each and every window, and I was over-come with a desire to run through the door and shout the news, open some champagne, let the kids know they did have a grandfa-ther. My father's wary face in McCann's, warning me to hold my si-lence, flashed before me and the thought burst like a cartoon soap bubble.

I mounted the steps to the covered porch, stomping my feet on the worn mat, and took out my key. I steadied myself, turned the latch, and opened the door.

Marie, my seven-year-old daughter, streaked past with a shriek, followed closely by my twelve-year-old son, Nick. He was wearing the devilish grin that meant he was terrorizing his younger sister.

Judging from her giggle as she went around the corner, they were both enjoying every minute of it. He went past in a blur, tossing a "Hi, Dad!" over his shoulder.

The foyer was as hot and humid as a greenhouse. Tuesday's hatred of the cold was both genetic and environmental, and meant that the thermostat was pushed to the stop.

Before we'd met I would sleep with the bedroom window wide open, summer and winter. I loved the chill crisp air and enjoyed nothing more than lying in bed on a winter night beneath a pile of blankets. But no matter how I tried to help her love the winter and its beauty, her loathing for it never diminished. In the end, her suffering of winter was deeper than my love of it. As a result, I was coated with a constant sheen of perspiration all winter long. Even now, just in the front door, before I had time to rip off my coat, I'd started to sweat.

Whenever the humidity was this high, for it was enough to choke an orchid, it meant one of Tuesday's big pots of stew or curry had been bubbling forever, filling the house with exotically scented steam. Her mother had taught her that food needed to cook "until it was well and truly done." Because I've discovered that the Vietnamese have no real sense of time as we know it, "well and truly done" could mean anything from fifty minutes to several hours, depending on the cook's mood, the cut of beef, or the phase of the moon.

Nick and Marie screamed around the corner again. This time Marie stopped long enough to give me a breathless hug and kiss. Nick waited three steps back. When the kiss was over, Marie smoothed her pajama top, looked over at her brother with a happy grin, wailed, and took off. Nick smiled and shot after her.

The house was almost eighty years old and was the kind of small that allowed two small children to circle the entire ground floor before a man could take off his overcoat. It was the kind of small that enabled the nervous real estate agent who showed it to us to call it a "starter," as if it were the salad course for dinner.

There was a tiny living room, with equally minuscule kitchen and dinette along with a half bath on the ground floor. The second floor had three closet-size bedrooms and one bath at the head of the stairs. The basement held the boiler, water heater, a washer and drier, four battered suitcases, and a few cardboard boxes. There was little room for anything else.

It was also small enough to be cleaned top to bottom in one day, except Nicky's room—which hadn't been really cleaned in three years. The yard was shaded by a maple out front and a willow and handsome old oak in the back, and bordered by a wood on the east. The small lawn could be trimmed with my old push mower in under twenty minutes, and I let the leaves collect in the fall, raking only once in spring to let the crocuses bloom. Not only that, but the monthly upkeep—insurance, utilities, and all—was less than what some of my trendier neighbors paid for the lease on their foreign cars. I had rebuilt half the place and hoped to do the rest before I died. The end result was that the house was my safe haven and refuge.

The low overhead meant that Tuesday and I, parents and sub-urbanites, still acted a bit like Tinker Bell and Peter Pan; to wit, we never seemed to have grown up. For the past dozen years, our combined annual income had only once exceeded sixty thousand dollars, and that was a fluke resulting from a down-and-dirty show-room I built in the garment district—for cash. Usually we grossed a little below fifty. My small one-man show brought in about forty, Tuesday's dance teaching another seven to ten. By the standards of the community we were odd, eccentric, and poor. It was the truth but if I wasn't happy most of the time, at least I knew moments of rapture and joy with Tuesday and the kids. I had no illusions about the rest of it.

Tuesday came to the door of the kitchen. Her long, straight, jet-black hair was tied in a tight knot at the top of her head, a few er-rant strands gracefully framing her face. I was sure that she was the only woman in Port Washington that night not dressed in sheep-skin slippers and a sweater. Her legs poked from a pair of cut-off shorts, and her oversize New York Rangers T-shirt was tied, exposing her trim midriff. My heart beat just a little faster.

I smiled.

In return I received the look Nick often got when he came home after dark.

"I was worried." Her voice, thin and high, had steel in it, and the half-moon scar on her cheek flashed a little redder than usual.

"Safter called as I was about to leave," I lied. "Seems the missus needs more shelves for her shoes."

She laughed. "Maybe you should stop working for people with too much money."

I took her into my arms. I was fully a head taller, but we fit together like pieces of a puzzle. We kissed and held each other. The top of her head smelled musky.

"But they're lost," I explained. "They need me."

We were almost toppled as four sinewy arms locked around our legs.

Marie, still holding tight, started jumping up and down. "Daddy! Daddy! Daddy!"

"Marie! Marie! Marie!—Nicky! Nicky! Nicky!" I called back, dropping my arms to embrace them.

"I got an A on my spelling test!" Marie announced proudly as she disengaged.

"And I," Nick chimed in, mocking his sister, "received a D in fractions."

"So," I said gently, "the family average is about a C plus . . . Not bad."

Tuesday shot me one of those looks. Her opinion was that because her children were small, one-quarter Irish, one-quarter Jewish, and half Vietnamese, they had better study hard and do well in school, because not belonging anywhere in particular, they were targets of sideways glances from everywhere. They would have to make their way by wits and cunning, it was that simple.

I agreed but took a more laidback approach, often provoking

hot silences and sharp looks. I couldn't take any of that tonight. I tried to appease Tuesday without, I hoped, pressuring the kids.

"Maybe next week we can pull a solid B."

Tuesday's expression softened—a little. I was following orders. All was well. As small and delicate as she was, she ran the house, herding everyone around, myself included, like frisky puppies. I kind of liked it. I knew what was next: food.

"We're finished," she announced on cue, indicating she and the kids had eaten. "But there's still some stew for you."

"I'd love some."

To me, "Go wash." Then she turned to the children, who looked ready to start chasing each other again, and ordered, "Finish your homeworks."

"Homework," Nick corrected, allowing the wise guy in him out of the bag. "Not homeworks. It's singular, not plural."

Tuesday's eyes narrowed. Her back straightened. Her hands shot smartly to her hips. A vein pulsed in her neck. "So. If you're so smart, why did you get a D on fractions!"

I gave Nick a warning look, throwing all of my powers of telepathy into it. It was a red alert. "You're on thin ice here, buster," I screamed silently. "Can it."

Nick must have received the heads-up because he shrugged, turned away, and retreated for the stairs before the battle was joined. Marie followed two steps behind.

Tuesday's English was a sore point for her. She tried to reduce her accent and improve her grammar, but she could never completely eliminate the vestigial remnants of her singsong phrases and pidgin bar-girl grammar, and every once in a while it would come through. Most people thought her accent and occasional malaprops charming and cute, but Nick, who spoke with an accent somewhere between a Hell's Kitchen brogue and Locust Valley lockjaw, was becoming increasingly embarrassed by it. In the last year or so, he'd taken to correcting her. Tuesday usually accepted it with a sort of stoic masochism, but the hurt sometimes came through and she'd snap back. Nick, wise beyond his years, knew better but sometimes couldn't stop himself.

I followed Tuesday into the kitchen where the heat and humidity were, if possible, even higher. I washed at the kitchen sink, drying my hands on a damp dish cloth, then sat at the round wooden table in the alcove.

I could tell by the way the bowl hit the table that Tuesday was still smarting from Nicky's remark. But I'd learned to leave well enough alone. The few times I'd intervened I'd made a mess of it. She and Nick loved each other deeply. They'd work it out without me.

"So," I said, inhaling deeply from the steaming bowl of Vietnamese beef stew in front of me. "What's new?"

She was at the sink, back to me as she washed dishes. We had a dishwasher, but she didn't trust it, preferring to scrub things by hand in a sink full of steaming suds. From where I sat, she looked no older than sixteen, the age I think she was when I'd bought her.

"It was a hard day today," she said, not turning, arms working furiously. "The dress rehearsal was a mess. Two kids skipped. It's not going very well."

She was preparing a new dance she'd created with students from her class, scheduled to debut right after the New Year. She rented space in an aerobics studio just down the block from the larger, more established dance school and was still fighting to hold her own. The dance was going to be her first formal production, and she was putting everything she had into it.

"Don't worry. Your kids love you," I said through a mouthful of noodles and spicy beef. This was true. She made up for her lack of dance pedigree with firm discipline and unshakable faith in the kids. But she was still struggling in this her fifth year and was committed to making the production a success. I didn't even want to think about what would happen if it was a flop.

"Yes," she said, turning off the water and wiping her hands. "The children are great."

"It'll be fine. I know it."

She picked up a cup of tea and sat opposite me, smiling as she brushed a stray wisp of hair from her brow. "They're all working so hard."

A comfortable silence settled in. Neither of us were big talkers. We communicated in short, telegramlike phrases or expressive glances. I sometimes thought that because I'd bought her from the fat Chinaman, her love for me was a some kind of debt, maybe honor, maybe something else, one of those lifelong burdens Asians seemed to withstand with brooding stoicism. Once, when she was pregnant with Nick, and I'd had a little too much to drink, I'd asked her. Without pause and without a word, she slapped me hard enough to split my lip. I took this as a no and never asked the question again, though there were times I still wanted to. I often wondered just how well I knew her.

"A man came to the studio today," she said, looking down at her hands.

I looked up, waiting for more.

"He asked if I knew Sean Maguire."

I stopped chewing. Stopped breathing. My chopsticks, full of rice noodles and meat, stopped halfway to my mouth. Sean was my father's name. My heart pounded in my chest. She was still looking down at her hands, so fortunately she didn't notice my sudden paralysis.

"I told him my husband is Danny Maguire, Sean Maguire's son."

She looked up. "He asked if I'd seen your father."

She paused, looking at me, trying to read my expression. "I told him Sean has been dead for a very long time."

For Tuesday, death was a natural part of life. She had none of the fear or sense of mystery about it that most Occidentals do. Her parents and two younger brothers had been killed in front of her by a team of Viet Cong who suspected her father of being a South Vietnamese sympathizer. After the Viet Cong took turns with her, she was clubbed with a rifle butt and left for dead. She was thirteen. The beating had broken her leg near the hip. There were no doctors in her village, and the break healed badly, giving her a slight limp.

Like my love of winter, my reluctance to accept my father's death was one of those things about me that she accepted but didn't really understand and I was unable to fully explain.

I put down my chopsticks and wiped my mouth. "What else did he want to know?"

"Where you were."

"What did you say?"

"Working."

"And . . ."

"He left."

I sat back. This was happening too fast. My father's sudden appearance and grave warnings took on added weight. Whatever the hell was going on, it involved us all. They knew where I lived, where my wife worked, probably what classrooms the kids were in. "Danny?" Her voice was soft but firm.

My eyes snapped into focus and locked on hers. "What is it?"

He'd asked me to tell no one—ordered me to. But she was, if anything, twice as tough as me.

"He's alive," I said quietly, watching her reaction carefully. "He called me. We met in a bar just before I came home. It's why I was late."

She folded her hands on the table and nodded once. "So you were right. He never died."

It was a simple statement but confirmation that she didn't think I was crazy.

"What does it mean, Danny? Why are you so scared?"

"He told me we were in danger. All of us. You. The kids."

Her hand strayed briefly to the scar on her cheek, then ran through her hair. She looked up at me. Her eyes, naturally deep and black, became opaque. "Then the man at my studio is part of it?"

"Probably."

"What do we do?"

"I don't know. He told me to wait for his call. That we'd take care of things together. He said to tell no one."

"But you told me."

"Yes."

She nodded slowly, eyes locked on mine forming a silent question.

The fact that on the same day my father rushed out of the void of time with warnings of death another man had shown up on our doorstep asking about him wasn't very reassuring.

"My father told me he'd get in touch with me soon, let me know what to do. That until then I should act normally."

"But you're not sure?"

"No."

"The children," she said simply, looking to the ceiling.

My heart skipped.

"Right." The hell with my father and his coded instructions. We'd run.

"Get a bag together," I said, standing.

Tuesday was already on her feet when we heard the knock. At first I thought it was a branch rubbing on the back of the house, but then the pattern became clear. Two soft, quick raps, silence, then a single tap. It was coming from the kitchen door.

Without pausing, Tuesday picked up a cleaver from the kitchen counter. I held up my hand, motioning her to be quiet and still.

"It's him," I whispered.

"Who?" She was whispering too.

"My father."

"How do you know?"

"It's our old code."

I walked to the door, Tuesday behind me with the cleaver. The rear porch light was off, so I couldn't see anything through the small glass panes. No longer certain, I reached behind me and took the cleaver from Tuesday and cracked opened the door.

"It's me." My father's voice.

I stood back. He slid through the door silently, closing it softly behind him. He and Tuesday locked eyes, recognition passing at the speed of light.

"I am Danny's father," he said with a tight smile.

"Yes. I see."

"Are the children home?" Again, to her, not me.

She nodded.

"Dress them. We have to leave."

They looked at each other for a moment longer, then Tuesday turned and left the kitchen.

"Get on your coat and gloves and come out back with me," he said.

"What the hell's going on?"

"Seems they're a little faster than I thought they'd be."

"Who?"

"Later."

"Now!"

"Later!"

It was then that I noticed the slick stain on his gloves. I reached out and touched one. It felt like an electric shock. The slick was blood, still wet and red.

3

ICK AND MARIE sat in the back of the van with my father. Marie rested her head on his shoulder, her worn blankie clutched tightly to her cheek. Nicky was more suspicious and was keeping his distance. Because of the strong resemblance, the kids, just as their mother had done in the kitchen, immediately recognized the man in their house as my father, their grandfather. His magical appearance and the sudden unannounced road trip had the same effect on them as it had had in McCann's with me, a combination of awe and confusion.

Tuesday was looking straight ahead as we sped eastward. Because it seemed we had no control over what was going on or where we were headed, there was little to say. I hadn't told her about the body; there wasn't time.

While Tuesday filled two moldy suitcases from the basement and helped the children, my father had taken me behind the small shed in the rear corner of our property. The body was in a pile of leaves and small branches I'd never finished raking and bagging. He was leaning against the whitewashed shed in a sitting position, eyes open. He was about my age, with plain, almost bland features. There was a raw red hole on his cheekbone, just below his left eye. Most of the back of his head was gone.

I watched as my father quickly and expertly searched the body. Steam rose from the back of the man's head. In the light from the rear porch of the house I cataloged what he found: a worn leather wallet, key ring, ball-point pen, book of matches, cellular phone, beeper. After opening the man's jacket, he took a long automatic from a shoulder holster. On the man's ankle, above a pair of hiking boots, was a snub-nose revolver in a nylon holster. I noticed the grip of the gun was wrapped in duct tape. My father rolled him over and searched his back, finding a flat black dagger tucked into his waistband. Everything, including the man's watch, disappeared into my father's parka pockets. Finished, he stood.

"Get some garbage bags. Big ones," my father directed as he kicked at the pile of leaves, dispersing and covering the dark-brown stain of blood below the body.

I was paralyzed.

"Come on, Danny. He may have backup, though I doubt it. I think he was just the scout. I took the train right before yours, then hung around at the station in Port Washington. I saw you come off and this guy follow about a block behind. He snuck around back when you went into the house."

I shuddered. I hadn't sensed a thing. I caught my father's eye.

"Couldn't take a chance," he said.

I went to the shed and got two black plastic lawn bags. Keeping our gloves on, we put both bags over the man's head, one at a time. The body was still warm and supple. The bags reached to his waist, open and flapping slightly in the breeze. I went back to the shed and got some twine. Without thinking, I passed the twine under the body, looping it twice, then made a cinch and pulled it tight.

"Get the van. I'll be back in a minute," my father said, heading to the house.

My hands were shaking and the engine sounded very loud. I thought any minute one of my neighbors would come out to investigate the terrible roar. Leaving the headlights off, I backed up to the shed. As I stopped, the brake lights turned the scene a ghoulish red. I threw the van into park and took my foot off the brake, then went around to the back. I was lifting the tailgate just when my father appeared at my side.

Without a word, we lifted the body. It was heavy, loose, hard to control. I stumbled and lost my grip on his feet. The legs slapped the ground. My father, his hands under the man's armpits, the plastic bags rustling, waited patiently as I bent down. I gripped tighter this time, and we rolled the man into the van, folding him slightly at the waist. I was about to close the door when one leg flopped out. My father moved past me, shoved the leg at the knee, then quickly slammed the gate.

"Let's go," he said, guiding me gently by the elbow.

When we were settled he took out a cigar, lit it, and inhaled deeply.

"I told Tuesday we had to run out for a bit." He blew out a plume of smoke. "Head to Sands Point, past the Institute."

I put the van in gear and rolled slowly down the hill, out onto Main Street, past Louie's and the town dock, then made a left toward Manorhaven. The route was so familiar I could have done it with my eyes closed, which was just as well given the way my hands were shaking. My blood pressure must have been in the stratosphere because a high-pitched whine echoed through my head. We passed a few cars, and each time we did, I was certain it would be a cop with X-ray vision. I couldn't stop thinking about the body in the back.

Just past the narrow spit of beach near Sands Point, my father asked me to pull into a driveway on the opposite side of the road.

"Let's make this quick," he said, turning off the dome light before opening his door. "If someone comes along, let me do the talking. I'd like to do this differently, but there's no time for anything fancy."

We opened the back of the van and hefted the body, trotted across the narrow road into a tall stand of cattails, and dumped it there.

"They might never find him," my father said as we ran back to the van. We hopped in and were back on the road heading home. The whole thing had taken less than a minute. We didn't pass another car until we'd driven over two miles. I'd stopped sweating, but my heart was still racing.

"Luck of the Irish," my father said through the hiss in my head as he turned on the dome light and started to look through the man's possessions.

Whoever the man had been, my father had killed him, there was no doubt about that. Now I was an accessory—after the fact, true, not that it would help me in front of a judge and jury. But I'd killed before and gotten away with it, so maybe there was still hope, or just the lousy rotten luck of the Irish.

I WENT TO college because my mother was afraid I'd get drafted and end up in Vietnam. Which is exactly what I did after I flunked out. It was 1970, I was young and strong, and 1A all the way. So in spite of my mother's pleas, I enlisted in the army before I got drafted.

Summers working with my father had trained me to be a fairly decent carpenter, so after basic I managed to get picked up by the Corps of Engineers and spent four months training at Fort Belvoir, Virginia. Another four months at the NCO academy there and I was on my way to Vietnam as a Spec 5, Sergeant.

The first few weeks in country spooked me. We'd build forward fire bases, camps, and crap like that during the day, and that was fine. But it was the long nights cradling my M-16 that gave me the willies, particularly when someone freaked and we lit the sky with phosphorous and started to scream and empty our clips into the infinite void of the jungle. After two months I was getting buggy, wondering how I'd finish my tour without going completely round the bend.

And then a miracle happened. One day my "Old Man" the CO asks if I know anything about plastering. For a minute I thought he was making one of his bad jokes before I realized he was serious. One thing I did know was that if plastering was involved, it sure as hell wasn't in the jungle. So I did the only logical thing; I lied through my teeth, told him I was a master plasterer and my last job before entering the U.S. Army was the restoration of the Waldorf Astoria's plaster ceilings.

Fortunately for me my CO was from Alabama. And while everyone in the world (including him) had heard of the Waldorf, he didn't know whether it had plaster ceilings or not. Of course I had no idea either, but I felt opportunity knocking real hard and I wanted to open the door.

He told me to get my gear; I was going to Saigon on a TDY— Temporary Duty to work on the consulate office. A Washington bigwig was coming for a visit and they wanted the place tiptop. As he turned his back I looked skyward and told the man upstairs I owed him.

Two days later I was in Saigon with a bucket of wet white plaster and a trowel. The chief in charge of the construction knew immediately that I didn't know my ass from third base. But he was an older Irish guy, liked my last name and took pity on me. He gave me three days to get my shit together or go back to the fire base. With the speed and agility granted only the doomed, I worked forty-eight hours straight and plastered until my arms ached. On day three, the Chief watched me repair a section of wall and patted me on the back with a smile. The platoon sergeant made my TDY a permanent assignment—I'd made it! Big time.

I was now a REMF, or "Rear Echelon Mother Fucker," and happy as hell about it. I thought little of the thousands of pounds of explosive 20-millimeter phosphorous-tipped shells and napalm spilling from the bellies of planes and guns in the jungle.

Sure, I hoped my buddies were dry and alive, but I had bigger problems now; like whether the beer would be cold enough and the women cute enough at the strip joints, whorehouses, and clubs where I spent every off-duty hour.

Other men were up to their chins in mud and shit, but I plastered, stayed cool, got stoned, got laid, and thought Vietnam was a reasonable adventure. Until the night at the Red Dragon, a month before I was due to rotate home and be discharged.

The Red Dragon was hands down the best whorehouse in town, a real class act. An old two-story stucco building in the colonial style down near the river, the place was known for its ice-cold beer, live bands, and most important, young, clean girls.

The owner had a deal with a couple of *bac si* medics from the medical battalion. They'd give the girls their checkups and penicillin shots in return for some free poontang.

The cage dancers wore g-strings and bikini tops. The bar girls wore tube tops and hot pants and attached themselves like jungle leeches to the GIs as soon as they came in.

Beer was ordered by the bottle, joints by the stick, girls by their Americanized names. Upstairs were two floors of bedrooms. I was a twenty-one year old kid. To me, the place was Eden.

I was feeling flush that night. I had a giggling girl on each knee and was on my second Thai stick and third beer when I heard the scream. It had come from upstairs. No one but me seemed to hear it over the pounding bass. A lot went on in the Red Dragon, and I knew the smartest thing to do was to lay low and ignore it but the scream seemed to be directed at me.

Maybe I was just too stoned, but I got up, spilling a beer and one of the girls. I headed for the stairs past dozens of GIs and their girls, oblivious to everything but themselves.

I didn't meet anyone on the stairs or in the hall. The screams were coming from a room at the end of the dimly lit corridor. I knew it was nuts, but I pounded on the door like an MP. A high-pitched drunken voice with a thick Vietnamese accent told me to fuck off. My senses were returning and I was about to leave when I heard a loud slap and scream. I stepped back from the door and kicked it open.

A naked man loomed over a frail-looking girl backed into a corner. She wore a sequined g-string. Blood ran from a cut on her cheek, down her neck, and between her tiny breasts, which she tried to cover with her arm. In her other hand was a straight razor. Her face was tight. There was terror in her eyes but a dark heat too; she wouldn't go down without a fight.

A familiar uniform hung neatly on a chair. I noticed the white shirt and hat worn by the National Police of South Vietnam. That made the naked guy what we called a "White Mouse": the South Vietnamese National Police, SVNP. They were the most corrupt, venal bunch of parasites in the whole damned country. I never figured out why this group of bloodsuckers had such a damned important position in a country at war and never really gave a shit until now.

On the bed was another girl, naked, unfocused, staring eyes, her head at a crazy angle. Dead.

"Fuck you, GI," the Mouse slurred, keeping an eye on the girl with the razor.

Every instinct told me to leave. I was a happy plasterer, not some masked avenger. But the look on the girl's face stopped me cold. She was next. She knew it and so did I.

"Leave her alone," I'd said, asking myself who the hell I thought I was.

The man turned toward me. His eyes were crazy, calm crazy, nuts, around the bend. I noticed the K-Bar combat knife in his hand, the one he'd obviously cut the girl with.

"Leave her alone," I repeated, trapped in a loop.

A thin smile, more like a grimace, formed on his mouth. The naked man started at me, lowering into a crouch, knife swinging side to side.

I was a head taller and had at least forty pounds on him, but he had a knife and seemed to know how to use it. He was definitely going to cut me. Training and instinct kicked in. I snatched an old brass lamp from a dresser and waved it back and forth in front of me. I warned him off again.

He came faster, the knife slashing back and forth like a scythe, whistling through the air. I didn't stand a chance.

The girl behind him let out a growl and sprang. She slashed at him with the razor, causing him to straighten and turn toward her. As he turned, blood sprang from a line across his back, from shoulder to waist.

His back to me, I took one step forward and brought the lamp down with both hands in a sweeping arc, catching him just behind the ear. My whole body was behind the blow. It made a dull thud. He simply folded and fell forward, landing on his face. His right leg spasmed and jerked, then stopped.

I looked over at the girl. She still held the razor.

She stared at me for a moment longer, dropped the razor, and walked to the sink, suddenly unworried that her bare, small breasts were exposed. She washed the blood from her face and chest, holding a towel to her still-bleeding cheek. She put on a bikini top and pair of silk hot pants. It was then that she started trembling and wrapped her arms tightly around herself.

I looked at the body on the floor. A pool of blood lay beneath his face. It had come from his ear. I knelt down, felt his neck for a pulse. There was none.

"Just come with me," I told her. "Don't say anything. Understand?"

She nodded quickly. I didn't know what I was doing, but I was doing it anyway.

We left the room, closing the door behind us, and made our way back to the bar without passing a single soul. She stayed at my side like a dog at heel.

I led her to the obese Chinese man who ran the Red Dragon. He sat in a red velvet settee against the window facing the river, smoking a cigarette. I pushed the girl roughly, indicating I thought she was worthless but mine.

"I want this one."

"Twenty dollah, two hour."

"No," I said. "I want to buy her."

The man's eyes teared and his belly bounced as he laughed.

"Not for sale," he finally managed to say, wheezing and coughing.

"Five hundred dollars," I offered.

"She make that one week here."

"Not anymore," I said, pulling the towel from her face, letting him see the gash.

I looked more closely at the girl, and understood that he'd accepted her barely perceptible limp because she was beautiful in the kind of way that drove us GIs nuts: Oriental and French. Small but sultry. Most of the girls at the clubs were pretty, but I realized this one was a little more exotic than most, a special hybrid. The limp would be one thing; the scar, something else.

For a second I thought I'd made a mistake and he would have one of his goons take me out back and teach me a lesson for spoiling his merchandise. I could see him thinking it over, smiling a bit. I smiled back. I was on very thin ice. We both knew that with just a nod from him, I'd be gutted like a fish and thrown in the river. But if a GI got wasted, the U.S. Army's Military Police would come down on him like a ton of bricks. The SVNP were trouble, but at least they could be paid off. The MPs were a whole different ball game.

His eyes narrowed. "Five thousand dollah."

It was my turn to laugh.

"One five," I countered.

"Three thousand five hundred."

"Two."

This was crazy. I had three thousand dollars to my name and I was about to buy a whore for almost all of it. I looked at the girl. She was staring straight ahead with the same expression she'd faced the knife-wielding man with upstairs, but I saw her chest rise and fall in short rapid jumps.

If I left without her, the Chinaman would find out about the dead man and girl upstairs soon enough, put two and two together, and the limping girl would simply vanish.

"Done. I'll be back soon," I said, meaning it, knowing I'd have to hurry things up before someone stumbled on the bodies upstairs. "And don't let anyone touch her," I added, putting some menace in my voice, knowing the fat man would, if he could, turn her out a couple of more times before I returned, probably in the alley for the cook or a waiter.

"Anyone else touches her and the deal's off," I repeated.

He laughed, probably thinking the Americans were twice as crazy as the French, but the message got through. She was soiled goods. Selling her to me was a bonus, a comic dividend.

"Get your things and be ready," I said to the girl. She bowed slightly and limped away.

An hour later I was the proud owner of a Vietnamese prostitute. Everything she owned fit into a small cardboard box, which she carried under her arm. She had changed into a simple shirt and dress, washed off her mascara and makeup. She looked something like a schoolgirl after a rough day.

That night we found and rented a small, filthy apartment on the third floor of a rundown building a mile or so from the base perimeter. I did my best to clean and dress the cut on her cheek, knowing it should be stitched, but I dared not risk a trip to the base clinic. There was always one of the Vietnamese doctors' offices on the street, but chances were the cure would be worse than the cut. So I cleaned it with soap and water, then taped it as tightly and neatly as I could.

Before I left, she asked my name, and bowed when I said it. When I asked for hers, it was something full of consonants, impossible to pronounce.

"Today is Tuesday," I told her. "I'll call you Tuesday."

"Like Tuesday Weld."

"Right, like Tuesday Weld."

She smiled. "Okay."

"Wait here for me," I told her simply. "Don't go out, don't let anyone in but me."

She understood. The Chinaman would make up a story about the dead cop and girl, pay off the SVNP cops investigating the case, and leave us alone. If he told anyone about us it would just complicate things. The way I saw it, we just had to wait it out.

And all I had to do was figure out what the hell came next. Admitting I'd killed a man even under the given circumstances would, at the least, earn me a dishonorable discharge, at most a manslaughter conviction and ten years in Leavenworth. I was young and stupid, but not that young or that stupid. No one had seen Tuesday or me in the room, hall, or stairs, and the son of a bitch I'd brained didn't deserve my penance.

I came by the next day with food and clothes. The first thing she did was offer to "fuck me." I refused. Puzzled, she offered me a blow job. I turned that down too, telling her to eat the food I'd brought. After a moment's indecision, she attacked the food as if she hadn't eaten in a week, occasionally stealing a glance at me. I changed the dressing on her cheek before I left.

When I visited the third day, the small room was sparkling clean, and she was freshly showered and dressed in a simple cotton shift. She'd changed the bandage herself, and when I gently lifted it off, the cut was ragged, but uninfected and healing.

She took my shoes, smiled, and asked me to sit.

"Thank you," she said simply.

"You are welcome," I said, smiling back.

"You good man."

"Crazy is more like it."

"Good crazy man."

"Where are you from?" I asked.

"Small village. Far away."

"Can you go home?" I asked.

She shook her head slightly from side to side.

I looked at the ceiling.

"What the hell am I going to do?" I said aloud. I was a serious short-timer, due to rotate home. I told her this.

"Take me with you," she said quietly.

"What!"

"Take me America."

I shook my head back and forth.

Her smile faded. She wasn't asking for a trip to Disneyland, she

was asking for her life. There was no heaving of shoulders or running of her nose, but a single stream of tears ran down her cheek,
flowed behind the bandage and never emerged.

I didn't know if I could do anything at all, but I said, "All right,
I'll try."

I found out that like everything else in Vietnam, it could be
done—for a price. I started with the basics. I found a Catholic
priest too drunk to take confession but able to marry us the next
day. Any reservations he had disappeared when I showed him the
hundred-dollar bill and bottle of Rémy Martin. The next thing I
knew, I was married to a prostitute whose name I couldn't pronounce.

I went to the Old Man, my CO, with the Vietnamese marriage
certificate and lied to him that my new bride was pregnant. I cabled
my mother and asked her to forward five thousand dollars ASAP,
without telling why.

The consular officer in the American embassy took my three
thousand dollars in the plain white envelope, then processed Tuesday's visa application.

By the date of my rotation, I had a wife with papers and two
plane tickets from Honolulu to New York. The bandage was gone,
but the scar was livid and bright, even beneath the makeup she used
to hide it. I had to fly on the army chartered PanAm; she paid half
fare on the next scheduled flight.

After I was processed out and given leave, I found her in the airport, standing in a corner. She looked like she'd cried the whole
flight. She almost fell into my arms.

We checked into a cheap hotel in Waikiki, showered, and went
walking on the beach. She took my hand, and I felt the rhythm of
her body, accentuated by the limp.

After a few minutes, she pulled me to a stop, kissing me gently
on each cheek. She whispered in my ear. "Thank you, Danny."

The setting sun highlighted her cheekbones, made her deep,
dark eyes luminescent. She was beautiful. I never thought much

about the girls from the Red Dragon; we laughed, we screwed, I left. Now one was mine.

"When we get to New York," I told her, "you can be free. We'll get you a green card, then we can divorce, and you can make a life."

She looked at me with steady eyes. "I like you, Danny. No want divorce."

"But you don't know me. You—"

Her slender fingers touched my lips softly, making me stop.

"We see. We see," she said.

That night she came to me. I resisted, not wanting to take any more from her than had already been taken. I wanted her to know she wasn't mine, even if I had bought her.

"I not whore anymore, Danny. I want you. Not like bar girl, no fuckee-fuckee. As woman. As girl."

And she did. Bar girls giggled and hopped and moved like pneumatic machines, moaning and grunting. Tuesday didn't. We made love the way two people who want each other do. With the kind of forceful tenderness that puts it all on the line. And when it was over, she didn't rush to feed me another beer or Thai stick but lay quietly in my arms as I stroked her hair.

I LOOKED IN the rearview mirror. Nick and Marie were sound asleep. Marie's shoulder rested on my father's lap, Nick leaned heavily against his shoulder.

"Where to?" I asked quietly.

"Exit at Riverhead, then take twenty-five all the way to Southold."

"Where are we going?"

"I've got a small place there. Rented it about a month ago, after he missed me. We should be safe there for a while."

Something in me snapped. He was my father, he'd returned, just as I'd always dreamed, but the dream was a nightmare. I pounded the steering wheel.

"What the fuck is going on!" I said in an angry hiss. "Who

missed you! You show up and turn my life upside down. The guy at the beach . . ." My voice kept rising. I stopped myself just in time and skipped over the dead man. "My wife and kids are in it, whatever it is, and I want to know, and I want to know now!"

"You'll wake the children," Tuesday said simply.

"I don't give a shit!" I looked back at my father again. I wanted to pummel him. "If you don't start talking, I'm going to pull into the nearest police station, then try to save what little is left of my life. So let's have it!"

His features softened.

Some, but not all of my anger left me then. We were father and son, but I was no longer his little boy. I had my own family to protect.

He looked out of the window for a while before he started.

"Remember the dagger I once showed you, the one in the attic?" he asked.

I nodded. One Sunday when I was about fourteen, I'd found him in the attic wrapping something in oil-stained canvas. I'd surprised him. He hurried to finish but I'd already seen part of it and wanted to see the rest. He seemed torn, but finally unwrapped the canvas, revealing a shiny dagger about eight inches long. The blade was copper, but the hilt was decorated in gold, bearing a faded inscription I couldn't make out.

"I told you not to tell anyone about it, that it was our secret."

"And I never did. When we cleaned out the attic after Mom died, it was gone."

"I took it with me, when I . . . left," he said simply.

"So what does an old dagger have to do with now, tonight?"

"Everything. It's what this is all about."

I wanted answers, not elliptical non sequiturs. I was close to the edge again.

"Tell me," I demanded.

"It's a long story."

I shook my head. He'd have to do better.

"I took the dagger from a basement in Manhattan in August of 1943. I killed three people to get it. It was the night this whole thing started."

Unconsciously I jerked the steering wheel a little to the right. A horn erupted. I swung back into my lane.

"I thought you were in Greenland during the war—building a clinic?"

"Oh, I was. And I did. But I was in Maine, Nova Scotia, Boston, New York, Portsmouth, Norfolk. Hell, I saw all the Atlantic coast this side of the lake."

"What's the dagger have to do with any of that?"

"Everything. It may have belonged to one of the Hebrew Zealots. But not just any Zealot," he said. "A zealot named Judas Iscariot, Jesus' betrayer. If it's genuine, and I have no reason to believe it's not, it is almost two thousand years old, and obviously priceless."

"But . . ."

He held up a hand. "Turn right here. Go to the end, at the T, then make a left."

I was having a hard time following directions and digesting what he'd said at the same time.

"No! Left, not right!"

4

ＡFTER A FEW more wrong turns, my father finally directed us to a small Cape with a cracked concrete driveway. The little house seemed to sigh in the wash of the headlights. A single bare bulb spilled pale-yellow light over a faded front door.

I shut off the engine. The hum in my ears from the long ride east slowly gave way to a deep and heavy stillness. I felt a kinship with the sad, lost-looking house, its drooping shutters and black interior.

"I'll open her up, kick on the heat," my father said, slipping open the side door of the van. He closed the door quickly, but not fast enough to stop the heated air within from being sucked out and replaced with a damp chill. Nick and Marie stirred but didn't wake.

Tuesday and I watched silently as lights began to pop on in the house. Beyond faded lace curtains covering the bay window flanking the front door, dark-paneled walls decorated with small framed prints came into view.

With the lights on, the little house looked even more forlorn. I slumped forward, resting my chin on the steering wheel. Puffs of condensation formed on the windshield in time with my breathing. I wanted to say something comforting to Tuesday but nothing came to mind.

The side door of the van slid open again with a long screech.

"Let's get the kids inside," my father said, scooping Marie into his arms firmly but gently. His tone was cheerful, as it used to be when we returned late from a family outing.

Without looking my way, Tuesday opened her door, went to the back, and woke up Nick. Still groggy, he held Tuesday's hand as they followed my father into the house.

I stayed where I was. Images of McCann's smoky interior and my father's face got mixed up with the sounds and smells from hauling the dead man's body into the reeds. I tried to remember the dead man's face but couldn't. I must have been there a long time, drifting, because my feet were numb with cold, and ice crystals covered the inside of the windshield. I got out of the van.

The front door of the house creaked when I closed it. A malignant orange-and-black shag carpet ran from the front door all the way through the living room to a tiny dining alcove. Blue, flickering light came from round, bare fluorescent fixtures at the exact center of the ceiling in each room.

An oversize sofa and matching armchairs upholstered in gaudy gold, and a small metal and Formica coffee table were the only furniture in the room except for an old console TV with rabbit ears, sitting against the wall opposite the couch like a Buddhist shrine. The dining table and chairs were metal and plastic, beaten and frail.

The other room on the ground floor was an eight-by-ten kitchen with chipped metal cabinets, the same round fluorescent light, and an ancient, groaning refrigerator. My father's back was to me as he set a dented old kettle to boil on a huge stove that was easily as old as me.

"Tuesday's tucking in the kids," he said without turning. "I thought some tea would do the trick."

I didn't answer. He turned a dial on the stove, then stopped to withdraw a slim cigar from his breast pocket and light it. A cloud of dense, pungent smoke surrounded his head.

"Let's go to the living room," he announced once he'd taken a deep drag.

He reclined on the couch, threw his arms behind his head, and locked the cigar between his teeth. I backed into the armchair, descending through sagging springs and crumbled stuffing. By the time I came to rest, my rear end was below my knees, scraping the shag.

My father blew a large, thick smoke ring. It drifted smoothly toward the ceiling and the flickering fluorescent.

"Rented the place last month," he said. "Told them I was a writer, needed someplace with no distractions."

"*Amityville Horror* 6?" I asked, an edge to my voice. "*The Shining*— Part Two?"

"I'll admit it's not very cozy," he said, ignoring my sarcasm. "But it's out of the way. No neighbors within sight. Four months rent up front. No one's gonna bother us until this thing is over."

"So what's going on, Dad? Why are we sitting in a shitty little house when we should be drinking eggnog in front of a fire celebrating our father-and-son reunion?"

He blew another smoke ring and looked up at the ceiling. The kettle in the kitchen started to sing.

"It's a collision of past and present, a cosmic train wreck." He looked over at me. "Mostly it's about old deadly secrets coming out. It's complicated . . ."

He jumped off the couch to answer the kettle's screaming whistle. He moved with an athletic agility and grace and didn't seem at all like a seventy-five-year old man. The kettle continued to howl as he stopped and looked down at me.

I held his gaze. I wanted answers I could understand. The kind he sometimes used to give me as a kid. So far everything he said was as vague and insubstantial as the smoke rings drifting up to the ceiling and breaking apart. I wanted to know why he was turning my life upside down.

"So far it's all smoke and mirrors," I said. "Can't you do better?"

He seemed to sag a bit. "It's complicated."

"I'm used to complicated," I said a little sarcastically. "Try me."

He paused a beat, was about to say something more, when the kettle reached a fevered pitch and started to sound like a freight train. He held up a finger, asking me to hold on, then slipped into the kitchen.

A stair tread creaked. Tuesday rounded the hall corner, and walked past me. She moved as smoothly and silently as a cat, her limp barely noticeable. Sitting on the edge of the couch, she reached for the clip holding her hair, released it and shook her head, cascades of black shiny hair spilling like lake water at midnight. She gathered all the long strands, pushed them behind her, and finally looked at me.

Her eyes were lustrous, deep, black, impenetrable. Hard.

"The kids?" I asked.

"Asleep."

I wanted to tell her about the body in the reeds, find a way to let her know. Sounds of cabinet doors opening and closing and cups clattering came from the small kitchen.

We'd locked eyes and I was putting the words together in my head when my father came through the door smiling, placing a chipped metal tray on the coffee table. On it were three mismatched mugs full of steaming brown liquid, a jelly jar of milk, and a few packets of sugar.

"Earl Grey it's not," he said, putting some milk and two packets of sugar in one of the mugs. "But it'll serve."

He stirred his cup, then sat back on the sofa sipping noisily.

"There's a name for this, you know," I said to him as he enjoyed his tea. He didn't look up.

"It's called passive aggression," I continued.

He sat back and smiled at Tuesday.

"Like making people wait for no reason, or smiling instead of answering when someone asks you a question, or doing nothing when someone wants a reaction."

He put down his cup. It hit the table hard. A small pool of

spilled tea formed a moat around his mug. "You want me to pound my fists on the table? See me hurting?"

His voice was strong and clear, but there were a few hairline cracks around the edges.

"Well, son, you can forget it!" he said, voice rising. "I've done it, all of it—a hundred, no, make that a thousand times. All it did was hurt more."

Tuesday, the scar on her cheek a dull brown in the sickly blue light, took it all in. I saw her nod her head in agreement, just a millimeter, but a nod just the same. My father leaned back, exhaled loudly, and ran his hand through his hair.

His hand trembled about as much as Tuesday's head had nodded, almost invisible, but there nonetheless. Maybe it was just age, but I read it as a ripple of a deeper fear and loneliness.

Now that I'd gotten what I wanted, managed to force him to show me his age and anger, I wanted the other man, the pretender with the shallow, cheerful smile, glib answer, mug of hot tea.

"Sorry," I said.

"Forget it," he said, looking past me.

An uncomfortable silence grew, broken only when Tuesday filled the growing void by getting up and pouring tea for herself and me. A gust of wind rocked the little house, making it groan.

His hand, steady now, veins raised and pulsing like Michelangelo's David, went to his shirt pocket. He pulled out a tin of cigars, shook out the last few of the short, thin stogies, then carefully withdrew a folded wad of newsprint.

"Read these," he said, handing the clippings to me.

When I unfolded them, there were two articles, both from *The New York Times*. The first was dated October 18 of this year.

ARONSTEIN RECOMMENDS PROBE

WASHINGTON, October 18 (AP)—Senator Richard Aronstein, Democratic senator from New York, has recommended the appointment of a special investigative committee to look into activities of the United States' intelligence community during and shortly after the Second World War.

Aronstein says that he has recently uncovered information suggesting that agents of the Office of Strategic Services, the intelligence agency which became the CIA after the war, may have aided some Nazis in "buying their way out" of Europe in the final months of the war.

"The world already knows about our dubious role in the snatching of German rocket scientists like Werner von Braun, and Abwehr spies from the nooses of the gallows at Nuremburg," Aronstein stated. "But the people I'm talking about were the behind-the-scenes facilitators of Hitler's 'Final Solution'—war criminals."

Aronstein noted that many records have been lost or destroyed, while others are still classified 50 years after the war. "If necessary," Aronstein said, "I will subpoena both current and past members of the intelligence community to testify."

Aronstein is the chairman of the U.S. Holocaust Committee investigating the trail of Nazi plunder through neutral countries. The Senator will submit his preliminary findings to the full Senate after the Thanksgiving recess.

I handed the first article to Tuesday and started to read the second. It was dated November 4:

SENATOR ARONSTEIN FOUND DEAD

NEW YORK, November 4 (AP)—Senator Richard Aronstein, three-term Democratic senator from New York, was found dead in his Sutton Place apartment. Although details are being withheld at the request of the senator's family, the 66-year-old senator was a diabetic who recently had started dialysis treatments.

Funeral services will be held . . .

I stopped reading and looked over at my father as I passed the second article to Tuesday. His face was hidden behind a gray curtain of smoke from yet another little cigar.

"What does that," I said, pointing to the clippings Tuesday held, "have to do with us?"

He exhaled a jet of smoke, a horizontal mushroom cloud billowing over the rickety coffee table.

"Aronstein was killed."

I stole a glance at Tuesday. "The article says he died of natural causes."

My father laughed. "Of course. It's the kind of quality job I'd expect from a man of his experience."

"Whose experience?"

"The man who wants me dead too."

I felt a screaming headache coming on. Even my eyeballs hurt. I stood up and massaged my temples.

"Why would anyone want to kill you?" I asked, wondering if there was aspirin anywhere in the little shack. "And who would want to murder a U.S. Senator? Not to mention have the balls and resources to do it?"

"How about Francis Xavier Laughlin?" my father asked, his smile returning.

I looked hard to make sure it wasn't some kind of a joke, a little attempt at humor on a bleak winter's evening in a sad little house. My father became Groucho Marx, raised and lowered his eyebrows twice.

I sat down hard on the armchair with the sagging springs so hard my tail bone hit the carpet sending a bolt of pain to my already pulsing scalp.

Francis X. Laughlin was the handsome, rich, seventy-something former director of the CIA. He was a World War II vet and one of the last of that great generation of warriors still basking in the glow of the fading spotlight.

Rags-to-riches Laughlin was, according to all reports, still deeply involved in the intelligence community, making deals, pulling strings, his fingers still sensing the vibrations from the web he'd spun during his lifetime as a spymaster. Though officially retired, the man was one of President Hammer's and the CIA's advisors.

Time magazine called him one of the most powerful men in America, perhaps the world. *The Wall Street Journal* painted him as the last of the great spies, a kind of Godfather of Spookdom. He'd been credited with shadowy work that was keeping the crumbling Russian and East European intelligence communities from imploding. In short, the guy was a hero of sorts; a hero with a wide reach and tremendous influence.

"Yes," my father said, waiting until my shock seemed to set in, "Frankie 'X Marks the Spot' Laughlin."

"But what the hell could he have to fear from you?" I asked. "You've been 'dead' for almost thirty years, and even if you were still alive, which no one knows you are, you couldn't pick a smaller David than Sean Maguire to Laughlin's Goliath."

"David and Goliath . . . I like that. Ties in nicely with everything. But that's where you're wrong," he said, his voice hard again. "I'm Laughlin's worst nightmare, his pale rider, his nemesis. He could lose it all because of me. His power, wealth, fame, ultimately his freedom. Scary stuff for a man used to being on top of the world and having everything his way, right near the end of it all."

He lit yet another cigar, coughing this time, then went on. "He could have left me alone. Even after he killed Aronstein I thought we still had our deal. I would have let sleeping dogs lie. I ran, gave him the last three decades, thought that would be enough for him, but he couldn't let it go. He tried to kill me last week."

"Laughlin?"

"Or someone sent by him."

"How?"

"Not as pretty as Aronstein. A cab jumped the curb on Twenty-second Street. Actually clipped my pants."

"But why you?" Tuesday asked. "Why us?"

"Aronstein was on the right track; he was getting warm, close. Close enough to make Laughlin wonder if maybe someone was feeding Aronstein the information. Someone like Sean Maguire."

"Were you?" I asked, not grasping what my father might know that could make a man like Laughlin want to kill him.

He laughed. "No, and that's the hell of it. I don't know who Aronstein's source was, but it wasn't me."

The superficial smiles and jokes were gone. I looked into his eyes; they were as gray and depthless as a winter cloud.

I put my head in my hands and thought about the man in the backyard, the kids upstairs, and whether my father might be out of his mind.

"So what are we going to do?" I asked, not at all sure I wanted to hear the answer.

He looked at Tuesday and was suddenly all Irish charm and blarney again. "How about a little trip to Honolulu for you and the kids courtesy of gramps? Nice and warm there this time of year. I've got a condo right on Kalakaua Avenue, middle of Waikiki. A shame to leave it empty, don't you think?"

He got up, reached into his parka, pulled a manila envelope from an inside pocket, and placed it on the coffee table. His smile faded, and his brogue dropped away. He was all business again.

"There's three open tickets on American from New York to Honolulu, some documents for you and the kids, and ten thousand cash. I've had the condo for years. It's registered to a Mr. Ma, an old friend, but I own it. The papers are as good as I could put together on short notice but will have to do. The driver's license will hold. It's real, good till 2001, the photo close enough to you to work. Use it to open a bank account, all the rest. There are birth certificates for kids about Nicky and Marie's ages, made out as Nicholas and Marie Ma. You can use them to set up their Social Security numbers, get 'em in school, the whole shmear."

He was in his stride now.

"I could send you to a place I know on the coast of Maine, but

you'd stick out like a sore thumb. Hawaii's for you. There's thousands of mixed couples and mixed kids, Oriental, Caucasian, Poly-
nesian. No one will give any of you a second look."

Then he pulled a ring of keys from his parka and fingered each
one as he spoke. "Keys to the condo, a Honda in the garage, and
a safe deposit box at the Global Pacific Bank downtown branch."
He put the keys in the envelope then patted it.

"It's all written down for you. Burn your credit cards, license,
everything. That way you won't be tempted to use them."

Tuesday kept her eyes locked on my father. Her expression was
still, frozen.

"How long?" she asked.

"Danny and I will meet you there in a week. Two, three at the
outside. If it's not over by then . . ." He let that hang.

"What do I tell the children?"

"I don't know . . . that you're going on vacation. A present from
Grandpa."

"What about my rehearsals, the performance?"

"I'm sorry . . . There's nothing I can do," he said, his eyes older
again.

I broke in. "You mean we just disappear—poof! No word to
anyone?"

"Has to be."

"And if you and Danny don't come?" Tuesday asked. It was blunt
but effective. It slowed him down.

My father sipped his tea before he answered.

"There's a small black Bible in the safe deposit box. On the inside back cover there are two lines of numbers, just numbers, thirty-
two in a string. Starting backward, the first fifteen in a string are
telephone numbers, complete international numbers without the
011 prefix. The next seven are an account number, the following
eleven authorization codes. Those two accounts have, the last time
I checked, about four hundred thousand dollars each. They'll wire
it anywhere you want. . . ." His voice trailed off.

Tuesday looked over at me. A single tear rolled down her cheek, hit the horizontal dent of her scar, slid sideways an inch, and rolled to her chin. Her expression never softened.

I stood up and paced. For the moment I'd forget about the fact that I'd been busting my hump to scrape along all these years, while my father had numbered accounts and a condo in Hawaii. I'd deal with that later.

"Eight hundred thousand dollars could buy us all out—together. Hell! We could disappear in Spain, Portugal, anywhere! No one would ever find us," I said, holding his eyes, "not even Laughlin and his spooks."

My father shook his head. It seemed to take all of his strength to do it. "I don't think so. If I did, that's what we'd do. Coast of Brazil is almost two thousand miles long; good bargains in Scotland these days too."

"So?"

"So I don't think it would work. We'd leave a spoor somewhere; an old man smoking cigars, two half-and-half kids, you, an Oriental lady with a scar and a little limp. All it would take is one waiter with a good memory, a hungry stringer looking for a bounty, some tiny print in the mud. Then they'd find us, make us disappear."

I laughed once. It was more of a grunt. "So what do you propose?"

"I'm going to do what I should have done then. I'm going to rip out Laughlin's black heart and make him watch as I feed it to the lions. And God forgive me, but I need you to help."

5

A N OLD CHEVY station wagon with a small orange taxi sign on its roof stood in the driveway. Marie was crying, her little fingers wrapped tightly around my thigh like the talons of a small, frightened bird. Nick stood next to Tuesday. I noticed that his head was now even with her shoulder. He'd grown somehow, and I'd missed it.

The taxi's horn sounded.

"I'll see you in two weeks," I said. "Promise." The words tasted bitter, almost choking me.

I leaned in to kiss Nick, hug him. He stiffened, pulled back.

I lifted Marie and held her tightly. She buried her head on my shoulder. I felt her chest heaving. I whispered in her ear that I loved her, and between sobs, she managed to tell me she loved me too. Tuesday took her, Marie's fingertips tracing a path from my shoulders to my arm.

The front door opened, and my father stood on the stoop, his breath forming wispy trails in the chill morning air.

He took in the scene and put on his most charming smile.

"Time to go," he said. No one moved.

"Hey, now! We're talking two weeks in Hawaii! You'd think you were on your way to Cleveland!"

He tousled Nick's hair, then gently but firmly took Marie in his arms. I was angry that she trusted him, folded herself into his embrace.

"Come on. Planes don't wait," he said, and headed for the cab. Nick and I locked eyes.

"Two weeks, Nicky," I was whispering. "Just two weeks."

I opened my arms. A long moment passed and I was about to close them again, when something in him broke. He rushed forward, threw his arms around me, and squeezed tight.

I bent until my mouth rested above his ear. I inhaled deeply, closing my eyes for just a second, holding his scent.

"It will be all right, son," I whispered with what I hoped wasn't too much huskiness. "Take care of Mom and Marie."

He broke away, picked up his backpack, and walked outside without looking back. A survivor.

"I . . ."

Tuesday shook her head slowly, side to side. She came to me, stopping just inches from where I stood. She smelled of cheap soap and the morning's coffee. She kissed me once on the cheek. Her lips were cool, dry.

"Two weeks," she said. "I will see you in two weeks."

The taxi horn honked again. Longer this time, more insistent.

"Do you believe that?"

She shrugged. I passed my hand along her cheek, touched the scar. She didn't flinch.

"I believe in you—nothing else."

"If . . ."

Her fingers touched my lips, stopping me. Then her lips were on mine. It wasn't passion or comfort, it was longing. She broke the kiss, picked up her bag, and walked outside.

I moved to the front door, stood frozen there as the driver threw the Chevy into reverse with a loud clunk. My last glimpse as the cab moved forward was of my family in profile, eyes ahead. The next thing I knew, a small cloud of cigar smoke drifted past me.

With the smoke came my rage. My teeth were clenched, my

fists balled. I knew where almost a million dollars were. I could be away, follow Tuesday and the kids to Honolulu on the next flight. We could disappear, no problem. Let the old man take care of his problems by himself, just like he'd done since he'd left. And, if he died in the process, so fucking be it.

"Thinking of following them? Figure you can make it without me?"

His voice was behind me. I turned, slowly, the anger hot. "Crossed my mind. You going to stop me?"

He smiled. My rage turned crystal, subzero, brittle and sharp.

"No. Do what you please. Just think about this though: What would it take for you to leave them now, just let them go, never see them again? If you knew, I mean knew in your heart, your soul, that if you stayed with them one second longer, they'd be dead? Would you let your anger and hate weaken you enough to follow them, watch them die?"

He moved closer to me. He wasn't seventy, or twenty, he was timeless, primeval.

"How much would it take? How much love and fear to watch them go, leave them, sacrifice yourself for them?"

I didn't know. Couldn't answer. He turned and walked away. I closed the front door and followed him into the kitchen. The overhead fixture flickered.

"Just one thing," I asked his back. "Can we do it?"

He poured coffee from a dented electric percolator into two mismatched mugs. He handed me one that was burnished yellow from use. On its side was the New York Yankees logo.

His hands and eyes were steady now. Not a tremor. "It depends."

He sat at the dining table and looked out of the small double-hung window, the corners of the small panes of glass frosted over with condensation. His eyes were sad. I thought of my mother.

"A lot isn't what you think, Danny. I've done things . . . things I never wanted you to know, things I would never have done had I known then what I do now. You're going to have to see all of me.

I'll tell you what I can, how I can, when I can. But there's a lot you'll have to take on faith."

A blue jay flashed past the window. It darted to a tree and perched there. It seemed to be looking straight at me. The image of the man I'd killed, lying in his blood on the floor in the Red Dragon, flashed across my mind's eye.

"I'm no angel either, Dad," I said, the old memory suddenly fresh. "I have some things to tell you too. I . . ." I couldn't finish.

The silences were bringing us closer than ever before. There was so much to tell, so much I wanted to avoid, so much I'd waited a lifetime to share.

I took a sip of the hot black coffee, scalding my palate.

"I know all about faith," I said.

"Do you really?" His voice was calm. It wasn't meant as a challenge, but I took it as one.

"Yes."

"How?"

It was a fact of life, a given. "Because I am your son."

He looked at me, the space between us closing to a geometric point. I saw in his eyes exquisite, perfect pain, and intense, infinite love. When he spoke, it was as if his words had come from deep inside me. "Yes. And I'm sorry."

We stayed connected for a moment longer, and then we were two separate men again, but newly bound together in a timeless, primitive bond.

My rage was beginning to narrow and sharpen. I knew it was fear and maybe something worse, but it felt good. I was my father's son and he had returned. Our years apart were over. And now I knew that someone had taken them from us. Someone had taken my father, my mother, and a big part of myself. Now I had a name and a face. I knew who he was. Francis X. Laughlin. And there was still some time for what was left of us, however short, and I wanted it. Wanted it badly.

He ran one of his chiseled hands through his hair. "Then we can do it."

I looked out the window again. The jay was gone. Outside it was bleak; nothing but brown grass and skeletal trees. I thought about Nick and Marie. I knew exactly what they would feel like if I never came back. I remembered the many nights after my father disappeared, alone in my room, crying and cursing God.

My hatred became a glowing, brilliant thing. It pulsed with my heart, then cooled and became solid, hard. I turned to look at my father.

"Tell me," I said.

He nodded. "First I've got to back up a little. Start the story right."

I could see him searching for an opening to the past where he could enter and I could follow.

"I was a captain in the U.S. Army, you know that. Building support facilities at the southern tip of Greenland, a place called Narsaraq; you know that too. We'd taken it over in forty-one and were using it as a refueling and ferry point for the planes we were sending to England.

"I was helping build the hospital to handle the triage casualties anticipated from the long-planned invasion of Hitler's Europe—D-Day.

"And that's what I did do, mostly. Freezing my ass off, drinking pharmaceutical alcohol with the docs, screwing the nurses. Playing army. But that's another story."

This was pretty much familiar ground. I'd seen the old glossy photographs of my father and his army buddies, barren and raw glacial plains behind them.

"Back home, we were producing more tanks, planes, and uniforms than anyone thought possible. The problem was getting the stuff where it was needed.

"We were shipping millions of tons of equipment, tens of thousands of men; most to England, but some to our new allies, the Russians. Everything had to be put on ships to cross the North Atlantic. They traveled in groups—convoys—surrounded by light cruisers."

He stood and paced the small kitchen slowly. "You should have seen the piers on the West Side; it was wall to wall with ships of every size. Freighters, tankers, oilers, merchantmen mostly, filling up and getting ready for the trip.

"But the damned convoys, once they were out of port, were sitting ducks for the German U-Boats. And if one boat got hit, the others had to keep going. The last thing the survivors saw, if there were any, were the lights of the convoy as it steamed away."

I pictured this too. When I was a kid he and I would watch *Victory at Sea* every week. The show chronicled the sea war in the Atlantic and Pacific with dramatic black-and-white footage, somber commentary, and stirring music. The shows were riveting: ships plowing through waves the size of buildings as they crossed the Atlantic, invasions of faraway Pacific Islands, big guns flashing, flame-throwers spitting death. For a boy of ten it pushed all the right buttons. It made war romantic and noble, things my budding manhood accepted without question. Now I saw that my father's reasons for watching were more personal.

"That year we lost three million tons to the Wolf Packs; thousands of good men, half of them boys really. You didn't have to be a genius to see that the Germans had good intelligence on the ground; agents sending schedules, courses, and tonnages of the convoys to the Fatherland. The FBI nabbed one or two, but not enough. The docks and shipyards from Maine to Florida were like anthills. Placing an agent in one of the ports was child's play."

He tired of pacing and sat down again. He reached for another cigar, then stopped and just patted his pocket. "Ever heard of the OSS?"

I wasn't much of a history buff, but the OSS, the Office of Strategic Services, was one of those uniquely American stories from the country's glamour days.

"A little," I said. "The original spy boys from World War II."

"Well, the head of the OSS was a guy named William Donovan, ex–Wall Street lawyer, part of the aristocracy. But Wild Bill is what we called him."

"You were in the OSS?"

He nodded.

I thought about the movies I'd grown up with: Cary Grant, Jimmy Cagney, and others dropping behind German lines, blowing up bomb factories; kissing beautiful German agents, tortured by the Gestapo, laughing even as they died. I was confused.

"What does that have to do with Greenland or the convoys?"

"I'm getting there. Just hold on." He was annoyed.

"Like I said, the convoys were still being hammered. Donovan was convinced he could do something about it. He thought Hoover was nutty as a fruit cake and a fairy to boot, so he went to Roosevelt and asked permission to 'do a little field work' on his own. But U.S. territory was Hoover's domain, and he protected it like a mother bear protects her cubs.

"Donovan didn't give a shit, but Roosevelt did. He gave Donovan verbal approval but told Wild Bill that if anything ever came out, he'd cut Donovan loose, tell anyone and everyone he had nothing to do with it.

"For a guy like Donovan, that was all he needed to hear. He had teams on the ground within weeks. That's about the time I got involved."

I had questions now, ones I wasn't sure I wanted answers to.

"So you were"—I looked for words to make killing pleasant—"taking care of spies."

He looked straight at me but didn't speak.

"But they were the enemy," I offered.

"That's what I kept telling myself. I was convinced it had to be done, that if killing these guys meant one less American going to the bottom of the sea, it was all right with me.

"But they were crazy times, Danny. No one told me what the guy was supposed to have done, what the proof was. I was given a name and address. That's it. The guy was wasted. Now sometimes when I can't sleep I wonder, which ones were tagged wrong, which should have gone home to their wives or kids."

He was right, of course. But it made such perfect sense and

solved so many mysteries surrounding my father's wildly erratic personality and temperament, the fact that innocent people might have died paled in comparison. It also made him just as I'd always pictured him, larger than life, heroic. Big enough to soothe a lot of my own hurt.

"But that's war . . ."

He held up a hand. His palm was large and deeply lined. His voice changed, the words spewing out in a raging torrent.

"Now we're up to speed. The original sin. The night I lost whatever control of my life I might have had; the night I was seduced by two mistresses, greed and fear. It was an August night in New York, the kind without a breeze, ninety degrees, hundred percent humidity. It was 1943. I was just twenty years old, sweating, but my guts were ice. I'd just come down from Fall River, Mass., where I'd killed two men, Russian sailors, and dumped them in the harbor. I hadn't slept for two days. I was taking benzedrine and drinking and starting to see faces . . . faces of the men in Taunton, and others. Faces of men I'd killed. I was told they were the enemy, behind our lines. I believed it then. Think I still do."

If someone had told me this before today, I'd have called them a liar or worse. Now it made perfect sense. He lit one of his cigars. I watched the Zippo disappear in his hand.

"But that night, like others before and after, I was four days out on a made-up temporary duty assignment signed by a nonexistent general in Washington. First night I flew to Nova Scotia, where I left my uniform and gear, met up with the rest of my team who'd also been shipped from their normal duties on bullshit orders. We picked up new clothes. Used, dirty, cheap stuff. A man in a suit who never introduced himself gave us phony I.D.'s, throwaway pistols, knives, and some guitar wire."

His hands engulfed the coffee mug. His fingers knit and I saw his veins bulge. I waited for the cup to implode.

"Tools of my trade. The four of us were put on a transport plane. We landed in Taunton the middle of the night, were given a six-year-old Ford, two names, and three addresses."

Until he'd disappeared, my father was a builder by trade but sculpted with hammers and chisels every spare moment as though his very life depended on it. Once in a while I would sneak to the window of his small studio and watch, my heart pounding, as he attacked huge chunks of wood or stone with a ferocity verging on violence. What I saw fascinated me. His face would be beaded with sweat, his sleeves rolled up, revealing ropy forearms, his magnificent hands controlling the chisels and heavy hammer. When he was done, the result was always rough and abstract. Every once in a while, he'd gather the few chunks left and I'd help him scatter them on the beach, like driftwood.

As a child, I accepted things I couldn't or didn't understand and quickly forgot about them. But as my father talked about the killings, I became dizzy with knowledge. He paused and looked over at me. I was with him every step, felt his every sensation. I imagined myself in a car in the dead of night. I imagined my hands were his.

When he started again, it came out as the rest had; bits and pieces, smells, sensations more than fifty years old but as fresh to him as last night.

"We did the guys in Fall River and were back in Taunton before dawn.

"Sunrise we were put on another plane and landed in Mitchell Field, Long Island. A different civilian met us, gave us new names and addresses, the keys to another old car. We drove to New York and checked into a rooming house on the West Side. I spent that night drinking till I passed out, trying to forget what was going on, what was still ahead.

"Next day I slept off the hangover. We did things by the book; taking turns, going out separately to eat, walk around. After dark, we met in my room; me, Laughlin . . ."

My hand shot up. "Laughlin?"

"Yes."

"So . . ."

"Just listen," he said, too deep into his tale for interruptions.

"The other guys were Deere and Rosen. Deere was stationed at Fort Bragg but always met up with us. Walt Rosen was a doctor stationed in New York, an administration guy with the Medical Corps. Rosen gave us each a couple of bennies and some codeine pills just in case.

"Laughlin was the team leader. He prepped us for the last two men. He went over where we were going, who we were after, rendezvous points, fallbacks, then the location of the safe house in case things went wrong.

"The address was a railroad tenement on Forty-sixth off Ninth. A rundown five-floor walkup. We waited until ten.

"Laughlin and I went first. Deere and Rosen stayed outside to keep watch . . ."

He looked at me steadily and paused. He wanted to see if I still needed to know. I did. "Go on."

"Laughlin slipped the lock with a pocket knife; it was kids' play. In those days . . ." He let the thought drift off.

"A man was asleep on the couch. We jumped him. I held a knife to his throat with one hand, and a rag on his mouth with the other. Laughlin shoved a silenced Colt up the man's nose and whispered: 'Where's your buddy?'

"The guy's eyes were wild. He knew he was going to die. He held out a trembling hand. I understood, but before I lifted the rag from his mouth, I pressed the knife just hard enough to draw some blood.

" 'Don't kill me,' he said. 'I know what you want.'

"Laughlin and I looked at each other, figured what the hell?

" 'We'll see,' Laughlin said quietly. 'First. Where's your buddy?'

" 'Basement. Basement.'

"I slowly took the knife from the man's throat and Laughlin backed his pistol out of the man's nose. The man just started to smile when Laughlin shot him twice in the heart."

My father's voice never wavered or changed tempo. I got the

feeling he'd recited this before, probably to himself to make it all seem ordinary. But no matter how it came out, it wasn't. My palms were sweating.

"The door to the basement was unlocked and ajar, a dim glimmer of light coming up the stairs. The floor was packed dirt, the foundation old stone. It stank of rat shit and piss. A man's voice called out from under a bare bulb hanging from a twisted wire.

" 'John?'

"It was a big man's voice. He had a heavy Slavic accent. He was stooping over a small wooden box. When he saw I wasn't John, he straightened. He was a bearded giant.

" 'Who are you?' he asked, picking up a long pry bar and coming at me.

"I didn't answer but instead pulled out my knife. I heard Laughlin behind me, felt him move to my left so the big man had two targets, not one. Laughlin started talking to him then, telling him to put down the weapon if he wanted to live.

"Either the big man didn't understand or didn't believe him. He rushed forward. Laughlin was fast. He shot twice but that didn't stop the big guy. The pry bar came down on Laughlin's shoulder and knocked him down. It was raised in both of the giant's hands ready to come down again when I buried my knife up to the hilt where the giant's neck met his collar bone. Laughlin rolled away as the big man fell on his face.

" 'Let's get the fuck outta here,' I said, still shaking. I just wanted to get back to the car and leave.

"But Laughlin was different, He was like ice. If he could, he'd always give the place a toss, check things out, see if there was anything the higher-ups might want. Code books, radios, anything. But though we looked, we'd yet to find anything like that. He also scooped up any loose cash. No one else on the team had the balls or stomach for it, but Laughlin sure as hell did.

"The first couple of times we argued with him and he just shrugged. But one time he'd come away with over a thousand dollars. Back in Maine, he handed an envelope to each of us with two hundred fifty dollars . . ."

He must have seen the revulsion in my face.

"Yeah. That's when we crossed the line. And that's why we're here right now.

"That night, when Laughlin started looking through the box, we were already dirty."

"I was going through the big man's pockets, hoping to find something, anything, that made this guy my enemy. I took his wallet and a few coins. That was all. No Nazi party card. No swastika.

"Then Laughlin whistled softly. He held a small golden candelabra he'd taken from the box the giant had been bent over. He rummaged around some more and came out with a gold chalice. Every time his hand went in, it came out with something more beautiful than before.

" 'This stuff is worth a fortune,' he announced. 'Help me pack it back up and let's get out of here.'

"I hesitated. A few hundred dollars was one thing. Loot was another. That's the moment Laughlin dug his claws into me, sank them deep.

" 'You want to leave this stuff for the cops?' he asked me. 'Turn it in to Donovan and them? What do you think they'll do with it? Send it back? Grow up, man. I'm not coming out of this war just another bricklayer. I'm going somewhere and this is my ticket. If you want, you can come with me.'

"I still wavered.

"Laughlin smiled. It was scary.

" 'Listen, Maguire,' he said, 'listen good. Don't come off holier than thou with me; we're in this together. I go down, so do you.'

"'What about Rosen and Deere?' I'd asked, looking for any foothold at all.

" 'Leave them to me,' he said, pounding the cover of the small wooden crate back on.

"Back at the rooming house, Laughlin opened the box and laid everything out on the bed. Deere just about danced he was so excited. He was as greedy as Laughlin, just not as smart; they made a good team.

"Rosen picked up each piece in turn, handling them as gently as if they were newborn babies, then sat on the bed and held his head in his hands.

" 'What's wrong, Rosen?' Laughlin taunted, 'I thought all Jews wanted to be rich.'

"Rosen was big and strong, but thoughtful and gentle; almost too thoughtful, too gentle. There was something about his being with us that just didn't fit.

"Rosen just growled, and the next thing we knew Laughlin was against the wall, Rosen's thick forearm across Laughlin's neck.

"By the time Deere and I got Rosen off him, Laughlin's face was blue and he couldn't speak. Rosen towered over Laughlin ready to strike again.

" 'You ever say anything like that again, you greedy little shit, and I'll kill you where you stand.'

"He picked up the candelabra, shook it inches from Laughlin's head.

" 'You know what this is, you ignorant Mick? This is a menorah. We dirty Kikes use it to celebrate Hanukkah, the Festival of Lights.'

"He threw the menorah on the bed and picked up a delicate, intricately carved piece of silver with a tiny, delicate hand formed at one end.

" 'And this. You know what this is?' he said, a miniature finger almost in Laughlin's eye. 'Us Hebes use it to read from the Torah, the Holy Torah!'

"Still holding the little pointer, Rosen started to pace the small room.

" 'You guys never understood. Never knew why I was here—the good Jewish doctor slitting throats. It's because I'm the only one of you assholes with a personal stake in this fucking war! I'm the one with uncles and cousins I don't even know who are being shoved into ovens, just because they're Jews. Like me.'

"We'd all heard rumors of the camps, the ovens, the slaughter. But until that moment, surrounded by what I knew were valuable and cherished items, I thought it was just wartime propaganda, like the stories about the Japs bayonetting babies."

My father rubbed his eyes.

"But the proof was in front of us and we couldn't deny it. Everything on the bed was the worst kind of spoils. Each was covered in blood; not only of the men we'd killed that night, but from nameless, faceless families an ocean away.

"Rosen told us that he was going to take the box and everything in it and give it to someone he trusted. He said if anyone wanted to stop him, they'd have to kill him. I told Rosen that his taking the stuff was just fine with me. But Laughlin and Deere hesitated. They weighed things out, figuring the odds. Like I said, Rosen was a big man and he was possessed, so the odds weren't good.

"Rosen repacked the box, tucked it under his arm, and left. I thought that was that. But I'd underestimated Laughlin.

"As soon as Rosen left, he pulled out a small piece of paper.

" 'Let that Jew bastard take the box,' he said. 'If I'm right, it's just the tip of the iceberg. This, my boys,' he said, waving the scrap of paper, 'will take us to the mother lode.'

"He passed it around, told us it was the shipping label he'd pulled off the box. It was addressed to a gallery on Madison Avenue."

My father's story was making my head pound. I was having trouble meeting his eyes. I wasn't sure how much more I could take, and I could tell it was only the beginning. So when a muffled beep came from the living room I was relieved.

"Shit!" my father said. "I thought I'd shut that damn thing off!"

He jumped from the table and trotted into the living room. The beeping stopped. He came back into the kitchen, sat down again, and slid the pager across the table. It spun once before I picked it up, reading three digits where seven should have been.

"Code," I said.

"We have to move," my father said as he stood. "When they don't hear back from him, they'll start looking."

"No way they'll find him." I thought about the body deep in the marsh. It might never be discovered.

"Probably not," he said, pointing at the pager. "But when he doesn't respond, they'll start looking for that."

"But this thing only receives."

"True. But they work on cellular sites, like the phones. A message is transmitted, then the network broadcasts a packet of digital information, looking for the pager's address. When it finds the pager, it sends the packet, the pager acknowledges receipt, and the system clears."

At this point, I wasn't surprised by anything the old man knew.

"So if they want, they'll know the cell site that transmitted the signal?"

"Right. Then they can triangulate, narrow the search to about a mile radius," he said. "There's another car in the garage. Take it out and put the van in its place."

He unplugged the percolator, put his mug in the sink, and checked to make sure the stove was off.

"Meet you out front in ten," he said, moving to the living room.

6

T HE SKY HAD turned an opalescent gray. The air was still and smelled like snow. I put the van in the garage, thinking it might be the last time I laid eyes on it. I smiled. Most men I knew loved cars almost as much as women. The more exotic, lean, or sexy, the hotter it was, the more it became an object of desire. But from the time I got my license, all I could afford had been a succession of used heaps.

The van had been no different. A used rental, it smelled like a wet dog and was in the shop almost as much as on the road. I'd hated the damn thing from the day we picked it up. Leaving it in a sad Cape in Nowheresville on a bleak winter day had poetic resonance.

As I got ready to slam the creaking door for the last time, Nick's soccer ball rolled out. I picked it up, saw Nick smiling as he kicked a hard one. I rolled the ball around in my hands and gently placed it on the front seat. It was then I noticed the other assorted family artifacts: a bead necklace Marie made hanging from the rearview mirror, stubs from Tuesday's ever-present joss sticks askew in the ashtray. And Marie's blankie on the backseat. Always by her side, she must hae left it behind in the confusion. I reached in, held the smooth cotton, soft as angel's hair from a thousand washings, against my face, and inhaled deeply of its scent. I stuffed it in my parka.

I closed the door slowly. I rubbed its side, took a final look. Like so many things realized too late, I knew the hated van had been a part of my family as surely as if it were a living thing. And now it was time to say good-bye.

"Pull yourself together, asshole," I said aloud. My family was gone less than half an hour, and I was already getting misty-eyed. I'd have to do better.

The other car in the garage was a gray Ford sedan, probably about two years old. Neutral and nondescript, no sex appeal at all. But she was clean, smelled okay, and started on the first crank. I laughed in spite of myself—she was my kind of girl.

I backed out of the garage, then closed the overhead door. My father and I got in the Ford at the same moment. Tiny snowflakes started to fall on the windshield.

I retraced our route from last night. My father hadn't said where we were going. It didn't really matter. Wherever we were headed, the LIE, the infamous Long Island Expressway, a six-lane gash cutting the island in half, would be the beginning.

We picked up speed. The snow blew past the windshield without touching it.

A silence grew. My father pulled another cheroot from his seemingly endless supply and lit it. I pushed the heater up a notch. My father and I cracked open our windows one after the other. He lowered his a notch more, tossed the dead man's pager out of the window and smiled.

"Let Laughlin find that," he said.

The years peeled away. It felt good, almost too good. It was good to be a father's son again. And now, after a lifetime apart, separated by mere feet, we were surrounded by the same full silence. The snow was sticking on the shoulder. Traffic started to slow. The flakes, larger now, were melting on the windshield. I put on the wipers and headlights. It felt fine.

"Time to see how smart I am," he said, taking the dead man's cell phone out and powering it up. He studied the buttons, pushed one. He turned to me and said, "Redial."

"Yes. Hello. No . . . Tell Laughlin that Sean Maguire called," he said breezily, then flipped the bottom of the phone shut.

"Laughlin's cut-out number," he explained. "They're finding him now."

A minute later the phone chirped. My father let it ring a few times before slowly opening the phone and putting it to his ear. He didn't say hello. He nodded his head twice.

"Fuck you too, Frank."

He listened a little more. I could see the heat within him rising.

"A few things first. Your man in Port Washington has been re-tired. Two. My son and his kids are far, far away. Three. By the time you narrow down where I called you from, I'll be long gone too. Four. You broke our deal. Now everything is on my terms; I talk, you listen."

He seemed to be interrupted. He lit another cigar as he listened.

"Yeah, sure. Protecting me and my family. Cute. It's bullshit, Frank, and you know it. Want to hear how I see it? Aronstein was finally getting close. *Too* close. So you give the word, and he has a heart attack. Maybe tell Osborne to start cleaning up the files too. But there's only one little problem; you don't know who Aronstein's source is, so you figure maybe it's Sean Maguire."

Another interruption.

"Yeah. Sure. And I'm the Tooth Fairy. I would have let you alone, Frank, honest to God. But you wouldn't let me be. You're just too paranoid, spent too long with the spooks . . ."

My father pounded the dash. "Shut up! Just shut the fuck up and listen good. I've still got the letter from Rosen that tells the whole stinking story. It's signed, sealed, and witnessed . . ."

"Oh, there's a letter, all right. Remember when Deere and his kids died in that 'accident'? Well, Rosen and I figured we'd be next. We did what we could, exchanged confessions. Next thing I hear, Rosen blows his brains out. You remember, don't you? That's when I took a powder."

There it was. The answer to my oldest question. I looked over at him, but he was staring straight ahead.

His eyes widened and he jabbed his finger frantically at the windshield. I hit the brakes and skidded until I was inches from the bumper of the car in front of us. He rolled his eyes.

"Remember our deal, Frankie? I called you from the airport. Told you if anything happened to my wife or kid I'd spill it all, the consequences be damned. I held up my end but you blew it last week when that cab clipped me."

My father stopped to listen again. He laughed. "Not you? C'mon, Frankie—then who?"

My father's brow knit in concentration as he listened.

"Nice try, but no dice. You've got two choices; you either find me and kill me or you do what I want and I give you Rosen's letter . . .

"No. Not that way. You still playing poker? . . . Good, then after I've given you some time to sweat a little, figure your odds, I'll deal the next card. And, oh yeah. Don't call me, I'll call you."

He shut off the phone, folded it, and slipped it back in his pocket.

I needed some answers in a hurry. "Where's Rosen's letter?"

"There is no letter."

"What!"

"Even if he thinks I'm bluffing, Laughlin can't risk it. I did go to see Rosen after I heard Deere and his family bought it in an accident. Knowing Laughlin, we figured we were next. We were going to do something but just weren't quick enough. Rosen was found two days later in his study with his brains on the ceiling and a .38 in his hand. No note, no nothing."

I chewed on that for a while. I didn't like the taste.

"And if he calls your bluff, wants to see your cards, have a look at the letter before he deals?"

I saw my father look over at me from the corner of my eye.

"There aren't going to be any more deals," he said. His meaning was unmistakable, but I wanted to hear him spell it out.

"What do you mean?"

"Just like I said. No more deals. We're going to kill him."

I stared straight ahead, pretending to concentrate on my driving. I replayed the simple statement in my head. The condo in Hawaii started to look good again.

"Wait a minute," I said. I searched for a way to move this whole thing somewhere else. "How do you figure to get to him? He's Mr. Spy. This is his turf we're playing on." Then I remembered something else from the one-sided conversation with Laughlin. "And who the hell is this guy Osborne and what does he have to do with things?"

"Osborne is Laughlin's man at the Agency."

"As in the Central Intelligence Agency?"

"Yes. He's Laughlin's protégé. A career spook, ranked just high enough to know things or find them out, but just low enough to be damn near invisible," my father said, nodding in appreciation. "When Laughlin needs the inside scoop on what's going on in Langley, he calls Osborne. If Osborne was working for the other side he'd be called a mole. But the way it is, he's just a source."

Great, I thought. Now we had Laughlin and his man in the CIA looking for us.

"So," I said, squinting through the storm, still waiting for the answer to the first part of my question. "What did you have in mind?"

"We won't go to him. Too risky. He'd outflank us somehow. We have to get Laughlin to come to us. On our terms; when and where I say. He can't chance it not to."

"What about Osborne?"

"Osborne has to use more discretion than Laughlin. He's Laughlin's lapdog but still on a pretty tight leash. We'll have to keep an eye on him," he said, deep in thought. "But I'm more worried about Laughlin and the free-lance people he must be using."

I shook my head slowly side to side. The Maguires against Laughlin, the CIA, and a bunch of hired guns. I tried another approach.

"What did he say about the guy in the backyard?"

My father smiled thinly. "Laughlin is shoveling crap as fast as he can make it up. He said 'they're' after him too—whoever the hell 'they' are. Told me the guy in the backyard was there to protect you."

"Maybe we should listen to him. Maybe—"

He shook his head. "You're gonna have to trust me on this, Danny. Laughlin's a liar and a killer. I should know."

With that he lit another of his cigars.

I needed some time to sort things out. I turned the radio on and tuned in the all-news station.

The announcer said the National Weather Service was predicting up to a foot of snow, maybe more. People were being advised to get off the roads. Airports from Philadelphia to Boston were getting blanketed; how long they would remain open was anyone's guess.

Things were turning to shit in a hurry.

A few more miles. A few more minutes. Slower traffic. More snow. Slicker roads. Still no bright ideas. Another cigar.

My father's fist bounced off the dashboard. I jumped.

"We've got to get Tuesday and the kids," he said.

"What!"

"What time was the plane?"

"Noon."

"No way that flight's taking off in this weather. I don't want them hanging around the airport. Laughlin's men might be watching," he said, rubbing his unshaven chin. "They're only half an hour or so ahead of us. Their cab's in the same mess we are."

"So?"

"Let's beat him to the airport."

"And how the hell you figure we're going to do that?" I said, sliding sideways a bit as I tapped the brakes to avoid the bumper in front of me.

"Cabbie's going to stay on the main roads. We'll take the back way."

His fingers drummed the dash. "Get off here."

I slid down the off ramp. We were just across the city line on Springfield Boulevard. It was less crowded but the snow was deeper. I started to stop for a light.

"Run it!" he shouted.

I did, narrowly missing a delivery truck. The rest became a blur of side streets and near misses as I ran red lights and we hurtled south and west. He knew every back street and alley in Queens and Brooklyn. To tell the truth, I was impressed.

Even with the defrost on high and the wipers at top speed, visibility was zilch.

"Almost there," he said.

I turned to look at him, a smile forming on my lips when I heard the shriek of an air horn. A sander was bearing down on me. I hit the gas and spun out left. The sander was inching toward us, the driver shouting and making obscene gestures through his open window.

"Move it!" It was my father again.

I pushed the gas pedal, more gently this time. The wheels spun then gripped. I fishtailed down the street.

"Keep your eyes on the damn road. Okay?"

"You wanna drive!"

"Damn right, but we don't have the time to switch. Here! Turn left!"

We were at the airport's fringe. More rapid-fire directions: left, right, right, left. I was totally disoriented when all of a sudden we were on the main entry road. Traffic was crawling.

"Pull over," he said. I did.

"I thought we wanted to catch them."

"No way they got here before us."

He lit another cigar.

"Every worry about cancer?"

"I've had bigger things on my mind."

I looked out at the sea of red lights. Ten minutes crept past.

"There he is," my father said, jumping out of the car.

I followed him out. Sure enough, there was the beat-up cab with the orange sign in the right lane crawling along in the slow-moving traffic. When he saw us, the driver's expression transformed from bored and pissed off to baffled shock, eyebrows raised, jaw dropped. I had to laugh.

My father waved him to the shoulder.

Marie jumped out of the passenger door and ran to me. Her face was red and splotchy. She must have cried the whole trip. I remembered the blankie, pulled it out of my coat where I'd stuffed it, and handed it to her with a smile.

Next out was Nick. No holding back this time, he threw his arms around me too. Tuesday came to my side, touched my cheek.

"Get in the car," I said, seeing the stares we were getting.

"But . . ." It was Nick.

"I'll explain later."

Tuesday picked Marie up and gently nudged Nick's shoulder. I saw my father drop the suitcases in the trunk, then peel off two hundreds for the stunned cabby. I think the driver would have stayed there until he froze if my father hadn't told him to get lost.

My father hopped into the front seat.

Both kids started asking questions at the same time. I held up my hand. "Whoa. Hey. So first things first. How was Hawaii?"

They broke into nervous laughter.

I squeezed left through three lanes of traffic. Horns honked, lights flashed. I made an illegal U-turn at an opening in the guard rail and we were moving again. Traffic leaving the airport was light.

My father put on his best smile.

"Sorry about that," he said. "There's been a change in plans. Hawaii will have to wait." He was making it up as he went. "Your dad and me thought maybe—"

"Can we go home now?"

It was Marie. Her voice was small and afraid. The question hung just a moment too long, and she started to cry again.

"No, darling," I said. "Not yet. But soon."

I caught Nick's eye in the mirror. He was afraid too. I winked, letting him know it was just between us. His features softened a little. He winked back.

I looked at Tuesday. Her expression was neutral but I thought I saw an echo of a smile in her eyes. Maybe she felt as I did right now: that whatever happened, at least we were all together. Maybe it was something else. She was hard to read.

The snow was coming down heavier than before. My father was lost in thought.

"Where to?" I asked.

"Give me a minute," he said.

"Sure."

It was more like five.

"Hang a right."

He led me through every side street from Kennedy north. Marie had fallen asleep, her head on Tuesday's lap. Nick looked from my father to me and back. I could tell he was comparing us, probably thinking about how he fit into this generational stew.

We were in no rush now, so I drove cautiously through ever-deepening snow. My father smoked and gave directions. Soon Tuesday and Nick were sleeping too.

I whispered, "What now?"

"Laughlin is good. Real good. Cocky too. He figures time is on his side." His voice was hushed. "But now he's pissed. He knows his man won't be coming back and thinks you and the kids are gone. He doesn't like it. He'll put more men in the field."

"Does he really have that kind of manpower?"

My father laughed. "Just like the old days. He's got money and access to men with training and available for a price. If he can find us, then poof! we disappear."

"As easy as that?"

"No. Not that easy at all. But he's done it before. And don't forget, I was there. I was one of them."

I concentrated on my driving.

"First thing is that we still have to get them somewhere safe," he said, jerking his head lightly at the backseat. "Just won't be Hawaii."

"Do you have someplace else?"

He did the Groucho thing with his eyebrows. "Not to fret, laddy. I've still got a few tricks up these tattered sleeves."

I smiled weakly. I was exhausted from the roller coaster he'd strapped me into. All I could think of was sleep. He read my mind.

"Pull over. I'll drive for a while."

Maybe I should have argued with him. After all, he was a senior citizen. Instead I pulled to the curb and we changed places. I felt the car gently accelerate and I was instantly asleep.

7

I FELT A gentle push on the shoulder and turned deeper into the armrest, mumbling for it to go away. But the hand found me again. It seemed as if I were rising up from some great depth. I was stiff. I couldn't catch and hold the dream I was having, it was lost forever in the rush of remembering where I was. The inside of the car was cold, a soft glow from the streetlights coming through a blanket of snow covering the windows. My father held a finger to his lips.

I turned slowly and saw Tuesday and the kids in a pile on the backseat, still fast asleep.

"How long was I out?" I asked him, my voice thick and gritty.

"About an hour," he said, steam escaping with his words.

"Where are we?"

"Cobble Hill, Brooklyn. Four blocks from my place."

Three feet away in the eerie yellow light, the lines defining the boundaries of his body were blurred. He was ghostlike.

I rubbed the inside of the windshield. It had a thin coat of ice. "The kids must be freezing."

He looked back at my family. "They're fine, Danny." His voice was raspy, just above a whisper. "I'm just thinking things through."

I heard a hint of doubt, a breath of fear. "I thought this place of yours was safe."

There was no mistaking the tone of accusation in my voice.

He leaned a little closer, his eyes as cold as stones.

"When you sleep with the devil, and God have mercy but I have, you start to be able to sense when he's near, can feel it. And right now the hair on the back of my neck is standing up, and I smell something rancid. He's not far away."

"Then let's just keep going. Outrun him."

He just looked at me and shook his head.

There was a rustle in the backset. Nick coughed. Marie turned over. Tuesday's eyes opened but she didn't move. I reached over the seat. Her dry hand slipped into mine and squeezed.

My father turned to her.

"We're going to give my place the once-over. Make sure everything is all right," he whispered. "One of us will be back to get you and the kids. If we're not back in an hour, it means something went wrong. Take the kids and get as far away as you can, as fast as you can. Train maybe. Change the tickets, get to Hawaii. You'll be safe there."

He turned to me. "Ready?"

"All set."

He reached up and unscrewed the dome light, took out the bulb, and left the car quickly. A blast of dry snow swirled in his wake.

I looked at Tuesday. If she was afraid, I didn't see it. I couldn't stand another good-bye. I leaned over, kissed her hand, and left the car.

On any other night, my soul would have soared at the wild beauty of the raging winter storm. The snow was virgin and untouched. Majestic drifts covered the city with great democracy, dainty sloped rooftops and ugly cankers alike. Not a car was rolling, not a soul was in sight. Snowflakes sparkled in the streetlights. All was muffled and quiet. Lights shone from apartment windows where inside, families were warm and safe.

My father came to my side and led me to the narrow and darkened entryway of a closed store.

"Here," he said, slipping the revolver he'd taken from the body in my yard to me. "Let's hope we don't need it."

We started walking. The gun felt heavy in my coat pocket. We turned the corner.

"My place is on Baltic Street. It's an old three-story walkup. I'm president of the Delaware corporation that owns it. A management company handles it. No one—not the other tenants or the managers—know it's old Mr. Hennessey on the third floor that owns the place. Keeps things simple."

"Hennessey?" I said, unable to stop myself from grinning. "As in VSOP?"

"I knew I raised you right."

I looked skyward. "Lord save us."

"That would be nice, but don't hold your breath."

When we turned the corner of Baltic Street, something caught my eye. I took him by the elbow and led him behind a white behemoth that was once an ordinary van.

"Car halfway down the block, right side. Windshield."

He inched slowly past the rear of the van, looked, then stood beside me.

He exhaled slowly and nodded. "They're here."

Halfway down the street was a car that, like all the rest, was covered with snow. What caught my eye was that the shelf of snow had broken off and slid down just enough to expose a sliver of windshield. It was the kind of thing you'd never notice if you weren't studying shadows and waiting for someone to jump from behind a tree and garrote you.

"Looks like they ran the engine just long enough to heat it up inside," I said. "Defrost must have been on."

"Good spot too. Right in front of the house. Bet the passenger window's cracked open an inch. We'd have walked right into them."

"Let's get the hell out of here."

"Can't."

"Why not! They're waiting on your damned doorstep."

"Agreed. This place is blown. But there's something I've got to get."

I looked at him.

"A few things we might need, some papers that might be useful."

"But you said no one would listen."

"They probably won't. But without them we've got less than zero; no hope at all."

We couldn't get around the car without being seen. The snow was turning fine and dustlike, the wind slowing. Soon the cross-country skiers and kids on sleds would come out to enjoy the blizzard, before the plows and sanders came through, turning the beautiful white blanket into a gray, slushy mess.

"Is there another way in?"

He shook his head.

I peeked around the end of the van and looked at the car. The engine was back on, exhaust streaming from the tailpipe.

"Either these guys are just plain stupid, or . . ."

"Or what?"

I paused, a frightening thought occurring to me. "Maybe they're a couple of kids necking."

My father shook his head slowly. His hand emerged from his pocket, holding the automatic pistol from the dead man in Port Washington. From his other pocket he took a short metal tube and began to thread it onto the gun. "Can't chance it." His voice was tired.

"But . . . if?"

"Then you've lost your soul and a stone hangs on your heart forever."

"And?"

He straightened. "You live with it. You chase the demons. Sometimes you drink it away and stumble along."

I pictured myself in his shoes, living with ghosts for more than fifty years, carrying an infinite weight on an endless journey. I shuddered.

The snow had almost stopped now. My father looked at his watch, then at me. "Now or never, Danny."

"How do you want to do it?" I asked, wrapping my fingers around the butt of the revolver in my pocket. My hand was shaking.

"We'll split up. You walk around, slowlike, let them see you. I'll come from behind, take them from the passenger side."

It was backward. He was the better bait, me the better for what had to be done. I told him so as I reached for the silenced pistol.

"And if you're right?" he asked quietly. "If it's just a couple of kids?"

We locked eyes. My heart was racing. I was crossing a bottom-less chasm on a one-way span. I formed the words slowly.

"Then the sins of the fathers are truly visited upon the sons."

I'D CIRCLED AROUND the block until I was on the same side of the street as the car. As soon as my father saw me, he crossed under the streetlight and started walking, head down, moving haltingly on the deep snow. He was giving me time to be at the passenger door moments before he was at the stoop. The winter silence was deep enough for me to hear the blood rushing through my body and every breath I took.

When I was one car back, I went into a crouch, pulled the silenced pistol from my jacket, and moved forward slowly, the snow up to my knees. I stopped at the car's rear bumper. The engine was off now but, sure enough, just as my father predicted, the passenger window was cracked an inch. My heart galloped.

When my father's foot was on the stoop and his back was to the car, the passenger door clicked and started to open.

I rushed forward, pulled open the door, and shoved the pistol in the car, pulling the trigger twice.

A young woman fell to the snow, her eyes wide with pain and terror. I froze.

"God!" I said. "Oh, God!"

I'd been right! Young lovers on a winter's night in a dark car.

My father turned, started back down the steps, faster now, sure of his footing. I was still staring at the woman when a loud pop escaped the car, followed quickly by two more. From the corner of my eye, I saw my father fall.

I howled and rolled over the woman, firing into the car as fast as I could pull the trigger until the gun was empty. Gasping for breath, I looked inside. A man, no older than the woman in the snow, lay slumped over the steering wheel. The driver's window was shattered. Broken glass and snow clung to the man's bloody face.

My father was next to me now, holding his side, grimacing in pain. He leaned against the car.

"Get her."

I looked around me. No one was peering from a window, no one walked the streets. The whole thing had gone unnoticed. I moved as fast as I could, grabbing the man by his collar and pulling him down. I reached for the woman, lifted her under her shoulders, and threw her on the dead man, faceup. She was still alive, her breath coming in bubbling gulps. Blood was dripping from her nose. She wouldn't last long. I wanted to feel something: pity, regret—some human emotion. I felt nothing.

I slammed the door.

My father pushed himself away from the car, handed me some keys. He threw his arm around my shoulder and we mounted the stoop.

"Big key with the green plastic cover," he said.

My body still quivering, I fumbled and dropped the keys. I cursed as I dug frantically at the snow. Nothing. I was about to panic when I found them. Standing, I shook the snow off, twisted the key and pushed open the door. We tumbled inside the overheated vestibule. There was another locked door.

"Same key."

The door opened on a tidy little hall with a wide staircase covered with faded and worn carpeting in a vaguely Oriental pattern. I started for the steps up.

My father held me back.

"Basement," he said.

"I thought . . ."

"Basement," he repeated, tapping the keys. "Red plastic cover."

Still holding my father, we walked to the end of the hall and found the door to the basement stairs. On it was a large hasp and padlock. The door opened with a loud creak.

We both held our breath. The moment passed.

"The light switch is on the right."

I found the switch. A bare bulb hanging from zip cord lit the steps and basement beyond. The odor of mothballs and insecticide assaulted my nostrils. The stairs were too narrow for us to descend side by side, so I went first, my father behind me, one of his large hands on my shoulders.

Like the hall, even the low-ceilinged basement was broom clean and neat. Little storage cages made of two-by-fours and chicken wire filled with strollers, skis, and cardboard boxes lined the rear wall.

"Which one?" I asked my father.

He shook his head slowly. "The boiler."

We approached the hissing beast. It was running full out. I started to sweat. I was wondering how the hell you hid something in a boiler when my father spoke again.

"The old flue. Take the cover off."

The sheet-metal boiler flue went into a brick chimney about three feet wide. Next to the boiler flue was a dull metal cover where another flue must once have entered.

I pulled at the cover. It was fastened tight.

"There are tools at the back," he said, leaning against the wall.

A small workbench sat in the corner. Tools were neatly arranged on a pegboard. I trotted over, found a small crowbar, and started in on the flue cover.

The mortar was dry and flaky. It crumbled as the screws pulled loose. I was pulling hard when it finally gave way. My momentum threw me off balance and the back of my hand hit the boiler flue. There was the sudden smell of burning hair and flesh. I stifled a scream as I pulled my hand away from the searing metal. The red raw patch of burn started to ooze. I ran back to the workbench and took the cleanest rag I could find and ripped it in half. I found a roll of gray duct tape and bound my hand. I took the other half of the rag and roll of tape back to my father.

He was reaching into the hole behind where I'd ripped off the sheet metal. His hand came out with an old olive-drab knapsack. He laid it gently on the floor.

"That it?"

"That's it."

I held up the rag and tape. "Let's see it," I said.

"Lousy shot," he said, lifting his coat and turtleneck with obvious pain. "Fires three rounds. Only got me once."

Blood seeped from a round hole just above his hip on what little flab there was on his middle. He was trim and fit, but his skin was translucent and smooth. I looked at his back. There was a matching hole there.

"Clean through," I said.

"I would have used hollowpoints," he answered.

I ignored him.

"Hold this on your front," I said, tearing the rag in half again.

He took the cloth and placed it against the wound. I pulled the rest of the improvised bandage to his back, wrapping the tape around his midsection. I kept wrapping until the roll was empty.

"I can hardly breathe," he said, pulling down his turtleneck and smoothing his coat.

"I've got to stop the bleeding."

I took stock. The small rips the bullet had made in his coat were hardly noticeable; what little blood had seeped through simply made a darker spot on the dark-gray fabric. I hefted the knapsack and slung it on one shoulder, then slipped a glove on my good hand. I drew a deep breath as I tugged the other glove over the burn.

"Can you make it?" I asked. I looked at my watch. We'd been

gone just over an hour. I didn't know how long Tuesday and the kids would wait.

"Yeah," he said. "Give me a hand."

We reversed our steps. Standing on the stoop, we caught our breath and gave the block the once-over. A bunch of older kids down the street were hurling snowballs and laughing. No one was near the car in front of us, the one with the dead bodies.

We walked. Slowly. I was more alert than I'd been since those first few weeks in Vietnam. I now considered everyone and everything a threat.

As we turned the corner a teenage couple passed us, rosy-cheeked and arm in arm, their eyes clear and bright.

"Merry Christmas," the girl said.

I stiffened. My hand found the revolver in my pocket.

My father squeezed my arm.

"And to you too, my dear," he replied in his best brogue, a smile on his face. "Such a fine night for a walk."

The girl pulled closer to her boyfriend, making way for us with exaggerated deference. I knew what she was thinking: How wonderful, father and son enjoying a walk on a beautiful winter's night.

I relaxed my grip on the pistol. If she only knew.

8

I HURRIED MY father along as much as I dared, hoping Tuesday was using her Vietnamese senses, ignoring the hour and a half we'd been gone, letting her feelings rather than the clock judge the flow of time.

When we got into the car Marie's head was against Tuesday's shoulder, and Tuesday was singing her a lullaby. Nick sat with his knees to his chest staring blankly ahead.

Marie leaped from her seat and into my arms. She landed on my bad hand. I pulled back, accidentally flipping her off my lap. She shrank away from me.

I gently pulled her close, stroking her hair. I didn't trust myself to speak, my heart was still racing, the dying woman's eyes flashing before me. My hand was throbbing.

"You okay, Dad?"

It was Nick.

"Yeah. Just a little burn."

"Burn?"

"I'll explain later."

My father turned on the engine, pushed the heater to high, opened his window a bit, and laid his head on the back of the seat. He closed his eyes and I thought for a moment he'd fallen asleep.

"I have a friend," he said. He sounded weary.

"Where?"

He looked over at me, then turned away. "Not far. Columbia Heights on the promenade. Mile or two."

I thought about the drifting snow outside. "No way we can drive. Can you walk it?"

"I'll have to."

"Can we trust this friend?"

He looked at me again, held my eyes for a long moment. There was something in his silence but what it was I couldn't tell. He kissed Marie's forehead. A few more seconds passed.

"We better go," he said, opening his door.

Everyone zipped coats and put on caps and pulled on gloves.

THE STORM WAS spent. People were out. Industrious types were sweeping the snow from their cars and starting to shovel. The rest were taking advantage of the early Christmas gift. Parents pulled bundled tots on sleds. Apartment dogs bounded frantically. People who probably hadn't said hello to each other in years were smiling and waving. We started walking; just another family out on a stroll.

My father and Nick took the lead. Tuesday and I followed side by side. The snow was up to Marie's knees so I carried her, my father's knapsack bouncing on my shoulders.

Nick and my father were talking. I wondered what these two people, linked by blood but separated by two lifetimes, had to say to each other.

Tuesday and I walked in silence. I wanted to tell her about the couple in the car, the man in the backyard. I wanted to hold her tight and let her know how afraid I was of losing them. But though Marie's eyes were closed, I knew she was still awake and would hear every word. I recalled the ironic boast I used to make to anyone who'd listen that I'd kill for my family. Tonight it had become real.

The worst of it was that we seemed to be losing ground with every step. So far, all my father's plans had disintegrated. I'd just killed two people. My family was trudging through drifts of snow, running from an enemy who seemed to be waiting for us at every turn. But I was overwhelmed with joy. I knew it was perverse and twisted but we were together, all of us. I found new happiness in every step. I started to whistle my mother's favorite song, "Greensleeves."

My father slowed and looked back at me. I saw the same mad glimmer in his eyes that must have been in mine. He was hurting, but once in his stride, his hand on Nick's shoulder, he began to sing as I whistled, his baritone strong and clear.

We ran through the song, then walked on in silence again. The wind began to pick up and the temperature started to drop. I was breathing hard. Marie was now asleep, and it was hard keeping her head on my shoulder as I navigated the deep snow. We turned the corner of Columbia Heights. The windy chill had pushed everyone but a few teenagers back inside.

My father stopped in front of the most stately building on the street full of elegant brownstones. In spite of my exhaustion, the builder in me knew a gem when I saw one. It was three full stories, capped by a steeply pitched slate roof dotted with copper-clad oval windows. Everything about the house was balanced and perfectly proportioned. It stood serene and confident, making no apologies for being the most beautiful belle at the ball.

My father started to climb the wide stone steps. He stumbled. Nick, fast in the way only twelve-year-old boys can be, managed to stabilize him and help him the rest of the way. Tuesday and I followed.

"Ring the bell, Nicholas," my father said softly. I'd stopped calling my son Nicholas two years ago. For whatever reason, he'd all of a sudden started to hate being called by his full name and would bridle every time he heard it uttered. I noted that he responded immediately to my father without a trace of anger, a courtesy he would never have allowed me.

A bell sounded softly from within. A woman's voice, clear and well modulated, escaped a modern intercom discreetly installed near the door's sidelight.

"Who is it?"

"It's me, Lita. John."

John?

"Let me in, Lita. We have to talk."

"I thought we'd already done that."

"Please . . ."

A dozen heartbeats later, the latch on the tall oak and glass door clicked. My father pushed in, holding it open for the rest of us. We hurried in, happy to be free of the biting wind.

If anything, the inside of the house was more beautiful than the outside. The tall ceilings were trimmed with robust moldings. Champagne-yellow walls topped apricot wainscoting. Oriental rugs laid on polished oak floors. Old oils of schooners hung in gilt frames lit by brass lamps.

There was the rustle of silk. Muted footsteps came from the stairway directly in front of us. We all looked. The outline of a figure in a pale-pink robe descended the stair, moving with an easy grace. She stopped at the last step, put a slender hand on the rail post, and looked us over.

The woman and the house were one and the same; both were born beautiful and had aged magnificently. While the house had a century or so on her, I guessed the woman in front of me to be somewhere between fifty and sixty. The robe accentuated her small waist, full hips and breasts. She had thick auburn hair that just brushed her square shoulders. I knew she still caused men's heads to turn in appreciation.

She studied my father, waiting for him to speak. When he didn't, her clear green eyes locked on mine, lingering a moment before taking in Nick, Tuesday, and Marie.

My father started to walk to her. He held out a hand. "Lita . . ."

He staggered, bracing himself against the wall. His hand dropped and he slid to the floor.

The woman hurried to his side. I handed a still-sleeping Marie to Tuesday and knelt beside the woman and my father. She took his pulse with one hand and held back his eyelid with the other, looking at his pupil.

"He's been shot," I offered.

She didn't flinch or take her eyes off him. "Where?"

I held up his sweater and showed her the bandage.

She stood.

"Help me," she said, picking up his ankles.

I put my hands under his arms and lifted with her.

"In here," she said, jerking her head to a library near the hall.

While I was having trouble supporting what I guessed was my father's two hundred pounds with my injured hand, the woman handled him firmly and without apparent effort.

"The couch," she said.

We placed him gently on a red leather sofa facing a huge fireplace.

A light sheen of sweat coated her forehead. She walked to the phone, picked it up and punched 911.

"Hello? Police?"

I lunged for the phone, took it from her, and hung up. Her eyes blazed.

"He needs to go to the hospital!"

"No hospital," I said with more conviction than I felt.

It must have hit her then. The uncanny resemblances between my father, Nick, and I. She cocked her head slightly to the side.

The phone rang. She picked it up slowly and kept her eyes on mine.

"Oh. No, Officer. I'm sorry. It was a mistake. I thought someone was trying to get in the house but it was just some children throwing snowballs. No . . . that won't be necessary. But thank you for offering. Yes . . . Good night."

She put the phone back in its cradle. "Who are you?"

She knew the answer but needed to hear me tell her.

"His son." I turned to the doorway where Tuesday stood with the children. "And that's my wife and our children, his grandchildren."

She nodded slowly. Then her face seemed to crumble, her eyes growing moist. She took a deep breath, fought for control and won. "Why can't we take him to the hospital?"

"It's not safe."

"What?" She looked baffled.

I lost it.

"Listen, damn it! I don't even get it myself! He said you could help. If you can't or you don't want us here, give the word and we're gone." I laughed. "Shit, even if he dies I'll know how to handle it. He's done it before. . . ."

I felt a hand on mine. It was Tuesday silently telling me to be quiet. She looked at the woman for a long while before speaking.

"My children haven't eaten all day. They need some food, maybe a warm bath. Sleep. Danny and his father . . . all of us are in danger. We need your help."

As the woman studied Tuesday, Marie started to cry softly. Nick put his arm protectively around his sister. The woman turned to me.

"There's a black satchel on the shelf upstairs in my study," she said without taking her eyes from mine. "Third door on the right. Get it."

I didn't move. "Listen . . ."

"Lita. Lita Ward."

"Okay, Lita. My father needs a doctor . . ."

Her green eyes were steady.

"I *am* a doctor. If you want him to live, you'll get the bag—and hurry it up."

She turned to Tuesday. "The kitchen's down the hall at the back. Put up two big pots of water. Bring them to boiling."

Tuesday nodded and left, holding Marie's hand.

I took the steps two at a time. When I came back, Lita was cutting away my father's turtleneck with a pair of scissors. I set the black leather case at her feet.

She opened the old-fashioned satchel, took out a bunch of instruments, and handed them to me. She pulled a pair of reading glasses from the pocket of her robe and perched them on her nose.

"Give these to your wife," she said, looking over the top of her glasses. "Have her boil them."

"Are you a surgeon?"

She laughed. "Hell, no. I'm an neuropharmacologist. Can't stand the sight of blood. I close my eyes when I get a flu shot. Got out of medical school by the skin of my teeth. I haven't opened this case in years. The only reason I keep it on the shelf is to remind me that drugs are better than the knife."

As she was talking she cut away the last of the bandage. He was still bleeding. She probed around the wound gently. My father moaned.

"We've got to stop the bleeding. Get some clean towels from the hall linen closet upstairs. Lots of them."

When I came back with the linens, Tuesday was standing in the library.

"I'll help her," she said, reaching out and taking the towels from my hands. "You feed the kids."

"But . . ."

Lita took a cloth from Tuesday and handed it to me.

"We have to sterilize these instruments," she told me calmly. "There's rubbing alcohol in the pantry. Pour some on the towel. Boil the instruments for ten minutes, then pour out the water and drop the instruments on the towel. Bring it back to me with the bottle of alcohol."

She looked carefully at Tuesday, her glance lingering on the scar. "Ready?"

Tuesday nodded.

"Then let's scrub up the best we can." She stood. "We've got to clean him, suture him, and hope the bullet missed anything important."

I put the towels on the couch and started to leave.

Lita put her hand on my arm. Her skin was warm and dry, her voice a little shaky.

"One thing," she asked.

"Okay."

"His name. His real name."

I knew instantly that I hadn't been the only one who had been lied to and cheated by my father. He'd done the same to her. I wondered about my mother. Had he cheated her as well?

"Well, before he disappeared twenty-nine years ago I called him dad. Everyone else called him Sean. Sean Maguire. But maybe it's really Hennessey. Or Jones. Or Smith. We'll have to ask him."

"Yes," she said. "Let's."

9

THE BROWNSTONE'S KITCHEN was big and modern. And from my practiced eye, the custom glass-fronted cabinetry and commercial-quality appliances cost more than I'd paid for our little house.

The pan I was turning the ham and cheese omelets in was French. The plates I slid them onto English. Looking across the six-burner stainless steel stove, lower Manhattan sparkled brightly through crystal-clear floor-to-ceiling glass fronting the breakfast room.

I placed the steaming plates on the glass-topped table where Nick and Marie waited. This was their second serving.

"Can I have more rye toast?"

"Is there more orange juice?"

"Yes and yes. Hold on."

I dropped four slices of rye in the German toaster and poured another glass of fresh-squeezed orange juice. My hands started to shake.

I imagined my father and Lita eating caviar and drinking champagne in this very same kitchen while my mother was sitting cold and alone in hers, sipping weak tea. Then I pictured my father and Lita lying in each other's arms under expensive comforters awash in postcoital endorphins while my mother cried herself to sleep.

The plate and cup of juice hit the glass table harder than I'd wanted.

"You kids eat. I'll be right back."

I walked to the front library, fists clenched.

Blood-soaked towels lay on the floor. Tuesday adjusted the aim on the desk lamp as Lita stitched the wound in my father's back. I moved closer.

"When did you meet my father?"

"Why?"

"Just answer the question."

My voice was tight. Tuesday and Lita looked up at me for a moment before returning to their work.

"A few years ago."

"How many is a few?"

"Does it matter?"

I controlled myself as best I could. "Yes. It does."

Tuesday poured some alcohol on a towel and dabbed the wound clean. In spite of what she'd said earlier, the small curved needle in Lita's hand moved with a sure swiftness as she placed another suture.

"Until tonight, I thought John Hennessey, or Sean Maguire, or whoever he is, was a childless widower I'd fallen in love with but had left my life forever."

"That doesn't answer my question."

"June 4, 1992."

I had her now.

"A minute ago it was 'a few years ago.' Now it's a date. How can you be so sure?"

She didn't stop or look up at me.

"It was my birthday. I was sitting on a bench on the promenade, wondering whether I should jump over the rail and onto the BQE or not, whether anyone would care if I did.

"A man sat near me. 'Can't be that bad,' he said, spreading his arms wide. 'It's a fine spring day. You're beautiful and alive. It's a sin to ask for more.'

"I looked at him. He was smiling but his eyes betrayed him. There was a sadness deeper and heavier than my own. And he'd let me know it with just one glance. It was frightening to be read so easily and quickly by someone. To have him display his pain to me just as effortlessly. I wiped the tears from my eyes and ran home without a word to him."

She checked her work, then put down the needle. Her hands rummaged in the medical kit and came out with a pack of gauze and white tape.

"The next day I was eating breakfast and looked out at the happy young couples and children on the promenade. And there he was, sitting at the same bench, hands on his knees. I watched him watching the families, saw his head following parents and children. I wanted to see him again. I ran upstairs, changed, and hurried outside. When I got back, he was gone."

"I looked for him every morning all spring but he never returned."

My father's eyes opened groggily. He looked first at me, then at her, then closed his eyes again. Lita ran a hand lovingly along his stubbled cheek and stood.

"By the end of the summer I'd stopped looking for him. Then one September morning, there he was. I didn't bother to change. I ran outside in my robe and slippers.

"I sat next to him, breathless. He smiled. If anything his eyes were sadder than the first time I'd seen him. I'd waited months for this moment but was suddenly speechless.

" 'Ah, the mystery woman,' he said. Though I must have looked like a madwoman in my robe and slippers, it didn't even faze him. 'I see you're feeling better. That's good. I wondered whether I'd see you again.'

"I finally found my voice.

" 'I saw you the next day, watched you. By the time I came out, you were gone.'

"He shook his head slowly from side to side.

" 'I knew someone was watching. Just didn't know it was you.'

" 'Is that why you didn't come back? Because you thought you were being watched?'

"The sadness in his eyes was replaced by something else. He reached out for me. I tried to pull away but his grip tightened. His eyes became hard.

" 'Why were you watching me?'

"It wasn't a question. It was an accusation. I was afraid. I'd been a fool to dream about a man on a park bench, and now I knew he was paranoid and had a quick and dangerous side. He saw my fear. His grip loosened. I pulled my hand away.

" 'I'm sorry,' he said, and started to walk away."

She looked over at my father, held herself tightly. "But it had been so long since . . . since someone . . . and . . ."

She stopped abruptly and looked at me, her eyes hooded.

"I think I've told you enough," she said.

She was right. I'd heard more than I wanted. She studied me for a long moment then walked past me and went upstairs.

Tuesday shut off the desk lamp and pulled a soft cotton blanket over my father. His breathing was deep and steady. She took me by the elbow, leading me to the kitchen.

"Why were you so cold, Danny? She's a good woman. I think she loves your father."

She took me by the arm, turned me to her. "Your mother was already dead, Danny."

I pictured myself without Tuesday or the kids, without anyone for years. Thought about Lita Ward alone, crying on a park bench. Would I be able to resist? Would I want to? I looked down at Tuesday, brought her to me and folded myself around her.

"So my father mourned my mother six years before he met Lita. Or did he? Were there other women before her . . . during . . . Is six years enough . . . ?"

"Your father's not a saint, Danny," she whispered in my ear. "He's just a man. Like you."

"Is that all? Just a man."

She looked up at me, smiling. "Just a man as I am just a woman."

"But you're not 'just' a woman. You're . . ."

She held a finger to my lips.

"You and Nick," she said, shaking her head. "Always looking for more when what is in front of you is enough. Thinking of yesterday—or tomorrow, missing today. Making what is clear cloudy."

I kissed her gently, buried my head in her hair.

"What would I do without you?" I whispered in her ear.

"What I would do without you?" she said, her tone calm but steady. "Miss you. Think of you. Honor your memory. Raise our children. Live."

I felt the silkiness of her hair, imagined myself dead and gone, someone else holding her, running his hands in the soft musty hollows of her body I knew so well.

I nudged her gently away, held her at arm's length.

"Well, you can forget that," I said more to myself than her. "I'm not going anywhere. And neither are you."

We started to walk to the kitchen.

"See," she said, smiling. "Like I said. A man."

The kids took quick showers and then we tucked them in the guest-room beds. Exhausted and confused, they were asleep before I shut off the light and closed the door.

LITA WAS IN the breakfast room, blowing softly over a steaming cup of what looked like tea, looking at the skyline across the East River. A stack of sandwiches sat neatly in the center of the table.

She saw our reflection and turned to face us. "I made you something to eat."

The towers of Manhattan seemed to float on the inky black river. The wind roared off the water and buffeted the building, but the kitchen was warm and cozy. We sat at either end of the table, bookends with Lita between us.

"John needs a unit of blood, maybe two, some IV fluids and antibiotics," she said. "I'm on staff at Long Island College Hospital. It's around the corner. I could check him in under a different name . . ."

Her voice was husky. Maybe she'd been crying.

"It's the first place they'd look."

"Who? The Mafia?" She tilted her head, smiling sarcastically. "Tell me, damn it."

We were now intimate strangers, linked together across the boundaries of time and place by the man I knew as my father and she knew as John Hennessey. And like me, I also knew she was wondering about the lies he'd told her and where the truth really was.

"He called it a cosmic train wreck. It has to do with the war."

"Our war? The Second World War?"

"Right."

"After all these years." She laughed. It sounded thin and brittle.

"I'll be blunt. I know a little more than nothing at all. But what I do know is that we're in some pretty deep shit."

It felt good saying what I'd been thinking since last night. "And we've got a few problems. Tonight I shot and killed two people. And last night I helped throw the body of a man my father killed into some marshes at Sands Point."

I was on a roll now. Tuesday covered my good hand with her own, held it tightly.

"And if my father is right, just running won't save us. I know it's hard to believe, but if you put him in the hospital, it wouldn't take them long to find him. Then you. Then us. It's a risk I'm not prepared to take."

Lita sat back in her chair as if pushed. I'd seen her flinch when I told her about the killings.

She fidgeted with her mug, working hard at avoiding my eyes. If she was anything like me, right now she was trying to figure out whether we were all crazy or not. I knew she'd seen my bandaged hand before, but now it was a perfect and well-needed distraction.

"What happened to your hand?"

"It got burned."

She hurried out of the kitchen.

I started to stand. I wanted to follow her, see that she didn't do something logical and sane like call the police again. Tuesday seemed to read my mind.

"Don't worry, Danny. Trust her. For now."

Lita came back with her old medical kit, sat, put her glasses back on, and took my damaged hand. She cut the silvery duct tape and peeled away the bandage in a swift steady motion. I couldn't help but cry out. The wound was ugly. Clear liquid started to ooze from deep pockets.

She whistled.

"Fill a big mixing bowl with water and ice," she told Tuesday. "Boil these instruments again. Go back to the library and bring me the reading lamp."

Something was happening between the two women. I might not agree or understand, but they were already a team.

"This burn should be properly debrided and cleaned. If you or your father's wounds get infected and you go septic on me . . ." She didn't finish the thought.

Tuesday brought the bowl and the lamp, and put them on the table. Lita gently lifted my hand and put it in the freezing water. It started to numb. The throbbing decreased.

Lita lifted my hand from the water, looked at the wound, and put it back in again.

Then she held her mug to her lips and looked over it at me. Her voice was soft, almost childlike. "Can I ask you something?"

"Go ahead," I encouraged her. "I think we'd both better get used to a lot of questions."

There was a short pause, then it came out in a rush. "Is there a Mrs. Maguire?"

I'd been wondering when she'd ask, figured maybe she'd take the easy way out and ask Tuesday. Asking me took guts.

"Her name was Olivia."

"And . . ."

"If you met my father in '92 she'd have been dead for six years."

She let out a long breath I wasn't aware she had been holding. "That's why you wanted to know when we met."

I nodded.

It wasn't much. But it was enough. She sat a bit taller and wasn't afraid to look at me now.

Tuesday came back with the sterilized instruments.

Lita picked up a small scalpel and took my hand from the ice water. "Where's your pain threshold?"

"A little lower than your gore tolerance."

She smiled. "Then you should be happy. We'll both suffer. Cleaning burns is disgusting work. And it hurts like hell."

"Wow. Thanks, Doc. I feel better already."

"I could give you some pain medication, a drink."

I thought about the bodies in the car. They'd soon be missed. We were safe—for now. But I didn't want to be doped up and dreamy if any new threats arrived.

I shook my head. Tuesday held my forearm to the table. Her hands were small and delicate but sinewy and strong like the rest of her. I took a deep breath and looked out the window. A tug was navigating the river, its running lights bobbing. I tried to imagine who was on the sturdy little boat, where they were going this freezing winter evening and why.

Her first probes of the wound were tentative and hurt no worse than the throbbing. But soon she started to clean the burned flesh and dirty cloth from my hand with firm and concentrated motions. I tried to keep thinking about the little tug, but her every move sent jolts of pain all the way to my ears. Even the soft wash of her exhalations on the wound made me want to scream. My vision started to blur.

Tuesday put a clean towel in my mouth. I bit it with all my strength. I knew I passed out once or twice because each time I did, I woke screaming through the clenched towel.

I must have fainted one final time, because the next thing I knew, Lita was wrapping clean gauze gently around my hand and the towel was out of my mouth. I was too exhausted to speak.

Lita stood, took off her glasses, collected her instruments of torture, and went wearily to one of the cabinets. She returned with a bottle of aspirin, took my good hand, and shook a small pile of the white pills into it.

I swallowed them dry.

"I'll sleep in the library," she said. "Keep an eye on John . . . him. You two can use my bed. It's the room at the end of the hall. There are more towels and robes in the bathroom linen closet."

I stood shakily, the pain from my hand unbearable.

"If I'm not here when you wake up it's because I went to the hospital. I need equipment. Surgical kits, oral and topical antibiotics, medications, IV drips."

My face must have betrayed my paranoia.

"Don't worry. I have the keys for the main supply room in the basement, away from the nurses' stations. No one will know."

All I had strength to do was nod. If she was going to run or call the police, I could do nothing to stop her.

Tuesday helped me up the stairs. I lowered myself on the king-size bed and tried to pull off a shoe. It was too hard. I lay down and closed my eyes.

10

I SAT BOLT upright, soaked in a cold sweat, fighting for breath, my hand throbbing. Tuesday lay beside me, breathing deeply. The small clock on the nightstand read 4:13 A.M. Usually when I slept anywhere but my own bed I awoke disoriented and momentarily lost. Not now. I knew exactly where I was and why.

I got up as smoothly as I could. Tuesday rolled to her side but didn't wake. I was dressed in a man's flannel pajamas. I had a vague memory of Tuesday taking off my socks before I fell unconscious. I notched up the fact that she had managed to undress me and get the pajamas on my inert body to her years of practice with the kids. It wasn't that I was clumsy, but every time I tried to change a sleeping child from street clothes to PJs, the result was a hysterical kid. But Tuesday could not only change the kids' clothes as they slept, she could also give them a sponge bath and trim their nails.

The house was quiet and still. My footsteps were hushed on the deep carpeting. I looked in on the kids. Nick hadn't moved an inch; he never did. Marie, on the other hand, was an active and light sleeper. Her covers lay in a pile on the floor. Moving with as much stealth as I could muster, I put the blankets back on her. She rolled once. I held my breath. Then she buried her head on the pillow, still asleep. I backed out slowly.

Embers of the fire still crackled in the library fireplace. Lita was curled like a cat in a large leather armchair she'd moved next to the couch. Her legs were tucked beneath her. It wasn't hard to imagine her as a young girl doing the same.

I looked closely at my father. A thin sheen of perspiration coated his forehead. His breathing was slow and steady.

I walked to the kitchen, rummaged around, and found the coffee, filters, and coffeemaker. I started to pour water into the top of the machine. Someone was close behind me.

I almost swung the pitcher at the sound. I stopped myself just in time when I realized it was Lita. Some water splashed on the tile floor.

"Can't sleep?" she asked.

I emptied the rest of the water into the coffee machine. "What I'd love to do is wake up and find out this was all just a very bad dream," I said, then turned to face her. "When we first showed up you said you two were done talking. I got the feeling you meant it."

"I did."

"And?"

"It wasn't me who walked away," she answered.

"Me either."

"So then you must know what I mean."

She was right, but it didn't give me any comfort comparing who he'd hurt more.

I took a mug from the cabinet, filled it, and poured in some milk and sugar, slamming doors and drawers as I went. I walked to the breakfast table with the pitcher of coffee and sat with my back to her, hoping she'd just leave me the hell alone.

She sat opposite me with her own mug and filled it with coffee. I looked past her.

"I . . ."

Her voice trailed off. The way she was stammering made it obvious she rarely made apologies; something I'd become a master at, primarily because I'd had so much practice.

"I'm sorry," she said. "Forgive me?"

I thought about all she'd done for us, all the chances she'd had to throw us out or call the police.

I nodded.

I heard a soft rustle and Tuesday's hands on my shoulders. She leaned in and kissed me on the nape of the neck. She smelled sleepy.

"I reached out for you and you were gone," she said, then sat next to me.

It was time to fill Lita and Tuesday in. I started telling them everything I could remember from the moment my father called me at the office until we arrived at her doorstep, without leaving anything out. I narrated it as though it had all happened to someone else.

Lita was as good a listener as Tuesday, and they gave me all the time I needed, particularly when it came to the killings, which were becoming less real with each passing hour. I left out the part of the conversation where my father told me his plan to kill Laughlin. I wasn't sure they would be ready for it. I sure as hell wasn't.

By the time I finished, my voice was raspy and it was dawn. They seemed as tired as I was, maybe more. We'd all learned too much, too quickly.

"What's next?" Lita asked.

I remembered my father's pack.

"Hold on," I said as I stood. "I'll be right back."

It was at the front door, right where I'd dropped it. It seemed heavier now. Maybe it was the added weight of the souls of the people I'd killed to get it.

I placed the pack on the table and sat again. It was olive drab with canvas straps and worn brass buckles. You could pick one just like it up in any surplus store, but I knew it had a more interesting history. From my story, Lita and Tuesday also knew what it was, where it had come from, and what I'd had to do to get it. And we all knew that whatever was inside was bound to reveal new truths we might not want to hear. We looked at it as though it were a cobra, coiled and ready to strike.

Lita stood, keeping a wary eye on the pack. "I'm going to check on John, then run down to the hospital to pick up the supplies."

"And I think I'll check on the children," Tuesday said, also getting to her feet.

It was either their respect for me or relief at having such convenient excuses to distance themselves from whatever surprises lay inside the worn cloth.

I had no excuses, so sat there regarding the lumpy form on the table. My hands stayed on my lap.

"Be back in an hour," Lita said from the doorway.

"Okay," I said without turning.

I sat looking out at the skyline until I heard the front door open and close. The house was absolutely silent.

The pack was as soft as worn flannel. The straps rustled as I slid them open, the brass ends making a dull clink as they passed through the buckles.

I reached inside slowly, half expecting something to jump out and bite me. I felt four distinct packages; each a different size, each wrapped in heavy oilcloth and tied with waxy twine.

I pulled them out one at a time and laid them side by side. They were unmarked. Knowing my father as I did, I was sure they were not assembled randomly but were somehow linked together. Each package would be a separate chapter in the story. But without him to explain there was no way of knowing the order, which to open first, which to save for last.

I chose the one nearest me and pulled it closer. The bow on the twine opened smoothly. I turned the bundle over and opened each flap of the thick cloth. Inside was a large old cigar box. I flipped the lid open. Surrounded by smaller individually wrapped packages was a larger one. I picked it out of the box and knew what it was even before I finished unwrapping it. I could feel the bold form beneath the cloth, knew it was the dagger from the attic. It felt just as heavy and lethal as I'd remembered as a boy, maybe even heavier. The cloth unfolded like the petals of a flower.

The knife, worn smooth by so many hands, caught the winter sun and gleamed. I refolded the cloth and put it back in the box.

The next bundle I opened contained a small fragment of gold. Though beautifully carved, its shape was abstract and indecipherable. I turned it this way and that, held it near, then far. I was about to give up trying to make sense of it when I felt a growing shiver run from my toes to my scalp. I suddenly pictured an angel with forward-stretched wings, the piece in my hand forming the last few feathers of one of them. Making the mental adjustment for scale and placement, I guessed the whole angel might have been eighteen or twenty inches long; just the right size for one of the cherubim facing each other across the Mercy Seat on the Ark of the Covenant. I shivered again as I placed the small golden wing back in the box, nestled in its wrapping.

I couldn't resist opening just one more package. This one was richer than either the dagger or the angel's wing. It was an intricate geometric golden pendant about three inches tall and an inch across. There was something distinctly modern about the piece, but I could tell it was very old. It was three interlocking pyramids, connected by golden rods that formed additional lines and angles between them. Each node of it contained a sparkling jewel. It was beautifully crafted and glinted in the morning sun. Each of the branchlike rods was inscribed in a tiny hand. I looked closer still, noting that the symbols were Hebrew characters. Even though I had no idea what it was, it was wrought as if by a magician's hands. Like the tip of the angel's wing, I knew it was worth more than just money to whoever knew what it represented. It felt warm and vibrant in my hand, mysterious and familiar at the same time. I slipped it in the pants pocket of my pajamas.

If, as my father had said, a dagger that once belonged to Judas Iscariot was priceless, what value could the tip of an angel wing from the time of Moses have? And the golden pendant, delicate and full of mystery, what of it? And the other packages in the box? How did you estimate the value of things beyond measure?

I closed the cigar box and pushed it reverently to the side; chose another of the packages at random.

As I opened it, the unmistakable must of old paper escaped. Folders and manila envelopes lay neatly stacked, one upon the other in descending order of size, like a truncated pyramid, the whole thing neatly tied with another length of waxed twine, which I opened with care.

On top was a slim three-by-five-inch notebook bound in black leather. I picked it up, opened it gently. A small piece of folded yellow legal paper slid to the table.

I unfolded it. The creases were sharp and well set. Lines of my father's unmistakable bold script ran across the page:

My Dearest Danny:
If you are reading this, I am dead. Perhaps when you are done, you will understand that I did what I had to do.
They say the truth will set you free. This is my final wish for you. If you can't forgive me, pray for my soul. And remember; love is stronger than time.
Your Father, Sean Maguire.

11

I WAS THE only person who could decipher my father's handwriting. Like everything else about him, the style was unique, a combination of slashing strokes and quirky loops. He loathed ballpoints and always used the same old Parker pen filled with royal-blue ink, saying that only a fountain pen could give the written word the same variations in inflection and tone as the spoken word.

He also felt written words had twice the power of those spoken; that thoughts committed to paper could never be retracted or forgotten. True to his word, he was a great note and letter writer. Many mornings I'd awaken long after he'd left for work to find a short note with my name on it sitting on the breakfast table. Usually he would just wish me a good day. Occasionally there would be more; instructions for a chore, or words of encouragement if he knew I was troubled or down. My mother, whose script was as beautiful and perfectly formed as a Palmer lesson book, asked him to write to her in block letters. When he didn't, she needed me to unscramble the message.

I'd saved many of the notes, kept them in a shoe box on a shelf in my closet. Sometimes when I felt strong enough, I would take the box down and reread them slowly, the memories bitter sweet.

Before I began reading again I checked in on my father. Tuesday must have beaten me to it because he looked serene and a fresh blanket had been carefully tucked around him.

I headed back to the kitchen and sat. As I began to read his journal, for a journal was what it was, it was as if he were speaking directly to me.

The first entry was dated 15 March 1942:

> I made up my mind. Art school will have to wait. The whole world's in a lot of trouble, and now we're finally in it all the way. I went down to Lafayette St. and joined up. The line was around the block, filled with guys from sixteen all the way up to forty-year-old geezers. Everyone was smoking, talking about how they couldn't wait to get in it, kill some Japs or Krauts. Me too.

The next twenty pages or so had short descriptions of his basic training in Fort Bragg, North Carolina. I learned about his new army buddies. They had nicknames like Butch, Walker, and Jonesy. Most of the entries had at least a few complaints about rotten food, night marches, and the lack of female companionship—things familiar from my own days of basic.

Then in August of that same year the entries became shorter, the gaps between them sometimes as long as two weeks. He noted his assignment to Engineering, the training, his new orders to Greenland.

His descriptions of Greenland were spare and terse. The isolation and long polar nights were taking their toll. I read about the air base in Narsarsuaq at the southern tip of Greenland, code-named Bluie West One—BW1, and the construction of the thousand-bed hospital and clinic. It was just as he'd told me when I was a child. He described the Inuits as taciturn and unbathed, the majestic scenery harsh and forbidding, the lack of diversions numbing, and his desire to fight, not build.

Then there was nothing until an entry from 22 November 1942. Everything about it was strikingly different, from the words to his handwriting, which was smaller and tighter. The entry ran for several pages, another change.

Back from special training in VA. I'm not supposed to keep any notes at all, I could be kicked out—or worse!—if they found out. But maybe one day my kids will want to know about their dad—if I ever have the chance to have any, that is—and what he did in the war.

I anxiously scanned the page.

It all started when this bunch of civilians showed up at BW1. About twenty of us were asked to assemble in the mess. The top banana, a tall distinguished gent with gray hair, asked for volunteers. DiMarco, the base clown, shouted out "Does it involve any dames?"

The gray-haired man pointed at DiMarco and told him to leave. That shut the rest of us up. This guy meant business and wasn't going to take any guff.

Then he passed out a form. It was official-looking, just a paragraph long. He said that before he told us anything else, we had to sign, and anyone who didn't want to could leave. Half the guys just got up and left, muttering under their breath about more army bullshit.

Now there were just six of us. I think the only reason I stayed was that I was so damned bored, I would have volunteered for ballet lessons!

They kept me and the other guys separate from everyone else for three days. They gave us IQ tests, reaction tests, PT runs, everything (and I'm not making this up) from giving a speech to checking our table manners. They kept asking us about the war, what we thought about the

Nazis and Japs, the Russians, Poles, even the French and
Irish. It was almost like a game, and more fun than I'd had
in months, even if it was the weirdest three days I've ever
spent.

Day four the tests were over. I found out that only me
and this guy Laughlin were left. He's from New York City
too, on the building crew—just like me. Worked as a
bricklayer till he enlisted. Laughlin's an okay guy, even if
he is real quiet and keeps to himself—kind of standoffish.
But he's always got some booze—I don't know how!—is a
hell of a poker player, and has the quickest hands I've ever
seen. Anyway, the gray-haired guy with the glasses comes
back and gives us a speech. His name is William Donovan
and he's head of the Office of Strategic Services, the country's secret operations group. He tells us being part of the
OSS will be dangerous, but if we want in, we're ready for
the next step. It was the most exciting moment of my life.
Me and Laughlin say "yes, sir," and out comes a new form,
longer than the first. It was a Secrecy Agreement. The long
and short of it is that if I ever tell anyone anything about
the OSS, the tests, the training, the people—anything,
then it's jail. I looked over at Laughlin. We shrugged and
signed the damn things.

Donovan takes the forms back and puts them into his
coat pocket. Then he shakes our hands, looking us each
right in the eye. He tells us he's proud to have us on board
and the country needs us.

Two days later Laughlin and me are on the next plane
out. It took us another three days to get to the Marine
Base at Quantico, Va.

Everything about the OSS is real hush-hush. We entered the base at night through a side gate. Our barracks
were on a fenced-off part of the base on about three hundred acres. Laughlin and me were put in separate sections.
Everyone was in civvies, so no one pulled rank.

It was six weeks that made basic look like kid stuff. We trained from before dawn until well after dark, sometimes all night long. Half the instructors were Limeys, and let me tell you, even with those accents, the Brits are tougher than nails. They gave us crash courses in just about everything: radio repair, codes and ciphers, dead-drops, poisons, advanced hand-to-hand, special weapons—you name it! We jumped out of planes at midnight, then would spend days in the field on survival missions, eating mushrooms and snared rabbits, practicing evasion techniques while other teams hunted us with dogs.

Even though we didn't ask too much about each other, I could tell most of the guys were college boys, not carpenters and bricklayers like Laughlin and me.

Not that it mattered. We were all on level ground; you screwed up, you were gone. One day I saw this guy Jack—a real hard case if you ever saw one—hesitate before he made one of the parachute jumps. The lost time made us miss our target. We had to circle back around to the drop point. Next day Jack was gone. It seemed every week another batch disappeared, always at night, never a good-bye. That's how the OSS works.

By the time training was over, there were 22 of us left from what I guessed were originally over 150 men. I was glad to see Laughlin made it too, even if he isn't exactly a pal. There wasn't an official graduation or anything. We were reminded to keep our traps shut and wait for orders. Three days later Laughlin and I were back at Bluie West One. Everyone wants to know where we were, what all the secrecy was about. If they find out it won't be from me—Loose Lips Sink Ships!

I don't want anyone to see me writing in this little black book, so I'll do it only when I can and keep it tucked tight and away so no one finds it. Shouldn't be too hard now that I know all the tricks!

I put the journal down and closed my eyes. I could see my father scribbling secretly in his little black book, a young man with reddish hair, firm muscles, and shining eyes, his hands smoother, less lined, more like Michelangelo's David than a real man's. How I wished I knew him then, when he seemed so innocent and carefree.

I closed the notebook then, wanting to hold onto the image of a young Sean Maguire, full of hope. My hand rested on the worn leather cover, knowing that whatever had cast the shadows plunging his heart into a cold darkness were inside, waiting for me to uncover.

I picked up the next neatly wrapped package. It was a thin legal-size folder, yellowed with age. Inside were brittle sheets of newsprint, each an official duplicate of some part of my father's army life. Written in the jargon of the day, it chronicled his induction to the army until his discharge at the end of '45. I wondered what was so special about the faded, crumbling papers he'd bothered to save for so long. I was about to go to the next pile when it hit me.

My father had said there would be no proof, no records at all of what had gone on, but here in front of me were what amounted to transport orders for unidentified TDYs—temporary duty assignments. Laughlin and my father left Greenland for destinations including Camp Myles Standish, Taunton, Massachusetts, Camp Upton, New York, Presque Isle, Maine, and New York City. Knowing what I did, I also understood the orders for Rest, Recuperation and Recovery so closely following the other orders. These would be the periods after their forays when they were given free rein to drink away the ghosts; just like my days in Vietnam when the SOG heavies were given R&R in Bangkok after action up north or Laos and Cambodia. If nothing else, these papers, meaningless in every other way, were official, stamped, and dated records that could be tied to real events.

And by putting together what I knew from history and what my father had already revealed, the rest of the possibilities tumbled out. I knew that after the war, the OSS was officially disbanded but never died. After several executive orders, it morphed into the CIA. And Laughlin had been there in the Agency's early days, climbed the ladder, became its chief.

If Laughlin was at the center of it and wanted things from his OSS days erased, it wasn't hard to imagine him carefully editing and cleansing official records, perhaps even destroying many, so no hard facts could be found. Also, if Osborne was Laughlin's inside man, I could see where information about a past sooner forgotten might be somehow "lost." And if a guy like Senator Aronstein was getting close to the truth, Laughlin wouldn't hesitate having him killed.

I heard the front door open and close. Muffled sounds began filtering through the stillness of the big old house. I quickly put everything back in the pack except the small black notebook, which I slipped into the breast pocket of my pajamas. As I stood, I felt the pendant with the jewels rub gently against my thigh as if to remind me of its presence.

I had just placed the pack on the bottom shelf of the pantry and closed the door when Lita and Tuesday came into the kitchen. Lita looked as if she'd seen a ghost. The hair on the back of my neck stood up.

"What's wrong?"

"You were right," she said, holding eye contact as she put a piece of paper on the table. "If I'd have brought him to the hospital, he . . . we'd all be . . ." She didn't bother finishing the sentence.

It was a computer printout. On top were photographs of my father and me. I was in three-quarter profile. I wasn't looking at the camera but somewhere past it. The image was flat and depthless, the kind long telephoto lenses produce. I had no idea who took the picture but knew that it was taken recently.

"This is only a few weeks old," Tuesday said, pointing at my picture and turning it so Lita could see. "See the coat? I bought it last month."

The image of my father was head on and had a surreal quality to it. The resemblance was strong, but the details were wrong; the lines of his jaw were paunchier, his eyes puffier.

"It's him, and it's not him," I said. "Laughlin probably took the last photo of him they had and had someone digitally 'age' it."

Lita didn't seem to hear me.

"Things were quiet when I got to the hospital this morning," she said. "Snowstorms usually keep the drunks and gang-bangers home. Last night was no different. I picked up what I wanted from the storeroom then went to my office to check my e-mail. I signed on and there at the top of the lab reports, memos, and that kind of stuff was a flashing red 'stat' message to selected staff—the kind of broadcast alert we use only for things like strep outbreaks, quarantines . . . medical emergencies that affect the whole hospital but we don't want posted on the bulletin board to scare the rest of the hospital personnel and patients."

Beneath the photographs were our names. A one-paragraph statement below said hospital personnel were being alerted to look out for the above individuals. It went on to say we might be injured and using different names, but that if either or both of us presented ourselves for treatment, we should be placed in isolation and the 800 number at the bottom of the sheet should be called immediately so that federal personnel could take over. Unspoken but implied was the warning that we were carrying some form of dangerous communicable disease.

It was just vague and official enough to be effective. Any doctor or nurse who ran into us most likely would escort us to a room, then make the call and run like hell to a shower with a gallon of Betadine.

The thing that struck me was that message lacked an agency logo or name and was unsigned. It meant my father had been correct; Laughlin was hunting us, all right, and he had the ways and the means, but he had some limits. Otherwise the memo would have been from someplace like the National Institute of Health.

I took my father's journal from my pocket and handed it to Tuesday.

"This is the beginning. His journal from the war. It was in the backpack. I think I understand a lot of it, but without his help it's going to be tough."

My hand instinctively reached for the pendant in my pocket.

"And this has something to do with it too," I said, giving it to Lita.

She held it to the cool winter sun, turning it this way and that, watching the light diffract through the prisms of the emeralds and rubies. "It's beautiful."

"There's more like it, in the pack."

"Like these?" she asked, handing it to Tuesday.

"One is a golden-hilted dagger my father said belonged to Judas Iscariot. And if I'm right, part of an angel's wing from the Ark of the Covenant."

There was something like wonder in her eyes.

I nodded.

"Right," I said.

"But the things you're talking about should be in museums, churches."

"I know. It all ties together—somehow. My father's 'suicide', Laughlin, the OSS, Aronstein's committee; his death. The religious icons. They're all connected."

I stood and took the pendant back from Tuesday. I closed my fingers around it, feeling its smooth edges, absorbing its warmth. I needed to think, and it was time to move.

12

THE UNMISTAKABLE SLAP of children's bare feet came from the hall. A moment later Nick and Marie raced into the kitchen and sat at the table, followed by Tuesday. The kids were out of breath and laughing about something that was obviously beyond adult understanding and not worth the effort of trying to explain. Instead they tossed off good mornings and asked what was for breakfast.

Lita excused herself to go check on my father. Tuesday and I swung into action, filling the space with a symphony of the everyday sounds and smells I'd started to take for granted: the magic of children's chatter, the smell of coffee and toast. I vowed that once this was all over, I'd do my damnedest to find hope and wonder with every sunrise.

After breakfast, Lita showed the kids the big-screen TV hidden artfully in the front parlor bookcase. Once they settled in, Tuesday and I went in to check on my father.

He was still unconscious. An IV was taped to his forearm, a drip bag hooked onto an umbrella stand.

"How's he doing?" I asked in a whisper.

"I'm not sure. His vitals are solid, but I'm worried about infection and what I can't see. Without some X rays, maybe a CT scan . . ." She let it trail off.

She took out her stethoscope and listened to his chest. She'd already replaced the makeshift bandages of last night with fresh hospital dressings, and I saw traces of brownish skin peeking from the gauze where he'd been swiped with disinfectant.

"He's holding on," she said quietly, giving his cheek a gentle caress.

I looked down at my father. His eyelids fluttered, threatened to open but didn't. His lips were chapped, his chin covered with stubble. I wondered if after all the years, these last forty-eight hours would be all we would have.

Under the bright beam of the banker's lamp Lita then changed the dressings on my hand and asked me if I was allergic to penicillin. I told her I wasn't and automatically lifted my sleeve to expose my arm. She filled a syringe from a small bottle, swabbed me down with an alcohol wipe, then gave me the injection. Unlike last night, the syringe and everything else came out of sterile hospital packages she'd filched from the storeroom.

Lita put her equipment away and sat next to my father. Tuesday came in a moment later, placing a tray of fresh coffee on the low table near the couch.

"What now?" Tuesday asked.

The more I thought, the more nervous I became. I had an image of Laughlin's men working the streets of Brooklyn, canvassing the area around the dead couple at Baltic Street in ever-widening circles, ready to intersect us. The walls of the brownstone, as thick and solid as they were, were starting to feel like a trap. I stopped pacing.

"Can you move him?" I asked Lita.

She looked at me like I was crazy. "Not without an ambulance and some EM techs."

Nine muted gongs came from the grandfather clock standing in the library. My father rolled slightly on the couch, groaned, then was quiet.

"Forget that," I said to Lita. "He'll have to stay with you." I looked at Tuesday. "But you and the kids have to get out of here," I said, envisioning innocent-looking couples with silencers and orders to kill.

"Maybe you can still make a flight to Hawaii."

My hand was on the phone when I heard my father's voice, croaky and weak.

"No. It's too late," he said, a labored breath between each word.

Lita rushed to his side. I was right behind her.

His eyes were bloodshot and unfocused, opening and closing in time to his breathing.

"Easy, John, easy," Lita said, rearranging his head on the pillow. "Dad?"

Somehow, he smiled.

"Just a scratch," he said slowly. "I'll be up in no—" His eyes closed.

"Damn!" I said, my balled fist hitting the sofa.

Lita took his pulse and nodded at me.

"Still with us," she said, adjusting the drip. "He'll probably go in and out like this for a while."

I started pacing again. Yesterday morning was one thing. But now Laughlin had lost another pair of hitters and had enough time to spread his net a little wider.

"He's right," I said. "We need someplace else. What with the storm, he knows we can't be far. He'll be watching the airports. Probably the train stations too. . . . They have to go someplace no one would think of, someplace we can get to on our own."

"My country place," Lita said matter-of-factly.

I turned to her. "Where is it?"

"Northwest Connecticut."

The way she saw it, even though Laughlin had obviously "found" John Hennessey, she was positive Laughlin could never tie him to her. She said the John Hennessey she knew was a loner with few acquaintances, none of whom he would swap stories with about a woman in Brooklyn Heights. As for herself, she said she kept pretty much to herself as well. I got the distinct impression her social life was quiet. And I was certain that none of the people she occasionally dined or went to the opera with were close enough to tell about her relationship with the mystery man from Cobble Hill. I couldn't help but think that their mutual exclusivity seemed to fit neatly into the rest of their odd relationship, built as it was on omission more than anything else.

Now that we had Lita with us, Hawaii became remote and un-necessary. It turned out that in addition to her Brooklyn brown-stone, she had a small apartment in Manhattan, her country place in Connecticut, and a small cottage in Negril, Jamaica.

The idea of having my family off the beaten track but within driving distance felt right. I said so.

Tuesday agreed and Lita immediately got on the telephone and made arrangements, putting the escape plan in motion with just three calls. The first was to her limo service, the next the charter company she always used arranging the flight from LaGuardia to the private airstrip just a few miles from the country house, and last a call to the live-in couple who watched the place. She told some-one named Alan that she was going to spend Christmas and New Year's there and wanted to be alone. She told him to stock up the house and take a couple of weeks off at the cottage in Negril, a kind of surprise holiday gift from her. It reminded me of a saying my mother used to use: "Rich or poor, it's nice to have money."

THE DAY WAS overcast but warmer. Steam rose from the river in huge white sheets. The dreamlike shapes were well formed and thick on the river, then thinned as they rose into wispy trails, finally disappearing against the light-blue sky. We sat at the breakfast table, finishing our plans.

Tuesday took notes as Lita explained the layout of the com-pound in Connecticut in detail: how to operate the heating system, where food and firewood were stored, whom to call for food de-liveries, and other details. Then they changed roles. Lita scribbled as Tuesday rattled off clothes sizes for us all, so Lita could replace the contents of the suitcases we'd left in the car near Baltic Street.

Then I instructed them in the same simple codes my father had drilled into me when I was a boy: two knocks then one, one ring, hang up, then redial, offsets for times and addresses. Next, Tuesday and I memorized the phone numbers for the house in Connecticut and the Brooklyn brownstone.

There was motion everywhere. Lita ducked out and went shopping for us. Tuesday did a quick load of laundry. The kids explored the attic. I took my father's pack into the library and, sitting near my still-unconscious father, spread the contents on the rug in front of me. Scattered everywhere on the ancient Oriental carpet were sparkling crosses, statuettes, talismans, and several old but still oiled handguns complete with boxes of ammunition.

I almost jumped out of my skin when I heard my father's voice.

"I'm parched," he said, his eyes now fully open and focused.

"Hold on."

I hurried to the kitchen and came back with a glass of water and a straw. He sipped it with his eyes closed, then opened them and looked around at the objects on the floor. He tried to sit up but didn't have the strength.

"Just lie still," I told him.

He nodded, closed his eyes, and was out again for a few minutes. I thought that was it, then his eyes opened again.

I picked up the angel's wing.

"Is this what I think it is?" I asked.

It was now four words for every breath.

"If you think that it's the last few feathers from one of . . . the cherubim on the Ark . . . then you're not alone."

"And this," I said, taking the pendant from my pocket and holding it up for him to see. His hand, the one with the IV, reached out weakly. I put the talisman in his palm. His fingers closed around it.

"The most powerful and mysterious of them all," he said, his voice growing stronger. "The rest may or not be as they are claimed, but of this there's no doubt. Its pedigree is pure."

"What is it?" I asked. I knew I was pushing him but I needed to know.

"The Tree of Life . . ."

"What does it mean?"

His voice dropped to a whisper. "Gershowitz . . ."

I leaned closer.

"What?"

"Rabbi . . . Isaac . . . Gershowitz. He can tell you . . ." he just managed to say before his fingers uncurled slowly and his eyelids drifted shut. I put my head to his chest. His pulse was agonizingly slow, and it must have been ten seconds before he finally took a deep, rattling breath.

I sat on the rug, the pendant in my hand. My own heart was racing. Regardless of what Lita had said, it seemed the distance between life or death for my father was getting shorter all the time. But at least I now had a name. Rabbi Isaac Gershowitz. A place to start.

I repacked the rucksack, except for the silenced automatic my father had lifted from the man in Port Washington. The face of the woman I'd shot with it last night flashed in front of me. I remembered my father's words, "tools of the trade," then shook off the image of the dying woman, ejected the clip, and reloaded it.

SOON LITA RETURNED from her shopping trip, her arms full of packages.

By noon we were ready to go. Two of Lita's suitcases were packed and in the front hall, the kids had their coats on, and a long black Lincoln sat waiting at the curb, engine idling. I took four of the ten thousand cash my father had given Tuesday and told her to hold on to the rest.

This was the third farewell in as many days. It's not that the good-bye hurt any less, it just didn't sting as much. Marie still cried, but not as hard or as long. Nick and Tuesday were stoic, straight-backed and in control.

I watched from the parlor window as the limo slid silently away on the slushy street. I tried to convince myself that like the fog on the river, all my troubles would soon disappear. That the snow-storm and killings were fragments of someone else's life. That my father was a hero and deserved to remain on the pedestal on which I'd placed him.

But the pain in my hand and the pendant pushing against my thigh made it impossible to enjoy even my boldest of lies. I dropped the curtain and got my coat from the hook in the hall.

Lita was with my father in the library, staring at the fire.

"Where are my father's things?" I asked quietly.

"There. By the desk."

I picked through his pockets, taking out the cigar tin with the folded articles and the cellular phone, and stuffed them in my parka. Then I picked up the rucksack and sat in the other arm-chair.

"Could I have the keys to your apartment in Manhattan?" I asked.

She got up and rummaged through her pocketbook. I heard the jingle of keys. She dropped them in my hand and gave me the address.

"What are you going to do?" she asked.

"I'm not sure," I answered, putting on my coat.

There was a loud pop from a log in the fireplace. My father stirred and moaned. I stroked his brow. He didn't react.

"How will I reach you if . . . ?"

"You won't," I said. "I'll call you."

I didn't want to answer any more questions. I wasn't sure of much, but the one thing I felt certain of was that I couldn't learn anything by sitting in a Brooklyn brownstone watching and wait-ing to see if my father died.

"Will you be coming back here?"

I shrugged.

I turned to leave but stopped short. I had a question of my own.

"It's hard for me to understand," I said.

"Understand what?"

"Why you'd risk all this," I said, my hand sweeping a wide arc meant to include everything in her domain, her position, her wealth, her life, "for someone who lied to you, someone you hardly really know."

"It's not that complicated, Danny. I love your father; loved him when all I knew was that he needed me as much as I needed him. And that's as much as I want. Maybe when this is over we'll have time . . ."

She didn't finish the thought. It was just as well. Today was hard enough; thinking about a future was asking too much.

We walked to the front door. I opened the pack, slipped out the automatic, and dropped it into my pocket.

"Remember," I said, my hand on the knob. "One ring, then two."

"Right."

There was one last thing. I zipped my coat and looked into her eyes. They were an iridescent jade.

"If you don't hear from me in a couple of days—whatever happens, promise me you'll do your best for my family."

"I promise."

I couldn't think of anything else to say. I left, the door closing behind me with a firm snap.

13

I T WAS SUNNY and warm, almost springlike. The only traces of the wild beauty of last night's winter storm were huge boulders of dirty gray snow lining the roads and thick rivers of sludge oozing into the sewers.

Every once in a while I'd stop to rearrange the pack, zip or unzip my coat, and look around to see if I was being followed. If I was, I didn't see them. Once in a while I'd touch the pistol as if it were some kind of charm.

I'd told Lita a half truth; I *did* have an idea of what I was going to do and where I was going to go. I had the name that my father had worked so hard to tell me: Gershowitz. Rabbi Isaac Gershowitz. It was obvious he knew some of the story. It would be my job to find out how much and why my father thought I should see him. I didn't want Lita or Tuesday to know because if worse came to worst, they couldn't tell what they didn't know. And I figured that if the shit did hit the fan, they might have a chance of surviving.

The subway was packed with the lunchtime crowd. The car was hot, the air fetid. Normally I would have found it claustrophobic and suffocating, but not today. I enjoyed a newfound comfort being surrounded by ordinary people doing everyday things.

The train's wheels screeched, the lights flickered on and off, and sparks jumped from the darkness. As the train rocketed through the tunnel under the East River, I found it hard to think about the things that had crept into my dreams last night.

I changed trains twice, ending up on the street just a few blocks from my office. After several tries, I finally found a pay phone that worked. There were two messages on my answering machine. The first was from Eleanor Safter. She wanted to talk about the color of the marble in *her* bath. The second was from Mr. Safter. He wanted me to know that the plasterers had waited for me all morning and finally gone home. He demanded I call him immediately, slamming the phone down for emphasis. I reset the machine.

I PICKED UP a paper and found a greasy spoon on Fifth, the kind that had probably once been Formica and fluorescents but was now all low-voltage lighting and granite tabletops. I settled into a booth near the rear, my back to the wall. The lunch crowd was long gone so I had the place to myself.

The menu the waiter brought was as big as some small-town newspapers. I gave it back to him without reading it and ordered eggs over easy, sausage, home fries, buttered rye, and coffee. He didn't even write it down.

Soon the table was cleared and my coffee cup refilled. I was the only customer and my meal was my ticket to linger. I reached in the pack and took out my father's diary, sat back and picked up where I left off.

After OSS training, the entries returned to telegram style; nurses he screwed, bourbon he drank, poker pots he won and lost. The long Arctic nights in Greenland.

Then there was a gap of several months before he picked up again. These new entries were different from any that came before, even down to the script, which alternated between his usual bold style to angry strokes and cramped scribbles. I didn't need a degree in handwriting analysis to recognize my father was having a hard time.

Each small sheet of the journal had two entries, which in itself was nothing new. The words themselves were neutral, almost meaningless.

18 Feb '43:   Now keeping this book in Greenland; don't want to lose it. X and me back from T. Mass. this night. 3X in Fall River. Week in Boston after.

12 June '43:   Back TDY NYC. X and me. 2X Brooklyn.
16 July '43:   Three weeks TDY. T.Mass, NY, P.I. Maine, 8X total. Two weeks Camp Upton. Back Greenland last night.

The code, if you could call it that, would be cryptic enough unless you knew what I did. It was a ledger, a record of assassinations. It told where and how many men had been killed. I knew that 2X meant two men, 4X, four.

I STOPPED READING. An image of Marie formed in my mind's eye. Tuesday and I had agreed that the children would never hear the story of the Red Dragon. No child needed the burden of such things. But if it ever did come out, with enough shading and embellishment "The Tale of the Red Dragon" could almost be made a fairy tale of sorts, albeit a twisted one.

But no matter how I candied and colored the rest, nothing could make last night, or June of 1943, more—or less—than it was. Would my daughter sleep as calmly and innocently if she knew I'd killed two people in cold blood, even if they were planning to kill me?

And would Nick, as full of the myth of manhood as myself, love and trust his grandfather once he knew what those big strong hands had done in Fall River or New York; the bodies in the harbor, the relics and icons looted from the doomed?

I knew the answer to both questions. Maybe one day, but I hoped that day came when I was already gone.

I read the next entry.

12 Aug. '43:   Back TDY NYC this night—4X. X, me, R,
and D fell into something. Could be big. X says to leave it
to him; we'll all be as rich as Rockefeller. Still, I'm not sure.
O . . .

I let out the breath I was holding. It wasn't the suddenly ex-
pansive description of something "big"; it was that one large capi-
talized letter O. I recognized the forceful O with the loop on top.
Knew it from my childhood, the thousand notes he'd addressed to
my mother when I'd been a boy. The "O" for Olivia. My mother.

Seeing it here in the journal could only mean one thing. He and
my mother met on the hot August night he'd described. It also
meant something else—that whatever he'd concealed from me, she
had as well.

I didn't know I was crying until my vision blurred and I tasted
the salty-sweet tears as they ran to my lips. At first I was angry with
myself, wiping my eyes and cursing myself for being weak. Then I
started crying again and didn't bother to try to stop. I had forced
myself not to cry the day of my father's memorial service; I was determined to be a man—whatever it took. And I promised myself
that day never to cry again. And I hadn't. Not even at my mother's
funeral. But I wept now.

I don't know how long I sat there crying, but it was long
enough to weep the tears of two generations of lies and secrets. I
stole a quick look at the waiter, hovering near the cash register,
talking with the owner in a low whisper. They must have seen, but
they didn't give me a second look. After all, they were New York-
ers, highly practiced in the art of ignoring the kinds of pain and
hopelessness that would make a man break out in tears in the middle of the day—it happened all the time. I took a deep shuddering
breath, wiped the end of my nose, then picked up the journal
again.

My father spent almost the entire summer and fall of '43 on
various TDYs all over the northeast. And at the bottom of all but
three was the large bold capital O with the loop at the top. With-

out a doubt it stood for my mother, Olivia, but there was never anything more. No note, no description—just her initial. I think I understood. While each X was another body, her name was mentioned each time he saw her. And although the journal was for his eyes only, he wouldn't include anything more for fear that she might somehow be sullied simply by being on the same page.

By the end of '44, the entries became routine again; apparently his OSS activities in the States were winding down as the Allies began to encircle and crush the disintegrating Nazi empire. By spring of '45, as the war was ending, the old Sean Maguire, the young man with the optimistic streak, seemed to reemerge. There were jokes about the nurses and drunken doctors; even a few about Frankie—X Marks the Spot—Laughlin.

The journal ended December '45 when he noted his return to Fort Dix, New Jersey, and discharge from active duty and with streaked exclamation marks. I flipped through the remaining pages. I found nothing but my father's doodles.

I put the journal back, closed the pack, and rubbed my eyes. Next I pulled out my father's cigar tin, retrieving and rereading the articles about Aronstein. As I was putting them back, another piece of newsprint peeked from under the foil wrapping.

It was from *The Wall Street Journal* and dated just four days ago:

ART DEALER ARRESTED FOR TRADE IN ICONS

New York—Jeffrey Lindquist, owner of Lindquist Galleries, was arrested early last evening at his home on Sutton Place. Police sources in the Special Projects Unit said the arrest is the culmination of a lengthy investigation into the international trade of rare and illegal artifacts. Recovered at Lindquist's home were several Russian icons dating from the early 1600s as well as four religious relics believed to have originated with one of the Messianic Hebrew cults.

Detective Sam Tarkan, chief investigator for the unit, noted that, if authentic, the items seized are international treasures and every attempt will be made to return the items to their rightful owners.

Last year Tarkan, in cooperation with agents of the Egyptian government, recovered 16 items stolen 50 years ago from the Egyptian National Museum in Cairo. The pieces were all from the tomb of the chief priest of Pharaoh Tuthmosis in the Valley of the Kings, discovered in 1909. Considered unique, they are some of the finest examples of the late Dynastic period. The recovered objects are now the center of a new display at the Cairo museum.

Tarkan describes the trade of such rare items as extremely profitable, very private, and, at times, very dangerous. "The network of dealers and buyers is very small and very exclusive," he said. "You have to remember that some of these pieces sell for amounts which make Christie's auctions of Picasso look like a garage sale. The people involved are the top of the food chain, the Great White Sharks of the art world."

Lindquist was declared a flight risk and denied bail. He is being held at the Rikers Island detention facility awaiting arraignment. According to Tarkan, Lindquist faces up to 20 years in jail, if convicted. Federal charges may also be filed.

Tarkan's name was underlined, and a pair of my father's squiggly question marks followed it. I carefully refolded the article from the paper and put it back in the tin with the others.

As I stood to leave, one arm half in my coat, a muted chirp came from the backpack. I reached in and pulled out the cell phone. The owner of the restaurant, a gray-haired man with a full mustache, looked my way, letting me know that empty or not, the restaurant wasn't my private office.

"Hello," I said, walking to the cash register.

"Maguire?"

I knew the voice from thousands of sound bites. It was Laughlin.

"Yeah," I said, pausing just long enough to drop a twenty on the counter and wave away the change.

"Nice try, kid," he said with a laugh. "Let me speak to your old man."

"He's not here," I said as I hustled to the door.

"Everything all right?" he asked.

"Ask your people on Baltic Street," I said, standing just outside the restaurant.

There was a long pause.

"That was a mistake," he said. "It won't happen again."

"Damn right it won't."

"You're in way over your head, young Danny Maguire. Have your father get in touch with me; we have some business to do."

I thought about my father and the IV drip, his bluff about Rosen's letter.

"I have Rosen's letter," I said. "You'll be dealing with me now."

There was a pause. "Fine. You get me Rosen's letter and you and your family walk. We'll let bygones be bygones."

"I don't think so."

"Think about it, kid," he said, voice rising. "This is the last time I'm going to make the offer."

I wasn't sure how to handle him yet, didn't know if his people were homing in on the cell phone right now. I had no idea whether my father was already dead and Laughlin was just cleaning up the rest of us. I needed time.

"Just stay near the phone," I said with barely controlled rage. "And wait for my call."

I hit the power button and slapped the phone shut with a curse.

IT WAS ANOTHER Manhattan rush hour as I walked down Sixth; endless lines of taillights blinking on and off, car horns, rushing pedestrians. The afternoon warmth was gone, replaced by a brittle chill and twinkling stars in a clear sky.

I opened the door to Charlotte's Web, a punk coffeeshop I

sometimes frequented, and was greeted with loud techno music and the smell of high-octane coffee.

I took off my pack and coat and went to the counter where Charlotte sat, smoking a clove cigarette. She was all rough-cut orange hair and heavy eye makeup. She had enough studs and earrings to set off a metal detector. She looked up at me and gave me what passed for her come-hither look.

I'd first stumbled on the place when Nick asked for a computer. At the time I was still using an old IBM Selectric for all my bills and letters, so it was like sending out an Eskimo to buy a surfboard. I was walking past the café early one morning and saw dozens of computers. I poked my head in. Charlotte gave me the once-over and invited me in, calling me Gramps.

I told her my problem. Charlotte said she had a soft spot for the technologically challenged and showed me the ropes. She then recommended what I should buy for Nick. After I'd bought the machine and learned to use it, I still stopped in once in a while for a cup of coffee and a chat. Most of all I'd watch the kids at Charlotte's place, trying to prepare myself for what I might encounter as Nick and Marie entered their next developmental phase. It made me shudder.

"Hey, Gramps," Charlotte said with a smile. "Kind of late for you, isn't it?"

"Yeah. I need to use one of your machines for a while. One hooked up to a printer."

"What's wrong with your kid's box?"

The lies just rolled off my tongue. "Hard disk crashed and my son's got a report due tomorrow."

"Ouch! Bummer," she said, getting up. "Follow me."

She was a little shorter than me but couldn't have weighed over a hundred pounds.

"Right here," she said, patting a monitor near an open station. "I call this baby Bertha. She's hot. She'll do full-motion video without a burp," she said with a smile and a wink.

"I just need to download some text," I told her.

"I ever told you I think you're cute, Gramps?"

"Yeah. Every time I see you."

"Well," she said, pouting. "You aren't getting any younger. Know what I mean?"

"We've been through all this before, Charlotte," I said, smiling.

"Have it your way," she said, the ritual complete. "Ten dollars an hour for the Web connection, fifteen cents a print."

"Thanks, doll," I teased.

"Doll?" she said, playing along as she walked away. "Wow. Love it!"

Now that we had a computer at home, I'd taken the time to learn how to use it. I wasn't a pro, but it didn't take me long to settle in. I called up my favorite browser and started cruising the information highway. Usually when the house was quiet and the kids were asleep, I wandered the Internet with no particular destination, just amazed at what was out there.

The difference tonight was that I knew where I wanted to go. I started with Office of Strategic Services and ended up with nothing much. Same for OSS. CIA yielded a lot, but in addition to a gonowhere home page of the agency itself, most of it was wannabe spies and militia kooks talking about the "New World Order."

There were a few interesting hits for Laughlin, but nothing new. Likewise the late Senator Aronstein.

Then I typed in a single word, an elemental four-letter word guaranteed to get results: Nazi. Screen after screen of hits rolled in, everything from the history of the real thing to American Nazis, femme-Nazis and Soup-Nazis. Too much to handle, too little focus.

I cleared the search and tried again, linking the only two words that seemed to describe the convergence of my father, the OSS, Laughlin, the CIA, the Nazis, and the pendant in my pocket. I typed "Nazi Loot" and when the screen filled, I knew I was where I wanted to be.

I made hard copies of about a dozen of the stories. By the time

I was done, Charlotte had had to refill the printer twice and I ended up with a stack of printouts two inches thick.

I took them to the counter where Charlotte tallied me up and put the prints in a large Tyvek envelope.

"Wanna have dinner with me?" she asked as she gave me my change.

"Charlotte . . ." I said with the same tone of voice I used when Nick or Marie whined.

"All right. All right. Can't blame a girl for trying."

I leaned over a gave her a peck on the cheek.

"Later, babe," I said.

She broke into hysterics.

"Babe! Oh, Gramps," she said. "Please . . . run away with me."

I flipped her the peace sign and walked out the door.

14

THERE WAS A bank of phones right outside the café.
I called Lita first. She reported that my father was improving;
still drifting in and out, but better—holding his own. I told her I'd
be in touch and hung up. I wanted to call Tuesday and the kids;
hear their voices. But I was getting more anxious with each passing
minute. It would have to wait.

Miraculously, the white pages on the chain beneath the cubicle
was intact. There was half a column of Gershowitzes but only one
Isaac. I took a deep breath and dialed. The phone rang five times
and I was about to give up when he answered.

"Hello?" The voice was garbled, as if my earpiece were covered
in mud.

"Rabbi Gershowitz?"

"Who is this?" the strange voice asked.

"Do you know a man named Maguire?"

There was a long silence.

"Who is this!" the voice demanded.

I hung up.

The address listed in the book was 70 West Seventy-sixth.

* * *

GERSHOWITZ'S BUILDING WAS one of those huge prewar apartment buildings a block west of Central Park. It had a faded grace enhanced by an old liveried doorman. He asked who I wanted to see.

"Rabbi Gershowitz," I said.

"Is he expecting you?" the gnomelike man wanted to know.

"I'm not sure."

"One minute, please," he said, eyeing me suspiciously and sliding behind his little desk. He put on a heavy pair of worn glasses and consulted a list before he made the call.

"Good evening, Rabbi, there's a gentleman here to see you."

He looked up. His eyes, magnified by the thick lenses, were as large as a night owl's.

"Your name?" he asked me.

"Danny Maguire."

He repeated it into the intercom, then nodded.

"Very well." He put down the phone and took off his glasses, his eyes blinking at me blindly.

"You can go up. Apartment 12C."

When the elevator arrived, I wasn't surprised to see another uniformed man at the controls. He so resembled the doorman, I knew they were related.

"Twelve, please."

The gate and door slid closed and we rode in silence. Large white numerals slid past as we ascended. The car stopped smoothly, the floor of the cab perfectly aligned with the landing.

"Twelfth floor," the operator announced, sliding the gate and door open in a fluid motion. I envied the obvious pride he took in this simple task, something he must have been doing for as many years as I had been alive.

The door to 12C opened before I rang the bell. A small black-clad figure retreated into the shadows. I followed.

It was hard to keep up as he scurried through the dark corridor, a cane tapping with every step. The walls were lined with stacked cardboard boxes. The place was a labyrinth of narrow halls and closed doors.

The phantom disappeared through an opening. When I walked in, the man I'd followed sat in an overstuffed armchair facing me, his back to windows covered with heavy velvet drapes.

The walls were lined with dusty books on slanting shelves.

When my eyes adjusted to the gloom, I looked at the man in the chair. Gershowitz was probably just a few years older than my father but looked a hundred more.

His face had been twisted by a stroke, the left half fixed in a perpetual drooping scowl, the right side lively, almost elfin. His eyes, a penetrating light blue, were mirror images of life and death.

When he spoke, only the right side of his lips moved.

My tongue twisted in sympathy as he formed each syllable. What came out was a rumbling kind of rasp that I remembered from the phone. It matched the rest of him.

"You look like him, you know," he said.

"So I've been told."

"And you have your mother's eyes."

It hit me hard. Not only did he know my father, he knew my mother too. The circles were intersecting, closing.

"You knew her?"

"She was the only one . . ." His voice trailed off in a cough that seemed to come from his shoes.

"The only one?"

"The only lamb among the wolves. The only one unblemished before man and God." He raised his stick in a shaking hand and pointed it at me. "My boy, what hasn't he told you?"

"Who?"

"Your father."

"My father is dead."

His good hand, spotted with age and gnarled by arthritis, gripped his wooden cane. His good eye closed, the lid of his stricken one fluttering, leaving half a bloodshot eye exposed. He took a deep wheezing breath. It came out as a shaking sigh. His eyes opened, one at a time.

"No, he's not," he said, staring hard at me. "I always knew he was still alive. I felt him. Watching. I knew he'd come for me one day. I've been waiting all these years . . ."

"Waiting for what?"

He draped the crook of his cane on the arm of the chair, and his hands dropped to his lap. His eyes, both of them, became wary.

"An accounting."

"What accounting?"

I could almost see the gears shift in his head. His voice became softer, gentler.

"Why are you here and not your father?"

"He couldn't make it. He gave me your name," I said, not knowing how much and what to tell this man. "And this."

I took the charm from my pocket, got up, and placed it in Gershowitz's lap. The old man's good eye fixed on it. His hand went to his shirt pocket with surprising agility and came out with a pair of reading glasses. Next he switched on a small reading lamp and picked up the talisman. The pendant came to life in the bright light. As he held the charm, his hand ceased its shaking. I could see half his mouth moving slightly as he silently read the tiny inscriptions on the rods joining the jewels.

The man who looked up was no longer a twisted shell. In his eyes I saw a younger man, vital and strong. And a glimpse of something else slipped through, just for a moment, but long enough for me to recognize it. Something I'd seen before. Pain. And maybe a touch of madness. Or both.

"Do you know what this is?" he said in a reverent hush.

I didn't answer.

He held it tightly and closed his eyes again, this time in a kind of rapture.

"This belonged to Rabbi Moses de Léon of Spain," he said, his eyes opening one after another. "He was the greatest student of the

Cabalah that ever lived. The author of the Zohar, if you believe some. Ironically, the charm was made for and given to him by his adoring Catholic mistress in the early 1300s."

He fell silent for what felt like a long time. Finally he stood, his whole body straining with the effort, and hobbled to the bookshelf. He ran his fingers slowly across one of the dusty shelves to a point where it intersected a vertical divider. His index finger disappeared around the side of the painted wood and I heard a soft *click*. A shallow false panel full of book spines swung away, revealing a glass-fronted cabinet lit softly from within. Unlike the rest of the warrenlike apartment, the cabinet was neat and dust-free, the glass clean. He then took a key from his pocket, slipped it into the cylinder and opened the door, taking out a small golden chalice and handing it to me. Like the pendant, it was simple and intricate at the same time, lovingly fashioned and adorned with several small rubies and emeralds.

"This is the Shabbes cup that belonged to de Léon," he said. "The pendant and the cup belong together."

I put the cup back in the cabinet and took out a small golden bowl that looked like it didn't belong with the glittering collection. It was plain and covered with small dents.

"And this?"

"Have you ever heard of the Essenes?" he said, taking the bowl from me and rubbing a hand over its worn side, his tone now relaxed.

I shook my head.

"Not too much is known about them, and what is can't be proved." He took another deep breath. The good half of his lips formed a smile. "They were a sect of Jews from the second century B.C. A Messianic cult; one of many in those days. They had communal property and believed in ceremonial purity. They dressed in white robes and paid strict observance to the Sabbath."

I turned the simple bowl in my hands as he spoke.

"That was one of their ritual bathing vessels," Gershowitz went on. "Especially reserved for the Sabbath. They believed in purity above all else, held baptisms, and," he said, taking a deep breath, "many think it was the cult that Jesus of Nazareth was born into. It is even possible that this was once used by him."

I passed the small bowl back to him. He handled it gently and put it back, locking the cabinet doors but keeping the false front open. I took another look at the objects inside—simple and elaborate, each polished and glistening. Like the things in my father's pack, they were all old, carefully wrought, obviously unique, priceless, and covered, I was sure, with blood.

I held out my hand. Reluctantly he returned the pendant to my open palm.

"I'm rotting," he said, hobbling slowly back to his armchair and sitting down with effort. "I have been for years. I pray every day for Him to end my suffering and take me, and yet I still live. So I ask you, young Maguire, tell me why? Why doesn't He hear me?"

I had a feeling the answer could be found in the cabinet of the priceless artifacts, their legacy and power. I heard the echo of his word: "accounting." I'd never given too much though to the Divine Plan, if there was one, but I thought a simple statement might answer his question.

"Maybe because the time hadn't yet come."

"The time for what?" he asked rhetorically, much, I imagined, as a rabbi might ask his student.

"The time for you to make things right," I said, suddenly sure of my every word.

His whole body seemed to sag, and I felt, for the first time, that somewhere, under the madness, beyond the disintegrating body, lay what was left of a soul.

He cocked his head to one side.

"And how do I do this?" he asked.

"My father told me part of the story. I need you to tell me the rest."

His eyes focused at a point behind me. "How much do you know?"

"I know that in August of 1943 four soldiers in the U.S. Army,

and OSS agents to boot, were illegally and secretly killing suspected spies in New York. Those four soldiers were Francis Laughlin, my father, a guy named Deere, and another named Rosen.
They stumbled on some Jewish artifacts looted in Europe by the
Nazis that had been sent to the U.S. to sell."

I had his full attention. Everything I'd said so far my father had
told me. Now I told him what I had guessed.

"Rosen took the artifacts to someone and I think that someone
was you." I paused to let that sink in. "And now, fifty-five years later,
all the secrets are coming out: the Swiss bankers, the Vatican, the
secret killings by the OSS, the artifacts, all of it. And Laughlin is
doing his damnedest to prevent it, including murdering Senator
Aronstein and, if he can, my father. And now that I know, me and
my family."

Gershowitz nodded his head side to side and grimaced.
Whether a smile or a sneer, I couldn't tell.

"If only it were that simple," he said.

I was stunned. "Simple?"

He settled farther back in his chair. His eyelids closed a fraction
of an inch but his good eye was bright and alive. His voice became
stronger, and just as my father had taken me into the past, Gershowitz took me back with him, back to the days when he was a
young man with all the energy and weakness of youth. He began
with an explanation.

"It didn't take us long to find out just how serious Herr Hitler
was about making the Fatherland *Judenrein*—'Jew Free,' " he said,
his gaze steady. "I was young. I was idealistic. I thought I could do
something. So I formed a group. I called it the Committee."

The way he told it, the Committee tried to convince the U.S.
government of what was happening in Europe, particularly what
was happening to the Jews. They had photographs and letters from
the victims, smuggled out of Germany at the cost of many lives.

"We even had a letter from a top-ranking Nazi begging the Allies to do something about what we now call the Holocaust," he
said. "And they could have. Hitler himself had asked early on. All

the Allies had to do was take the Jews off his hands and it would have been done. Hitler, Goebbels, even Ribbentrop, said 'Come. Take these dirty Jews! They're yours!' But no one accepted the offer."

He looked past me again, his voice losing some of its vibrancy. "So the Nazis concluded, rightly I might say, that no one gave a damn about the Jews. Or the Gypsies, or the Freemasons, or the feeble-minded. And that's when the real slaughter, the deportations, the camps, the ovens, began."

He went on to explain that it was not until Rosen showed up on his doorstep with the box that the Committee understood just how far along the genocide had progressed. With the artifacts, they finally had the kind of solid proof they'd been looking for.

"But by that time the government had bigger things to worry about than a few looted menorahs," the rabbi said, waving his hands in small circles on his lap. "Like waging and winning a war raging across both oceans. Keeping American soldiers alive to fight. Bombing factories, not lagers."

I knew something about this, the supposed indifference of the Allies to stopping the slaughter in the camps. But as the rabbi said, the first priorities were attacking and destroying the enemy's food, armaments, manufacturing, and oil wells—the things that keep an army able to fight, hitting them where it hurt. So while bombing concentration camps might have been noble, it would have done little to help win the war.

"We considered going to the press," Gershowitz said with a wheeze, "but there was strict wartime censorship, and the government wasn't interested in distracting the public with side issues. So I was elected by the Committee to approach the only other organization we could think of with the power to help: the Catholic church."

According to Gershowitz, the church was busy doing a tango with Hitler. In fact, the German clergy were as rabidly anti-Semitic as the Nazis.

"It was nothing new," the rabbi said in a tone that seemed at once sympathetic and condescending. "They were trying to prevent their faith from being swept away by the Nazi tidal wave. They knew that after the Jews, the Nazis were determined to destroy the church as well. They'd beaten tyrants before. Done it for a thousand years. Getting in bed with the Nazis was no different."

The representative of the church that met with Gershowitz in New York was a man named Peter—no last name, just Peter. Gershowitz said the Committee had dubbed him the Adjustor and that the Adjustor was more of a what than a who: a permanent position in the New York Diocese—a kind of secret cabinet post.

"The Adjustor," Gershowitz explained, "was the 'fixer' for the Diocese. If a priest has some trouble with an altar boy or a young widow, the Adjustor was notified and the priest, the boy, or the young lady moved to Tenafly or Tampa. If the Diocese needed some help for a parishioner, a little dirt on the alderman, the Adjustor was put on the case. I showed the artifacts to Peter."

"And . . .?" I asked.

"And nothing," the rabbi said.

"What do you mean, nothing?"

"Just that. Nothing. Oh," he said, "Peter was sympathetic, but he said he couldn't help. It was the things that came later that got him interested."

"What other things?"

His face seemed to cave in on itself again. "Trainloads of icons and artifacts from every religion known to man. Touchstones of faith and reverence. Some from the time of Moses; pillows slept on by Mohammed. A few, like the Essene bowl, thought to have been touched by Jesus. The property of whole villages and cities of Jews, Catholics, Copts, Russian Orthodox, Armenians, Gypsies . . ."

Then he fell silent and his eyes closed. I knew he wasn't sleeping but simply unwilling to tell the rest. The quiet was broken by the clang and sputter of the radiator. When the noise became a quiet hiss, I spoke.

"But you kept some of the artifacts," I said quietly. "And so did the church."

"Yes," he said wearily, eyes still closed.

I had to know. "Why?"

His eyes opened and he looked at me steadily. "We told ourselves that they were better in our possession than anyone else's." Then he looked to the hands folded on his lap. He said the rest slowly. "But the truth was that we were corrupted by their beauty, their power, their link to the divine."

I stood and walked over to the cabinet, suddenly restless. Looking at the artifacts, a part of me understood Gershowitz and his fall from grace. I could see how it might be easy for the devout to deceive themselves. But something was missing—something important.

"What happened when the war was over?" I asked.

He looked past me, his good eye misting over.

I walked over to him and lowered myself until we were eye to eye. "Tell me, Rabbi."

He took a deep, rattling breath.

"The trading went on," he said softly. "Artifacts for passports. Icons for visas."

"For who?" I asked, already knowing the answer but needing to hear him say it.

"For them!" he spat. "The Nazis. Butchers! Killers! Kommandants, Capos, 'Doctors' . . ."

"Why didn't you stop it?" I asked. "Expose them."

He looked at me sadly. "First I told myself that if I kept the artifacts, then one day I could return them, save them for the generations to come." He somehow managed a small, ironic smile. "And who better than me, a rabbi, to take the job? But each year that passed, I knew it was a lie. The truth was that I'd been seduced by the objects. Each time I held one I had the feeling that I was touching a part of God. It grew. Like a cancer of the soul. Until it consumed me."

It was hard to hold his gaze as he made his confession. But when our eyes met, the space between us closed. I shook my head in a gesture of understanding.

"But there were others," I said simply. "You were just one man. I need to know who else was involved."

His answer was a name. The name that ran through it all.

"Laughlin," he said. "Laughlin was the hub, the dealmaker. He promised Rosen and me that all the Jewish artifacts would be given to us. But in return we had to pledge our silence. And that," the Rabbi said, his face a mask of pain, "was when I turned my back on God."

I stood and turned away from him and looked again at the glass-fronted cabinet. In its own twisted way, it was perfect. Laughlin as Mephistopheles, sitting at the nucleus of the nebula that was to become the CIA. Trading safe havens for fleeing Nazis, using the excuse of buying information to his bosses, taking looted treasure under the table, having it both ways. I thought about Osborne. Might he be in on it too?

"Was Laughlin working alone?" I asked, my back still to him.

"I'm not sure," the rabbi said.

I faced him.

"What about the church?" I asked as I turned. "Was the Adjustor still involved?"

"I'm not sure but I always assumed he was."

"How do I get in touch with this Adjustor?"

"The 'Peter' I knew died a few years ago," he said. "I'm sure there is a new 'Peter,' but who he is," he said, his good shoulder giving a weak shrug, "I don't know."

I was certain that Gershowitz had told me all he knew. Maybe I was imagining it, but he looked even smaller and more frail. And his story had left me weaker too. I felt the walls closing in. I needed air and time to think.

I walked to the door.

"What are you going to do?" the old rabbi asked, still slumped in his chair.

I looked at the soft glow of the artifacts in their glass cage.

"What should have been done a long time ago," I said, realizing without a doubt that my father was right. I was going to rip Laughlin's heart out. "And you're going to help me."

"It's too late for me," he said, fingering his cane.

"No," I said with more anger than I'd intended. I wanted to feel

luxury

last chance to answer the cries of the dead. Your final hope for mercy and forgiveness."

He coughed again, a deep rattle that left his face red. A tear sprang from his bad eye.

"Can you do this, young Maguire?" he asked when he finally caught his breath. His voice was almost a plea. "Can you offer me these things?"

"I don't know, Rabbi. But I'm the only chance hope got."

I backtracked through the darkened apartment, closing the door on my way out.

15

THE CAB DROPPED me off on Park Avenue between Thirty-eighth and Thirty-ninth.

I was puzzled. I'd expected Lita's apartment to be as unique and imposing as the house on Columbia Heights. Instead it was a modest affair, a dull slab of building with all the personality of a cardboard box.

But I was in luck. There wasn't a doorman with questioning eyes or a collection of tenants sitting in the lobby, checking out the action. Using her keys, I eased my way in and made it to her unit on the seventh floor without seeing a soul.

I opened the door and walked through the apartment flipping on the lights, taking off my pack and coat when every light in the modest one-bedroom apartment was on. I took stock.

Everything about Lita's Brooklyn townhouse was expensive and of museum quality. It could have belonged to anyone with taste and the money to follow through. The apartment was a different story.

Bits and pieces of a real person were everywhere. Dog-eared paperbacks lined painted wood shelves. Simple furniture and a single armchair and ottoman. A cramped kitchenette, the cabinets half full. A blue-tiled bathroom, a terry robe on a hook, one pair of worn slippers on the floor. A queen-size bed with three pillows and a single nightstand. And photographs.

Some were color but most were old black-and-white prints. They hung in three small clusters, each a discrete grouping. In the first was Lita as an infant, then a child. In some she was with a stiff-looking couple I knew must have been her parents. Her father was handsome but remote with a trim mustache. Her mother, not as pretty as he~

~ unreadable—defiant.

Then a larger grouping. A radiant Lita, her arms around a tall man with curly black hair: in the park, in formal clothes, at the beach. Then Lita with a bundled infant, the unmistakable glow of motherhood in her eyes. The infant became a toddler, then a tow-headed little boy. The man and Lita always smiling and relaxed. The last picture showed the smiling man pulling the bundled tot on a sled down a snowy road. I roamed the other rooms, looking for more photographs. There were none.

The man? The child? Without doubt they were her husband and child. But where were the other pictures: the boy as an awkward teen, the graduations, the parties? The answer screamed out to me in the silent apartment. There were none because the man and boy were dead. Not just gone. Dead. Maybe a crash, a boating accident, or at the hands of a madman; it didn't matter. A girl had grown from a melancholy child to a beautiful young woman, fallen in love, had a child, then lost it all.

I rubbed my eyes and looked through the pictures again. I wondered how much, if any, my father knew. I guessed none, just as she'd known nothing about me or my mother. So two people who'd lost everything managed to find each other, bringing to it nothing but themselves. Because there was no past, there could be no excuses or unfulfilled expectations. And by joining us she'd stepped over an invisible line that would forever change things. She was risking what they already had for something they might never have.

MY HAND HURT but maybe that was good because otherwise I would have fallen asleep. Instead, I made a cup of jet-black instant coffee and sat in the armchair. I placed the Tree of Life in my lap, just below the neat stack of papers I'd printed out in Charlotte's Web. I started to read.

Some articles were a page or two, short news summaries. Others were full-length stories with footnotes and references for further reading. But what most of them shared was that they seemed to revolve around the Swiss.

I'd read a lot of it already. Hell, the stories had been everywhere for the last year or so. At first there was outrage and angry editorials. Then with each passing month the stories grew shorter and were moved farther and farther back as more urgent news filled the front pages. But now that it was part of me and I was part of it, I wanted to know it all.

The whole world now recognized that the Swiss had used their "neutrality" to launder Nazi gold, had known in fact since before the war even ended. But every day some new story emerged and another chink was made in the Swiss denials.

What was now being revealed was that the bullion accounts financed the German war machine and a lot of the Swiss economy. German money paid for Swiss-made war matériel, which was shipped back to Germany to be used against the Allies. It was a perpetual motion money and war machine.

Germany, broken and still reeling from reparations required by the Treaty of Versailles ending World War I, had only about three million dollars of gold reserves when World War II began. However, in spite of this, they sent almost ten times that to Switzerland. Where the extra gold came from was a pesky little accounting detail the Swiss chose to overlook.

But the discrepancy was obvious to anyone who had a grasp of even the most basic accounting skills. A lot of the gold that ended up as bars shipped to Switzerland embossed with the Reichsbank swastika had been stripped from the victims. It was a necklace here, a wedding band there, a gold filling from a fresh corpse there. Of course, when you added up the gram here and the ounce there from six million Jews, a million Gypsies, and a few million Russians "processed" in Hitler's Final Solution, it added up. But the Swiss, in their almost religious neutrality, conveniently ignored these facts.

But the cries of millions of dead never do go away, they just take time to be heard. And now it seemed the time had come. The survivors and children of the survivors of Treblinka, Matthausen, Auschwitz, and all the other camps, most now in their eighties, wanted the old debts settled, a *real* accounting.

The loudest and best organized were the ones the most: the Jews. They demanded to know what happened to the money in "Papa's" or "Aunt Sadie's" Swiss accounts, the ones Mama whispered frantically about in her children's ears as she was dragged to the edge of the pit or hurried naked down the chute to the "showers."

They had the gall to ask for a moral accounting as well. They wanted to know why the Swiss should go forward as if their hands were as clean as the alpine snow instead of covered with the blood of millions of torn lives.

But as usual, the real problem began with the denials, the stonewalling, the refusals. Sons whose fathers were sent to the sky in Poland as smoke from the chimneys of the crematoria were asked by the bankers for death certificates from Auschwitz. Daughters were asked for their mothers' birth certificates, marriage licenses, signatures, and last known addresses. If this failed and something was actually produced, they were asked for account numbers, passwords. If these too could be supplied, the by-now weary and hobbling survivor would be told that the account, dormant for more than ten years, had been closed and all records destroyed, in accordance with Swiss banking laws.

Soon the American Jews and politicians became more vocal. The Swiss were now boxed into a corner. And when they offered twenty million as a settlement, the gloves came off. If twenty million was put on the table without even a skirmish, the real number must be ten or a hundred times that high. The fight had just begun.

I read with a growing anger. The bounty of the Holocaust and the boundaries of greed seemed to know no limits. The millions in unpaid insurance policies. Art looted from Jewish collectors still hanging in the Louvre and private collections. Swedish Saabsters doing the "neutral cha-cha" with the Nazis, taking gold and supplying raw materials. The Portuguese. Perón in Argentina. The Boys from Brazil . . .

But amazingly, this was just the half of it. Even before the war ended, the Allies decided that the new enemy was the Soviets. And in a mind-bending shift of polarities, the Nazis, just months before a hated foe, became our new ally against the godless Communists. Nazi spymasters were secreted out of the Reich and set up in safe havens from Canada to Paraguay. Collaborators from Paris, Copenhagen, Budapest, and Minsk were given visas to the United States. It was madness.

The last article was the longest, least emotional, but most riveting piece I had downloaded. It was from a university in Copenhagen. A doctoral candidate named DeVrees had published his thesis, titled *The Economics of Death: How the Holocaust Financed European Unity*, on the university Web page in English and Danish. The piece was a dry, technical accounting of pre- and postwar Europe full of bar charts, graphs, and tables.

What it boiled down to was something basic and simple: Incredible wealth had been created during the war. The concept was clear enough; you simply remove six million Jews, a few million other "undesirables," then seize their assets as your own. Voilà!: death and destruction for the vanquished, a horn of plenty for the victors.

DeVrees's paper made note of the bank accounts and insurance policies, but what he concentrated on was what the others had overlooked: the communal guilt of the quiet millions who silently profited from the cumulative wealth of millions of dead. And not just a few of the victims were wealthy; owners of multinational businesses and banks, inheritors of family fortunes.

DeVrees's final pages became more pointed. He noted that each year that slips by another one of them, another of that generation, another potential witness, dies, history dying with him. But the author concluded it wasn't some grand conspiracy working against the survivors; it was a huge web of related but unconnected people and institutions: the Vatican, governments—villages in Poland all the way up to the mayors of Stockholm and Paris. Museums, banks, collectors. On and on. Each with a piece of hidden profit from the Holocaust. Yes, it was the big banks in Switzerland. But it also was individuals: Families. Companies. Each wanting the past to die with the survivors, counting the years.

He gave a series of hypothetical examples: a developer who builds a shopping center in Germany on land confiscated from a Berlin Communist turned to ash in Dachau. Or someone mining for gems in Africa on land once owned by a family of French Jews gassed in Auschwitz. Or a young man in Budapest turning out crystal vases in a factory confiscated by his father from a Hungarian Jew bulldozed into a pit. Or a potato farmer tilling the soil of the missing Jews from Minsk or Cracow.

I put the dissertation down and closed my eyes. I had images of packs of human vultures: the neighbors, friends, landlords, tenants of all the missing. Picking up what the Nazis and their lackeys left behind. Grabbing what they could after their Jewish or Communist or homosexual neighbor was hauled off in the dead of the night. Paintings, silver, furniture, antiques . . .

So it wasn't just a bunch of stone-faced Swiss bankers or fugitive Nazis wearing SS uniforms sitting under a portrait of the Führer somewhere in Brazil. It was a geometrically expanding network of common criminals and everyday cowards connected by guilt and silence. And if they waited long enough, the dull roar of the victims would become a murmur, then a whimper, and finally fade into silence as the entire generation died.

The implications were too big and unwieldy for me to get a

handle on. As a rule, I tried to stick with the things I could touch and feel, not the things ready to fall on me like a boulder from a cloudless sky.

I drifted into a kind of waking nightmare filled with disjointed images. I saw the shining objects in Gershowitz's hidden cabinet, the articles of faith in my father's pack, the millions of dead, the shattered homes and churches. I saw synagogues burning against the night sky. I saw a younger Gershowitz in his study, fondling Rosen's offerings, keeping the best for himself before giving the rest to the Committee. I saw bishops and cardinals running trembling hands over chalices and crucifixes. My father was in the dream too. He had Judas' dagger in his hand and a smile on his lips.

16

I AWOKE AT dawn, the printouts in a pile around my feet, the pendant clutched in my hand. I was physically and emotionally drained.

I stumbled into the bathroom. The face in the mirror looked wild and dangerous. I found a bottle of aspirin in the medicine cabinet, swallowed four, then took a long hot shower, shaving by touch in the steam.

I wrapped a towel around my middle and wiped the moisture from the mirror. Dripping wet, I looked cold and feral.

Still in my towel, I put water to boil and called Lita's. I used our signal; I rang once, hung up, and dialed again. No answer. I convinced myself she was giving my father a sponge bath or changing his IV.

I put everything, including the printouts, in the backpack and put on my coat. Right before I left I called Tuesday in Connecticut using the same simple code. She said she was fine and so were the kids, who were still sleeping. I was tempted to tell her how much I loved her and a lot more, but all I did was instruct her to hang tight and stay near the phone.

* * *

THE MORNING WAS sunny and cold. I found a diner near Madison and gulped down a cup of coffee.

I made the call from a pay phone in the restaurant. A man with an accent as brash and bold as all New York answered.

"Special Investigations."

"Lieutenant Tarkan, please."

"Speaking."

I don't know what I expected, but a man who sounded like a Bronx cabbie wasn't it. It took me a second to answer.

"You don't know me," I said over the noise on the street. "But I think we should meet."

"Why?"

"I read about Lindquist. I have something I think you might be interested in."

He answered deliberately. "I'm a busy man. You'll have to do better than that."

"Have you ever heard of the Hebrew Zealots?"

The answer rolled off his tongue as if someone asked him an obscure history question every half hour. "Sure. Hebrew religious and political faction, resisting Roman rule, first century A.D. Led by Judas of Galilee. Started the revolution against Roman rule of Judea. The Zealots held Massada for two years against the Roman Tenth Legion. They committed suicide instead of surrendering. . . . What about them?"

I paused a beat. "I have something that once belonged to one of them and a few other things you might find interesting."

It took awhile for him to answer. I realized he must have gotten dozens of calls after the newspaper article from people who wanted to show him a piece of the "true cross" or a handful of barbs from Jesus' crown of thorns.

"I don't like jokes or wild goose chases . . ."

I'd counted on his curiosity overcoming his cynicism. I was wrong. I had to sweeten the pot.

"I'm not joking, Lieutenant. I can also tell you where to find a golden bowl from the Essene sect . . ."

Silence.

"Are you still there, Tarkan?"

"I'm here," he said. I heard the squeak of a chair. "How do you want to do it?"

I WAS LOITERING in the last row of the reference stacks at the Public Library on Fifth and Forty-second Street, one eye on the book spines, the other on the aisle. The section was deserted and as still as a church on Saturday afternoon.

I'd told Tarkan to meet me here forty minutes, to the dot, after we hung up—alone. It was now an hour since we'd spoken and I was starting to sweat. A man came around the corner, saw me, and stopped. It had to be him.

"Tarkan?"

"Sorry I'm late. Traffic."

He started to walk toward me. With what had become second nature, I took the gun from my pocket and pointed it at his chest; it was a big target. He held his hands away from his sides, palms toward me.

"Easy now!" he said. "Just relax."

"Are you alone?"

He nodded slowly, his gaze steady. His eyes were a deep dark amber. He smiled. It was open and friendly, but he looked like the kind of guy who might smile as he caught you with an elbow to the gut. I kept the gun on him.

"Now listen up," he said, still smiling. "If I'd wanted to get the drop on you, you'd be on your belly already, a half-dozen detectives with the barrels of their nines up your ass. Now put the gun away and let's talk; you're making me nervous."

I put the gun in my pocket.

"That's better," he said, moving closer. "And," he said, his voice firm, "don't ever, I mean *never*, pull that kind of stunt on me again. I'm one of those old-fashioned cops. You know—shoot first and ask questions later."

Sam Tarkan was my height but wider, with a football player's

neck and thick wrists. He had longish dark-brown hair and laugh
lines at the corners of his mouth. I don't know why, but I'd expected him to be older and smaller. And with his thick city accent,
I'd somehow imagined him as an off-the-rack polyester type of guy.
Instead, he was dressed in a white oxford shirt and power tie, gray
flannel trousers, and a navy blazer. Brooks Brothers all the way.

He held out his hand. "Sam Tarkan, NYPD."

His grip was firm and dry.

"Danny."

"Danny . . . ?"

"That's all for now."

He shrugged. "If that's the way you want it. So," he said casually. "You called me . . ."

Before I left Lita's apartment, I'd taken the dagger from the pack
and put it in the inside pocket of my parka. I started reaching for
it but heard a *click* and looked up. Materializing from thin air,
Tarkan's gun was now in one of his steady hands and inches from
my stomach.

"Slow and easy," he said.

"It's not a gun."

"Call me crazy," he said with that smile. "But I'm not sure I
trust you."

I moved as slowly as I could, until the oilcloth package was between us.

"Now open it," he said.

I unfolded the stained canvas. The dagger was a deep yellow.
Tarkan looked at me for a moment, slipped his gun into the holster
at his back, and picked it up, edging closer to the light.

He studied it from every angle, then took a small magnifying
glass from his pocket, held it to his eye, and inspected the inscription. He went front to back several times.

"Do you know what this says?" he finally asked, looking at me.

"No."

"It's written in Hebrew," he said, looking back at the dagger.
"There are rumors that the Zealots had a group of extremists. They

were called the 'Sicarii,' or dagger men. They assassinated Romans and Jews who collaborated with Roman rule. Some say Judas Iscariot was a Sicarii, as was his father before him." His fingers traced the faded lines of the inscription.

"And," he said, handing the knife back to me, "inscribed on the hilt are the words 'Glory to the Lord.' Scratched underneath is the sign of the fish. An iconographic symbol of the early Christians, something Judas might have done after he betrayed Jesus but before he killed himself . . ."

He ran a hand through his hair and looked at me again, as if for the first time.

"Why did you call me?" he asked quietly.

A woman, her arms loaded with books, rounded the corner and almost jumped out of her skin when she saw us.

"She's looks like she's going to call the cops," Tarkan said sotto voce. "Do you like pastry?"

WE WALKED IN silence to a small restaurant on East Forty-fourth named Yerevan. Once inside, Tarkan spoke softly to the maître d', who whisked us to a small table in the corner.

"What language was that?" I asked.

"Armenian. Yerevan is the capital of Armenia."

"You're Armenian?" I said, thinking that only in New York could you find an Armenian cop who read Hebrew.

"Part. My father was. His name was Tarkanian. My mother wasn't," he said. "I changed my name."

A plate of assorted pastries and two Turkish coffees appeared.

"Try the round one," he said, pointing to a small cookie with chopped nuts on top. The topic of Tarkan was closed.

"So," he said, sitting back and wiping his mouth carefully with the linen napkin. "Give me a reason I shouldn't arrest you."

I looked straight at him feeling the same ice-cold fire that I did when my father told me I'd lost twenty-nine years because of Laughlin.

"I'll give you two," I said, my voice steady and filled with a men-

ace I hadn't planned but seemed to rise from a deep, dark place inside me.

"You're a big man, Tarkan, but that doesn't mean squat. I'm no
virgin. Know what I mean? Right now, right here, I'd say it'd be
about fifty-fifty who walked out that door. But I've got the edge.
Know why? Because killing you is the least of my troubles. Two," I
said, taking a breath, watching his eyes. "even if you did manage to
take me, that would be it. You'd get the dagger and nothing else.
And you'd be missing the chance to hit the mother lode, the
chance of a lifetime. A chance *I* can give you. Do we understand
each other?"

He rested his hands flat on the table. Maybe he was figuring the
odds, but I remembered my reflection in the mirror from this morning and didn't think so. He must have seen that I'd crossed a line
and wasn't playing by the rules anymore.

"Talk to me," he said.

I pulled out my father's cigar tin and handed him the article
about the Lindquist arrest I'd found behind the foil liner.

"Do you know where Lindquist got the icons?" I asked.

He scanned the article as if he'd memorized every line. "I have
some ideas. Nothing definite though."

"Then how did you bust him?"

"The truth?"

"I haven't got time for anything else."

He sipped his coffee. "Do you know how detectives work? Most
of the time we sit on our asses waiting for the phone to ring. The
call from a fink, the guy out to cut a deal with the DA. The jealous
wife or disgruntled employee anxious to whisper something to us,
drop the dime on someone who did them dirt. Like Lindquist's ex-
boyfriend did two weeks ago."

The detective gave a shrug as if to say that's the way it went.
"I'm not saying I don't have my sources or that I don't dig around,"
he went on. "But the people who deal in rare antiquities are very
rich and sometimes a little twisted."

I thought about Gershowitz and his locked cabinet.

"Some would call it natural," Tarkan continued. "The desire to hold a holy relic, to possess it. Others call it a form of compulsion. The kind of obsessive desire and madness that would make a man lock his lover in a room so no one else could gaze on her."

"What do you think?" I asked.

"I can see it both ways," he said, avoiding my eyes.

"And then there's the money," I said.

"As always. But compulsion drives it. Some of the 'collectors' I've met were actually happy when I arrested them. I remember one, the head of a brokerage firm, who pulled me into his temperature-controlled vault to see his collection of Mayan artifacts. Couldn't stop babbling about where he got them, or what they represented, and how he'd never shown them to anyone before." He shook his head. "That's the paradox: People who collect the kind of things we're talking about want to show the world but can't. The secret would spread and they'd lose what they love."

I took the pendant from my pocket and handed it to him.

Just as he'd done in the library, he looked at the pendant with unflinching concentration, again using his pocket magnifier to study the worn inscriptions.

"More Hebrew," he muttered. "Early Middle Ages. Ah. Here it is. Cabalist. Medieval Spain," he said, eye still glued to the magnifier. " 'The Book of Splendor,' and here, 'The Godhead is unknowable' . . . 'For Moses, Lion of Truth' . . . Moses de Léon!"

"Hebrew? Armenian? What other languages do you speak?" I asked, impressed.

He didn't take his eye from the pendant. "I've got a master's in archaeology from Fordham. Ancient languages are my avocation."

"How'd you end up a cop?"

"There's a reason for everything," he said by way of explanation, handing the pendant back to me.

Like his name change, I'd hit a subject he wasn't eager to talk about. He put his hands on the table and knit his fingers. He looked at me steadily, choosing his next words with care.

"You didn't call me to show me your collection, find out about my education or why I became a cop," he said. "I believe you when you say you'd kill me rather than have me arrest you, and maybe you're right and you'd make it. But maybe you wouldn't. I'm willing to let it happen. So either tell me what the hell is going on, or let's do it."

I measured the man across from me. I knew what I was willing to die for. But what was he? It sure as hell wasn't so he could arrest me, or the money, or even my naked challenge. I didn't know why, but as different as we were, I felt Tarkan and I were a lot alike. He was willing to put it all on the line. And what choice did I really have? I had myself, my father—who was out of commission—and a rabbi with one foot in the grave on my team. I needed all the help I could get, and Tarkan seemed like the kind of ally I could use.

"Can you promise to keep this between us?" I said. "That you won't file any reports? Won't open an investigation folder? Pretend you never met me."

He held my eyes and I could tell he was considering my offer carefully and didn't give his word lightly.

"Because once I tell you, if they find out, the most you could hope for is an end to your career; the worst and you're a dead man."

He leaned forward. He didn't scare easily. Another good sign. "Agreed . . . for now. Who are 'they'?"

I dropped my bombs all at once. "Francis X. Laughlin, the Catholic church, a group called the Committee, and if I'm right, the CIA. That's for starters."

I expected shock or disbelief but didn't get either. His expression was unchanged.

"Keep talking," he said.

I put together everything I had found out from my father's pack, plus what I'd learned yesterday. I told him about my visit to Gershowitz, slipping in my own theories whenever they fit. I trusted Tarkan but left out the part about the dead man in my backyard and the couple I'd shot in Brooklyn. Still, I was able to paint a picture that, though filled with blank spots, had a balance and the resonance of truth.

When I finished almost an hour later, Tarkan's expression hadn't changed.

"This is dangerous stuff, Danny," he said quietly.

"Are you saying you want out?"

"No. Not at all," he said, his dangerous smile returning, "in fact, I wouldn't miss it for the world."

"Good," I said, comfortable with the man across from me. "That's settled. Is there a phone in this joint?"

"Do you have a last name?"

"Maguire," I said. "Danny Maguire."

He nodded once then reached into his breast pocket and pulled out a slim cellular phone, passing it over to me. I dialed Lita's. Tarkan watched as I hung up and dialed again.

"Wrong number," I said, punching redial.

Still no answer. A chill ran through me. "Do you have a car?"

"Outside."

"Then let's go," I said, standing up and making for the door.

"Where?" he said, throwing some bills on the table and hurrying to catch up to me.

"Brooklyn."

17

Tarkan's dark-blue Chevy Suburban was parked in a loading zone on 41st, the NYPD "Official Business" placard on his flipped-down visor. He pulled into traffic.

"Brooklyn Heights," I said. "And let's move it."

We barreled down Broadway. Tarkan's driving fit his accent; he had the instincts of a cabbie. He drove with one hand on the wheel dodging and weaving. With his other hand he picked up his radiophone handset. He told someone named Franklin that he would be out of touch for a while. Then he was quiet, the phone glued to his ear.

"Who authorized the transfer!" Tarkan shouted, stealing a glance at me. "What! When do we get him back . . . ?

"I want you to keep me posted. Page me the minute you hear anything. Yeah. Right."

He slammed the receiver down.

"What happened?" I asked.

"Seems the feds took our pal Lindquist over to the Federal Building for questioning."

I thought about the article. "The *Times* mentioned something about federal charges."

"Yeah. But usually we get first crack, then call them. This is backward."

"Who took him?"

"That's the really strange part," he said looking at me. "Someone from the CIA. My aide Franklin says the reason on the form was 'national security.' "

"Laughlin," I said.

"He's retired."

"Not Laughlin himself," I said. "He's still got a man at the Agency. A guy named Osborne. It's the kind of thing he might be able to pull off."

Tarkan nodded as he swerved around a bus, only to be blocked by a sea of red taillights stretching ahead for blocks. He pulled his dome light from under the seat, rolled down his window, and slapped it on the roof. As he rolled up his window he hit the siren. A path slowly started to form in front of us. Tarkan put his fist on the horn and kept it there. The gap widened.

It wasn't until we were at the foot of the Brooklyn Bridge that he killed the siren and pulled down the light.

"Now that," he said with his kick-ass smile, "is one of the reasons I love being a cop."

The bridge was clear and we were at the brownstone in minutes. Tarkan parked across the street, two wheels on the curb, and flipped down his visor.

I ran up the wide stone steps. Tarkan came up behind me.

I was about to push the intercom when Tarkan put his hand on my shoulder and pointed to the latch.

"It's been jimmied," he said.

"Cover me," I said, taking out my gun and pushing open the door.

"Right behind you," Tarkan whispered, retrieving his own gun.

The house was quiet. I pointed to the library and put my finger to my lips. Tarkan nodded.

I crept into the room gun first. The couch was empty, embers from a fire still glowing in the fireplace. I saw the umbrella stand with the IV bags. The catheter tube was dripping into a small pool on the rug.

"I'll take the first floor," I told Tarkan, heading to the kitchen. "You check upstairs."

We met back in the library.

"Empty," he said, holstering his gun. "What the hell is going on?"

"Wait!" I said, picking up the phone and dialing Lita's place in Connecticut.

"If Laughlin found them"—I said as I let it ring once, hung up, and dialed again "—then he'll know about . . ." I didn't finish because Nick answered the phone.

"It's me, son," I said, doing my best to control my voice.

"Dad! Where are you? Are you coming up here? It's—"

I cut him off. "Where's Mom?"

"Outside with Marie," he said, feelings hurt.

"This is important, Nick," I said, looking over at Tarkan. "Get her."

"But . . ."

"Listen, Nicky, I don't have time to explain. Get Mommy. Now!"

He put the phone down. I looked at my watch, counting the seconds, wondering how much time I had before the noose closed on them too.

"Danny?" She was out of breath.

"Thank God you're home," I said. "Is there a car up there?"

"Yes. In the garage."

"Okay. Take it and get out of there. Now. This minute. Just take the money. Don't pack, don't shut off the lights. Just leave."

"Danny . . ."

I felt each passing second as if it were a sting. "Just listen to me! Go. Now."

"Where?"

I ran a hand through my hair.

"I don't know," I said. "Just get in the car and drive. Find a motel out of the way somewhere. Understand?"

"Yes," she said. Ready to hang up.

"Hold on!" I said.

"Give me your pager number," I told Tarkan.

He gave it to me and I repeated it to Tuesday. "Write it down. It's a pager number. Call me when you get settled so I know how to get in touch with you."

I made her repeat the number to make sure she got it right. "Good," I said. "Now don't wait another second."

No sooner had I hung up the phone than Tarkan's pager went off. I reached for the phone and was about to dial Tuesday when the detective pulled out his cell phone and held up a hand.

"My office," he said, pulling up the antenna.

"Tarkan here," he said. He looked at me, his expression unreadable. "What?" Another long pause as he listened. His head dropped and he ran his free hand across his face. "When? . . . Okay. . . . Thanks, Franklin," he said. "Start the paperwork for me. Tell the commander I'll check in as soon as I can."

He shut off the phone.

"Lindquist is dead," he said, looking into the fireplace. "Broke a window and jumped from the fourteenth floor of the Federal Building about half an hour ago. What the hell is going on?"

I took my cell phone from my pocket and turned it on.

Tarkan looked puzzled as I powered it up and pushed redial.

It was answered on the fifth ring.

"Where is he!" I demanded.

"Relax," Laughlin said. His voice was chatty.

"Don't tell me to relax! Let me talk to him."

"My, my. Aren't we testy?" he said.

"Fuck you, Laughlin!"

Tarkan's eyes narrowed.

"As usual, you've got it all wrong, kid. In case you hadn't noticed, things have changed. *I* am the fucker, and you are the fuckee." He laughed at his own joke. Then his voice became harsh, his words clipped.

"And I'm tired of you and your father's games. From now on you'll be following my instructions. To the tee. You with me?"

I didn't answer.

"Here's the way we're going to work it. I hope you're listening, because one screwup and your daddy dies—this time for real. And so does the lovely Lita. Can't for the life of me understand what she sees in your old man. . . ."

He was enjoying this.

"Ah well. Such is life. But where was I? Oh, yes. A trade: Rosen's letter for your father—"

"Let me speak with him."

"I haven't finished."

"And unless you put him on the phone, you won't. For all I know he's already dead. Now put him on!"

"You're pushing it, kid."

A few seconds passed.

"Danny?"

It was my father. His voice was almost a whisper. I closed my eyes then opened them.

"I'm here," I finally said.

"Sorry . . ."

"Forget it. Are you all right?"

"Fine. I'm fine." Then in a rush: "Run, Danny! Take the letter—"

There was the sound of a scuffle, the phone dropped. I held my breath.

Laughlin got back on. "Stupid! You still there, Maguire?"

"I'm here."

"Call me back in exactly two hours. Be ready to follow my instructions. And remember: Anything goes wrong and Daddy gets hurt."

The line went dead. I looked at my watch. It was half-past three. I put my head in my hands. When Tarkan spoke, his voice came from a million miles away.

"I know some people . . ."

"Think, Tarkan," I said as I stood. "Laughlin cut through the

NYPD like it was a ripe watermelon, ate it whole, and spit Lindquist out like a seed. Lindquist didn't jump from any window and you know it. Anyone else you tell is another potential leak. Forget it."

"Do you have a better idea?"

"Not yet," I said, walking up to him. "But if you're going to bail out, now is the time, because things can only get worse. If you do, it's okay. Just forget we ever met. In return, I'll promise to keep you out of it, make sure your name never comes up. Whatever happens."

His Cheshire cat grin returned.

"Punch out now?" he said. "Just when things are getting interesting? You've gotta be kidding. I'm in."

I smiled back. I'd chosen well.

WE WERE STOPPED on the Brooklyn Bridge in a traffic snarl that even Tarkan's siren, light, and horn could do nothing to ease. So like the rest of the victims, we inched our way across the span, the sparkling East River far below.

I took the pendant from my pocket and held it to the cool winter sun, turning it this way and that, watching the light diffract through the prisms of the jewels. I heard my father's voice on the phone, telling me to run. . . .

"What's this worth?" I asked.

"If you knew who to call, three hundred fifty thousand before dinner. Give it three days, put the word out, hold a telephone auction, you could easily double that, maybe even get a cool million."

"What about the dagger?"

He whistled.

"That's a tough one," he said. "It defines the word 'priceless.' It belongs in a museum."

"But if the word got out it was available?"

"Fifteen, maybe twenty million."

I thought about having almost thirty million dollars' worth of artifacts in my pockets and more in the worn backpack sitting on the backseat. If I listened to my father, I could catch up with Tuesday and the kids, start selling the artifacts, and we could run. Thirty million could buy a lot of space.

But it wouldn't work. My father had been right. No matter how far we ran, sooner or later Laughlin would find us. And I'd have sacrificed my father for nothing—something I wasn't ready to do.

"Is that what you want to do?" Tarkan said, reading my mind. "Sell the icons and run?"

I shook my head. "No. What I want is to get what's left of my life back. I want to wake up in my little house next to my wife, hear my kids laugh, watch them grow."

We were finally off the bridge.

"Do you like to gamble, Tarkan?"

He laughed. "You tell me."

"Point for Tarkan," I said, scratching a line on an imaginary slate. "Laughlin thinks I have a letter that tells the whole story . . ."

"But you're bluffing."

"Of course. If he knew, my father would already be dead."

"Knowing how to bluff is one thing," he said. "But sooner or later you'll have to show your cards. What else have you got?"

"Not much," I said honestly. "The artifacts. A few old papers, a diary no one but me can read or understand . . ."

The light bulb came on. "And Gershowitz!"

"The rabbi?"

"Right. I think it's time to see him again."

"What for?"

"Give him his chance to do the right thing. We'll take him with us, let Laughlin know he's got other problems. Up the ante."

"You've got another card too," he said, hitting the gas hard. "A wild card nobody knows is in the deck."

I fastened my seat belt. "What's that?"

"You're looking at him."

18

TARKAN PULLED TO the curb a few blocks from Gershowitz's building. I told him that the rabbi might not be ready for a New York cop and asked him to wait in the car. He agreed. Reluctantly.

Instead of the ancient doorman with the faded but regal uniform, a pallid young man with rose-tinted glasses opened the door.

"Can I help you?" he said without a smile.

"Rabbi Gershowitz, please."

I followed him to the tiny concierge desk and watched as he picked up the building phone and dialed. I recognized the thick-lensed glasses of the old doorman sitting atop a folded newspaper.

"Someone to see you," he said into the intercom. "Fine. You can go up," he said as he hung up. Walking to the elevator, I turned to look back. The surly young man's eyes were on me.

There was a different elevator operator too. He was a bit older than the man downstairs but wore the same empty expression. I stepped in.

As he slid the door closed and the elevator jerked to a start, all the alarm bells in my head sounded. The old doorman from my first visit would never have left his glasses behind. Today's doorman never asked who I was. The man running the elevator never bothered to ask which floor I wanted to go to because he already knew.

The elevator operator turned his head in my direction just as I reached for the gun in my pocket. His leg shot out in a sweeping arc. It was aimed for my knee. But as he made his move, he lost his grip on the control and the elevator jerked to a stop, throwing him slightly off balance. Still, when his heel connected with my hip, it felt like being hit with a baseball bat.

There was no room for me to back up, no time to pull the gun. I dropped into a crouch, his fist whistling past where my head had been.

I threw a straight left. Instead of connecting with his groin, where I'd aimed, my bandaged fist drove deep into his gut. As I screamed in pain, he grunted and backed up half a step. When he did, I drove my fist between his legs with everything I had. As he started to go down, I clubbed the back of his neck with my elbow, dropping with him, putting my whole body into it. I heard something crack.

I leaned against the elevator wall panting, cursing my stupidity, my hand a thousand points of pain. I was trapped. If I went down to the lobby the other man would be waiting. I had no idea what lay in store for me at Gershowitz's, but threw the switch forward. The elevator shot up with a jerk. I kept an eye on the body sprawled facedown on the floor just in case.

I missed twelve and had to reverse. I slid past the floor again on the way down and cursed. This time when the cab was within a foot of twelve I let go of the control and slid open the door. The man at my feet hadn't moved.

The hall was empty, but the door to Gershowitz's apartment was ajar. The gun now in my good hand, I slowly pushed open the door with my bad hand. A red stain was spreading across the bandage and every move hurt.

I eased into the catacomblike apartment, my gun leading the

way. Over the roaring sound of my own heart, I heard the unmistakable slap of skin on skin, then something that sounded like a cat's mewling.

I became still, not daring to take a breath. I stayed that way until my lungs screamed. Silence. I started forward again. The door to the study was half closed. Then there was the sound of another slap.

I held the gun straight out, took two quick breaths, and pushed the door the rest of the way open, my finger tightening on the trigger.

Gershowitz was in his chair, a man standing over him, his fist in a ball. The man had just turned to see me when the gun in my hand spat twice. The man fell over, a fountain of blood spurting from his neck.

I knelt beside the rabbi, trying not to look at the bloody mess of the man I'd shot. The still-living side of the rabbi's face was twisted in pain and a trickle of blood flowed from his nose. His good eye found mine.

"Can you move?" I asked him.

He nodded.

"Help me," he said, his cane trembling in his hand.

I heard a floorboard creak behind me and swiveled, the gun in both hands, my finger tightening on the trigger.

"Don't shoot!"

It was Tarkan. I lowered the gun. My hand was shaking.

He saw the man on the floor, his lifeblood surrounding his head like a halo.

"What are you doing here!" I shouted, my breathing ragged.

"I came in right after you. To keep an eye on your back. There was no one at the door and the elevator didn't respond so I started up the stairs. I heard someone ahead of me. I followed."

It made sense. When the elevator never came back, the doorman must have figured that I was already dead or something was wrong. Either way he had to go up to find out.

"I caught up to him," Tarkan said, his expression neutral.

"And . . . ?"

He fixed me with a blank expression that didn't need words; the man wouldn't be coming upstairs.

"Who is he?" Gershowitz managed to ask, his cane pointing at Tarkan.

"A friend. Come on. We've got to get out of here."

THE MAN I'D fought with in the elevator lay exactly where I'd left him. I hefted him under his arms and dragged him into the stairwell. From the way his head hung, I knew he was dead.

Tarkan scouted the lobby, making sure it was empty before he and I helped the limping Gershowitz into the backseat of the car.

Tarkan eased into traffic with uncharacteristic caution. A few blocks away, he pulled over and lay his head against the steering wheel. I knew what he was thinking.

"Listen, Sam," I said. "There's still time for you. Let us out here . . ."

"It's too late for that," he said without looking at me. "I just killed a man and walked away from a triple homicide! And . . ." He let it trail off. "Maybe if everything turns out all right," he said, not believing his own words. "Maybe then . . ."

I turned to look at Gershowitz. A nasty knot had formed over his bad eye.

"What did the man want from you?" I asked.

The good half of the rabbi's mouth twisted up into a smile.

"What you wanted. Information. Whether I'd seen you or your father. Whether I knew about Rosen's letter . . ."

He started to cough and rattled and wheezed for almost a minute before he could speak again.

"I told him I didn't know what he was talking about," he said, feeling his brow. "I don't think he believed me."

I looked at my watch. It was five. I pulled out the cell phone and dialed.

"You're early," Laughlin said as soon as he answered.

"There's been a slight change in plans, Laughlin," I said, making eye contact with Gershowitz.

"You're not in a position to change anything, Maguire."

"Enough!" I barked, the remainder of my adrenaline rush catching up to me. "There's someone I'd like you to talk to."

I held the phone to Gershowitz's ear.

"Laughlin," the old rabbi said, nodding his head. "Of course it's me. . . . No? . . . You can tell me all about it when we meet in hell."

I took back the phone and let a few seconds slip by.

"You still there, Laughlin?"

"You're dead!" Laughlin said, unable to control himself. "All of you! Dead!"

"Not yet we're not. Expect a call from me later. When I'm ready for the swap," I said.

Laughlin was silent.

"In the meantime," I said, "I suggest you clean up the mess at the rabbi's apartment; you'll need three body bags."

More silence.

"And, Laughlin? Take very good care of my father and Lita."

I didn't wait for an answer. I started to shake all over and just managed to get the car door open before I threw up.

TARKAN'S APARTMENT WAS on the second floor of an old railroad flat on Fifteenth Street just east of Third. Tarkan collected his mail and, together, we helped the old rabbi up the stairs.

"Lousy neighborhood," the detective explained after twisting the keys to three separate locks to open his apartment door. He stood aside and motioned for us to enter.

A big tabby cat rubbed against his leg. He picked it up.

"Hello, Pooh," he said, rubbing the cat under the chin. "I've had a rough day. How about you?"

The apartment was painfully austere and spare. There wasn't a photograph or painting on the wall. I knew without a word that except for the cat, Tarkan lived alone. The only hint that the flat was occupied by a living breathing human was a row of floor-to-ceiling shelves full of neatly organized books.

As I took off my coat and laid it on my father's backpack, Gershowitz hobbled over to the wall and studied the titles of the books.

Tarkan came back into the room. Instead of the cat, he was holding a bottle of Jack Daniel's and three tumblers.

"I don't entertain much," he said, putting the bottle and glasses down on a low table in front of a simple couch.

"You study," Gershowitz said as he turned.

"Yes."

"Art. History. Archaeology," the rabbi said, leaning heavily on his cane and sinking slowly onto the sofa. "Religion . . ."

Tarkan nodded and poured a fingerful of amber liquid into the glasses and handed us each one.

"And language," Gershowitz continued, his good eye following the detective's every move. "But not just any languages; Aramaic. Armenian. Hebrew. Latin . . ."

Tarkan sat in a worn black leather armchair, leaned back, and took a long sip of his drink.

"I'm a cop," Tarkan said easily. "I work in the art and fraud division. It helps me in my work."

Gershowitz raised a bony finger. "Ah. Perfect!" he said. "Very clever! No?" He took a measured sip from his glass. "Do you know what I see? A man who looks like he should play football, sounds like he should be selling peanuts at Yankee Stadium, is a New York detective, studies ancient cultures, and lives like a monk."

Tarkan shrugged as if to say "big deal."

Gershowitz flashed a crooked smile. "And who would be such a man?" he asked, not expecting an answer, his good eye twinkling.

I wasn't sure what he was leading up to. I looked over at Tarkan to see if he did. His features were set and unreadable.

"I can think of only one," Gershowitz finally said, taking his time with each word to make sure there was no misunderstanding. "Should I call you Simon? The Rock? Peter?—or the Adjustor?"

I let all of the whiskey slip over my tongue and down my throat. It traced a fiery path to my stomach.

I looked back and forth between Tarkan and Gershowitz to see who blinked first. Tarkan did.

I refilled my glass and threw back a second belt of whiskey. This was why Tarkan didn't haul me downtown; why he never asked where I got the artifacts; why he wasn't surprised by my last name and never pursued it; why he seemed to know where Gershowitz lived without my telling him: He already knew.

I stared at the detective. He returned my glare. "Why didn't you tell me?" I had been betrayed.

"I was going to . . ."

"Bullshit!"

He stood so we were eye to eye.

"Now you know," he said. "Does it matter?"

"That depends . . ."

"On what?"

"On whose side you're on."

"It's not about choosing sides. It's not just you and your father. Or me. Or Laughlin. Or him," he said looking over at the rabbi.

"The church?"

"Yes. And others."

He walked over to his books, ran a hand along the spines.

"If I'm gone someone will replace me," he said. "And when he's gone, someone will replace him. And on and on."

He wasn't afraid of me. He wasn't afraid of dying. He had a cause greater than himself, one he believed in. I had my wife and kids and now my father to kill for; I couldn't think of any other reason that would make me play chameleon or martyr. In a cockeyed way I envied his devotion.

He turned and looked at me, his dangerous smile returning. "Think it through," he said. "Although it was Providence that brought you to me, I knew who you were from the moment you called. If I wanted you and your father out of the way, it would have already happened." The threat was unmistakable, though it was delivered with something like regret.

"Then tell me, Peter," I said, filling my glass a third time. "Why haven't you?"

Gershowitz spoke before Tarkan could answer.

"Because," the rabbi said. "If you're dead you're of no use to him or the church."

"What do you mean?" I asked Gershowitz.

"Laughlin hasn't been blackmailing only me, he's threatened the church as well." His grin returned and he coughed a little, but I knew it was a chuckle. "The only person who managed to beat Laughlin at his own game is your father. He has eluded him all these years and still managed to keep a knife at his throat, as surely as Laughlin has held his to ours."

I finally understood. It was my father who really held it all together. By his strength and his pain. And now Laughlin had him and needed the one thing my father's years of cunning had kept from him, the letter from Rosen. The letter that didn't exist and never had. The letter Laughlin now thought I held in my hands.

"So as long as Laughlin thought my father was out there somewhere ready to expose him with the letter," I said, my rage beginning to show, "the church was safe as well. Is that it, Tarkan? You wanted my father out in the cold. Alone and untouchable! As long as he was keeping Laughlin in line, it kept your secrets too, made your job easier."

"It was the only way . . ." Tarkan said quietly.

I heard laughter and for a second didn't recognize it as my own.

"So my family was just another casualty, right? My father and mother. Me."

Tarkan avoided my eyes.

"Answer me, you son of a bitch!"

I sized him up. He'd taken off his holster. I could get the gun from my coat pocket and shoot him before he took three steps. I'd killed four people in two days, adding Peter to the count wouldn't make a difference. But then I envisioned my family and knew that even though he'd betrayed me once, I'd need this Tarkan, this Peter, if I were ever to return to them.

Gershowitz looked weary. Weary and ancient. Still, I needed all the help I could get. And right now all I had were the two men in front of me.

I roared and threw my glass. It passed inches from Tarkan's head and slammed into the wall shattering into a hundred pieces. The cat jumped three feet in the air and disappeared with a howl. Tarkan didn't flinch.

I had a thousand questions I wanted to ask him and I might have if his pager hadn't started its insistent beeping.

He pulled it from his belt.

"It's an 860 area code," he said, reading the display then passing it to me.

It had to be Tuesday.

THERE WERE THIRTEEN digits on the pager. I dialed the first ten, puzzled over the remaining three numbers until a gravelly voiced man answered.

"Riverside Motel," he said.

I looked back at the display and understood. I asked to be connected to room 318, the numbers that followed the ten-digit phone number.

When Tuesday answered, her voice sounded flat and distant. She said the motel was a drab affair about an hour south of Lita's country place, just off the Taconic Parkway. I asked about the kids. She said they were fine but I knew they were in the room with her and she was lying so as not to upset me or them. I told her Laughlin had Lita and my father.

"Just stay put," I said. "Okay?"

Tarkan was at my side, the cat in the crook of one of his arms. He held up a finger.

"Hold on," I told Tuesday, covering the mouthpiece and looking at Tarkan.

"I have a place for them to go where he can't find them," he said. "Someplace safe."

"Where?" I asked, no longer taking anything for granted.

"The Cloisters."

"On the Upper West Side?"

"Yes. I have a friend there. A man who can be trusted."

In that instant I had to again decide whether to believe the man who'd lied to me. A man already serving another master, one he'd devoted his life and soul to. A master that demanded complete and total loyalty. I held his gaze, watching for a momentary shift of his eyes telling me he was lying. They were steady and unblinking.

I pictured Tuesday and the kids in some cheap motel on the side of the highway, alone and afraid. I took my hand from the mouthpiece.

"Honey?"

"I'm here."

"Get a pencil and paper . . ."

19

AFTER I HUNG up the phone with Tuesday, Tarkan made a call and told the person on the other end to expect guests, a woman and two children. He gave instructions to make them comfortable and said he'd be there later. He did it all without a wasted word. I got the feeling it wasn't the first time he'd made a call like this.

I returned to the living room. Gershowitz was snoring deeply, his head thrown back on the couch, his mouth agape. I retrieved my gun, picked up my father's pack, shook out the ammunition box and reloaded the clip, then slipped it in my waistband like a bandito. The dull throb in my hand flared when the bandage, crusted now with dried blood, snagged on my pants.

"What are you going to do?" Tarkan asked from the doorway.

"Get my father back."

"And how do you plan to do it?"

"I don't know yet. Something will come to me."

"Lousy odds."

"Yeah. Well, I guess I'll just have to take my chances."

"I can even them up."

"You said it wasn't about choosing sides."

"Maybe I was wrong," he said.

The rabbi awoke with a snort, saw the gun in my pants, and nodded.

"Is it time?" he asked, his good eye darting from me to Tarkan then back.

"Soon, Rabbi," Tarkan said simply. "But first we need a plan—and something to eat."

Gershowitz started laughing and I was afraid he'd end up in another paroxysm of coughing, but he didn't.

"You sound like my mother," the old rabbi said.

"Then your mother was wise," Tarkan said, helping the old man to his feet. "An army, even one with God on its side, still marches on its stomach."

Like the rest of the apartment, the kitchen was unadorned and utilitarian. Our host carried two chairs from the living room and set them at a small table already flanked by a single chair.

As Gershowitz and I sat, Tarkan took a loaf of bread and a stick of butter and set them on the table. Next was a large bottle of a no-name Cabernet and three new glasses. Then the detective went to work with the efficiency of a short-order cook.

He boiled some pasta, stir-fried some vegetables in olive oil and garlic, then tossed it all together and sprinkled it with Parmesan. The aroma filled the little room, making my mouth water.

Tarkan placed the steaming bowl in the middle of the table and served us each. I was on my second mouthful when I noticed both Tarkan and Gershowitz, eyes closed, whispering to themselves in prayer. I figured they were covering all the bases, so I kept eating.

"Making a swap work depends on a lot of things," Tarkan said, after opening his eyes, and tearing off a piece of the bread.

"That's assuming both sides want a successful trade," I answered between bites. "But Laughlin doesn't. He'll do everything he can to get the letter *and* us. And you can bet he won't be alone. What we need is an edge," I said, remembering every movie and book I'd come across where a trade took place. "A way to keep him off guard and guessing where the meet is so he can't lay a trap for us."

"Someplace public," Tarkan said.

"I was thinking secluded," I responded. "Private and out of the way." I didn't add my reasoning. I didn't plan to complete the exchange either. If I could help it, Laughlin wouldn't be leaving alive.

I tried not to watch Gershowitz struggling as he ate and talked at the same time. "The shul," he said.

"What?"

"My temple. Beth Israel."

I thought Gershowitz might be drifting. But he wasn't.

"It's perfect," the old man continued, a small piece of pasta clinging to his drooping lower lip.

"Why is that?"

He carefully wiped his face with a napkin and pushed his plate away. "Because no one has the key but me. No one will be there, and he knows it well."

"How come?"

"It's where we met. The night he and Rosen came over."

"I thought it was just Rosen who came to you, a night in August of '43?"

"Right. It wasn't until the spring of 1945, right near the end of the war, that I actually met Laughlin." He waved a hand, wiping away the memories.

"But—"

"Your father can tell you," he said. "Later."

I wanted to know more and I could tell that Tarkan did too. But like so many things, it would have to wait.

"How long will it take to get there?" I asked.

"It's two blocks from my apartment."

I thought it over. It was just as Gershowitz said: perfect. I talked out loud, just to hear how it sounded.

"Let's do it like this. We'll head over to the temple, then I'll call

Laughlin and ask him to go to Lincoln Center, just him, Lita, and my father. Once he's there, I'll ask him to call again. Then I'll give him ten minutes to get to the temple, so he doesn't have time to set a trap. You and I will be inside," I said to Gershowitz. "You," I told Tarkan, "will be the outside man to see that he plays by the rules."

"And if he doesn't?" the detective wanted to know.

I found his eyes with mine. "We do what we have to."

TARKAN DROPPED US off in front of the temple, then took off to park around the block. We were expecting Laughlin to double cross us. Our only advantage was being able to dictate the place and time for the exchange. It would be nice if we had more backup, but Tarkan would have to serve.

Temple Beth Israel was a narrow three-story sandstone-faced building set incongruously mid-block in a row of five-story walk-ups. Like the rest of the neighborhood, the temple had seen better days and could have used a good cleaning. The front doors were blocked by an ugly accordion gate and padlock. The windows were covered with heavy woven steel mesh. I was about to take Gershowitz by the elbow and help lead him up the chipped stone steps when he pulled gently away from me and headed to the side of the building.

"The alley door," he explained. "That gate hasn't been opened in years."

A door was set in the side of the building. He took a key and handed it to me. It slipped into a gleaming chrome padlock holding a hasp on the door. The lock opened with a reassuring click, and the steel door opened soundlessly. I could tell that in spite of appearances, Gershowitz opened this door frequently.

Gershowitz's feet knew every inch of the old temple, and he was quickly ahead, calling after me. I put on lights wherever I found a switch. The feeble light that came from the low-wattage lamps cast a soft orange glow. The inside of the temple was cold, probably no more than sixty degrees.

We ended up in a small sanctuary with a dozen rows of narrow pews. Gershowitz, suddenly spry and with a quick step now that he was in his temple, stopped and pointed to a flickering flame near the Torah ark.

"The eternal flame," he said proudly. "Would you like to say kaddish for your mother?"

Kaddish was the Jewish prayer for the dead. I told the rabbi I could no more recite this most basic and essential Jewish prayer than I could quote Shakespeare.

He shook his head and put a bony hand on my shoulder. "This at least you should learn, young Maguire. For your mother."

I nodded and turned away, embarrassed. The extent of my religious education was limited to the two times my mother had taken me to synagogue and the one time my father had taken me to church. In the temple, my mother saw the eternal flame and cried. I asked her why, and she said she'd tell me later. There never was a later.

For his part, my father took me to St. Stephen's one Easter the year I was ten. I loved the bone-shaking organ, the ceremony, the holy water. My father saw my wide eyes and gave me his version of Catholicism, whispered during the Mass of the Resurrection:

"That's how they rope you in. They give you all the good stuff first; the pomp, the incense. Then, pow! it's on to sin, hell, and damnation."

So I was a kind of nondemoninational Judeo-Christian Frankenstein. And my own family didn't make things any easier. Tuesday was a sort of part-time Buddhist. Her only bow to tradition was making a yearly solo pilgrimage to a small Buddhist temple on the anniversary of her family's slaughter.

The rub was that the way things were going, I wanted to pray but didn't know who to ask or how, the same problem I'd had in Vietnam. Over there, when the mortar shells screamed in, all I could manage was to cover my head and say "oh shit, oh shit," over and over.

I took Laughlin's cell phone from my pocket and opened it.

"Here we go," I told Gershowitz.

"Tell him the door in the alley will be open," the rabbi said as he slipped past me, "and to meet us in the room where the mikvah is."

"The what?"

"The ritual bath in the basement," he said, doing his damnedest to cluck his tongue at me as he spoke. "He'll know. Just tell him. Now follow me."

Another steel door, another lock and key, and then we started to descend the stairs.

Laughlin answered the phone with silence.

"I know you're listening, Laughlin," I said. "But I have to make sure. What was your mother's maiden name?"

"Kiss my ass," he said.

"A little pissed," I said, twisting the screws as much as I dared. It felt good.

"You keep at it and I'll kill your father just for the hell of it."

"No you won't, Laughlin. In fact, I'd like to speak with him."

There was a rustle as the phone changed hands.

"Danny?" His voice was stronger.

"Are you all right?"

"I think I'll live to see another day," he said, just as the phone was snatched away from him.

"All right," Laughlin said. "Daddy's fine. Let's get this thing over with."

"How far are you from Lincoln Center?" I asked.

"Far enough."

"Wrong answer," I said. "Tell me. In minutes."

I knew he was debating whether he'd have to tip his hand by telling me.

"C'mon," I said. "It doesn't matter. You're coming to me."

"An hour. Maybe hour and a half."

"Good. Go to Lincoln Center. Pull in at the taxi lane. Just you, my father, and Dr. Ward. No one else."

"Listen—"

"I'm talking here, Laughlin. What kind of car will you be driving?"

"Black Mercedes sedan."

"Fine. Get there then call me back on this number," I said, and hung up.

THE BASEMENT OF the old temple was even colder than upstairs, the kind of damp cold that penetrated my shoes and traveled up my shins. But it didn't seem to bother Gershowitz.

"This is where we used to have Talmud sessions on the Sabbath," he said, flipping on the lights. "Me and the boys would sit around and argue, passing around a bottle of scotch . . ."

"Doesn't sound very scholarly," I said, looking at the stack of folding chairs. "Or pious."

"It wasn't. But that was the key," he said with his twisted smile.

I don't know if I'd just grown used to it or not but his voice no longer seemed as garbled or strained. I could now detect all the subtle nuances of inflection and cadence in his voice. Between the words I felt his sadness surrounding the memories of old friends long gone and a time when things were easier, simpler.

"It took me awhile to figure out that God had a sense of humor," he said. "And a sense of the absurd. How could you explain things otherwise?"

I could see him push these memories away, the implications too melancholy.

"I used to coach the kids for their Bar Mitzvahs down here too. I can't remember how many. And you know," he said with pride, "when the day came, and they stood in front of their families and the whole congregation, not one of them flubbed or faltered. . . . You know how?"

I shrugged.

"Bribes," he said, a twinkle in his eye. "I told each and every one of them there'd be twenty bucks in it for them if they didn't make a mistake."

He laughed one of those wheezing rumbling things that took a minute or so to pass.

"Come. I'll show you the mikvah," he said when he finally recovered.

I followed him as his cane tapped the linoleum floor in counterpoint to the scrape of his dragging foot.

The room was about twenty feet square with turquoise-blue ceramic tile walls and a white ceramic tile floor. In the corner was a square pool about four feet high, also covered with blue tile. It was full to the brim.

Large drops of water fell from a pipe poking from the wall into the pool. I dipped in the tips of my fingers. It was ice cold. I watched the ripples from the drips run across the glass-smooth surface and bounce from the tile walls then reflect and merge in an endlessly complex pattern.

"It looks like a baptismal."

"It is. The original model. It's what John the Baptist had in mind when he cleansed people's sins in the rivers of old Jerusalem," he said, running his hand along the tile.

"What do you mean?"

"The mikvah is a ritual cleansing bath. When someone converts to Judaism, they are immersed in the mikvah. Women use it after their menstrual cycle. It is so central and important to the practice of Judaism that many times a mikvah is constructed before a synagogue. But today, like so many other things, it is forgotten. . . ."

"Then why is it full if . . ." I didn't finish by saying "it wasn't used."

"It's a cistern," he said, his voice fading. "The mikvah must be filled with running water. In this case, rainwater. It's collected from the roof gutters, passed through a filter, and directed here, through that pipe. There is an overflow," he said, pointing without enthusiasm. "In the corner."

When he stopped talking, the only sound in the room was the rhythmic dripping of the water. The silence was palpable, threatening to engulf us. There were still things I wanted to know and now was as good a time as any.

"You told me my mother was 'the only one,' " I said quietly. "I'm not sure if I'll be leaving this building alive tonight, or if my father will either. I never understood my mother, never really knew her. And before I die I'd like to know. Please tell me the rest, Rabbi."

20

Gershowitz walked slowly to a long tiled bench and sat, motioning for me to sit next to him.

Looking at him in profile, the stroke-twisted side of his face hidden, I could imagine him as a younger man tending his flock in this place full of his faith's rich past. He focused on some distant point, took a deep, rasping breath and started talking.

I knew he was piecing together separate tales told by many people and that the story spanned decades, but he was a natural storyteller and the web he spun was as flawless as if he'd lived it all himself. It also became clear that there was little he didn't know.

He started his story the same place my father had started his: that hot summer night in August over five decades ago.

While Rosen was bringing the Judaica artifacts to this very temple, Laughlin showed Deere and my father a label he'd stripped from the cover of the small wooden box they'd taken from the basement. The address was for a gallery on Madison.

They went to the gallery in the small hours of the morning. It was a four-story brownstone. A light still shone from a top-floor window. Laughlin took the lead, slipping the lock on the front door. They quietly made their way to the top floor then rapped softly on the apartment door.

"A woman opened the door," Gershowitz said without turning toward me or looking my way. "The woman was your mother.

"The way your father told me later," Gershowitz continued, "he took one look at her and fell hopelessly in love. He said that even in the dead of night, facing three men with murder in their eyes, she was the most beautiful woman he'd ever seen. Thick wavy black hair, skin as white as cream, full lips, and the deepest brown eyes in creation. And," he said, turning toward me slightly, "according to your mother, the same thing had happened to her. She said that your father appeared to her as an avenging angel. The answer to her prayers.

"She asked who they were. Laughlin told her he'd ask the questions. She asked if they were Americans. Laughlin slapped her and drew back for another blow. Your father grabbed his arm and stopped him. She told them to do what they wanted with her and leave; she'd tell no one.

"By this time, she was begging," the rabbi told me, "and her accent got thicker and thicker."

I could hear it now, her voice soft, gentle, and high, but fringed with the exotic. When I was about five I first noticed her accent and asked her about it. She'd told me she had been born in Germany but sent as a young girl to go to school in the United States. Later, when I asked her why I didn't have a grandma and grandpa like my friends, she simply said that her parents had died in the war. Later still, after my father left and I pushed her to know more about my family, she explained that like millions of other European Jews, they'd been devoured by the Nazi death machine. She never seemed ready to offer me further details. There was enough pain and loss in our little family; dredging up more seemed cruel so I accepted her silence with love and understanding, maybe even gratitude. And as Gershowitz went on, I began to see the truth as far worse than I had imagined.

"Laughlin questioned her relentlessly," the old man said. My heart skipped a beat as I pictured my mother's fear.

"It didn't take long for her to break and the rest of the story to empty out of her. She was a Jewess, the daughter of well-to-do Berliners. Her father owned an auction house and gallery, her mother taught English, her brother Max was a law student."

My grandparents. My uncle.

"Your mother told me that her family were assimilated, secular Jews," Gershowitz said. "The type that thought Hitler was a funny-looking little man; that his Nazi party was a bunch of hooligans who'd soon stop their Jew baiting and rallies." He shifted slightly on the bench. "But when Max was kicked out of school in 1938 because he was a Jew, they knew they'd been wrong.

"The first thing they did was send your mother Olivia, just out of high school, to the U.S. It took all of their savings and then some for passage and bribes. She was accepted at Barnard as an art history major.

"For a while her parents managed to send her money, though their letters became less frequent and avoided all mention of the war or their lives.

"After Pearl Harbor, the letters from her family stopped and hers were returned unopened. She had no relatives in the U.S., no one to help. She soon ran out of money and quit school to work as an icer in a bakery.

"Then one day a letter from her mother arrived. It was post-marked Berne, Switzerland.

"Her mother wrote that she and her father and brother were safe but not to try to contact them. The letter went on to say that a man would be visiting her soon and that she should listen and do whatever he asked, that their lives depended on it."

Even in the chill damp of the basement, I was sweating. I got up, paced in front of Gershowitz. He was so engrossed in the story, he didn't even notice.

"The man arrived at her apartment one night unannounced. He

spoke flawless English and said he was Swiss, but she knew by his manner that he was German. He handed her another letter from her mother. Like the first, it was short and to the point, telling her to follow the instructions of her visitor.

"He called himself Jeffrey and told her he owned a small gallery trading in furniture and antiques and needed an assistant. He gave her the address. She was there the next morning.

"Jeffrey showed her how to open and close the store, answer the phone, the usual. He was only there for maybe half an hour a day, and usually spent that time on the phone in his little office at the rear of the cluttered shop.

"But your mother was confused. She knows her art, right? And the gallery is filled with junk not worth the wood or canvas it's made of."

He shook his head at the memory.

"And on the rare occasion a customer walks into the shop, they take one quick look and leave before she even gets a chance to greet them."

"Every other week Jeffrey hands her an envelope with her pay. When she felt comfortable with the routine, she gave him a letter and asked him to deliver it to her family. Two weeks later Jeffrey brings a return letter from her mother, letting Olivia know all is well.

"One afternoon, after a package was delivered, Jeffrey asked her into the back room. He opened the simple wooden crate and cleared away the wood shavings, then took out a cloth-wrapped bundle. He opened it, revealing a Bible covered with a solid gold front, back, and spine."

Gershowitz paused then and waited until I stopped pacing and looked at him.

"She told me she shivered when she read the Hebrew inscription on the front and her hands trembled as they leafed through the ancient parchment inscribed with handwritten Hebrew characters," he said, keeping me locked in his gaze. "She knew it was ancient and rare. She also knew it hadn't been given away or sold willingly. Just as Rosen had known the moment he'd seen the menorah, she understood, in a moment, and with complete certainty, that the Nazis were doing just as they'd said they would: They were eliminating the Jews—her friends, neighbors, and cousins. Not only their lives, but their faith. And that Jeffrey, and by extension she herself, was a part of it.

"She also knew that she was trapped. That the minute she ran or talked to anyone, Jeffrey would make a report and her family, like the people from whom the Bible had been taken, would die."

I started pacing again.

It was when Hitler's forces were in full retreat from Russia in the winter of '44 that the occasional shipments became a flood.

"Your mother told me that the packages started to arrive every day; some of the crates so big they had to be brought to the basement through the sidewalk elevator. And now it was no longer just Jewish artifacts but Christian, Copt, and Muslim as well."

Gershowitz took a deep breath and sat straighter.

"The German death machine was in full swing," he said, his voice stronger than before. If he could I'm sure he would have been shouting as he described the horrors that seemed as fresh to him as yesterday.

"There were killing fields from the North Sea to just outside Moscow. Whole villages were being rounded up and shot, or locked in their simple wooden synagogues and set afire by the mobile SS killing teams, German Police squads, and their willing local helpers. The camps like Auschwitz and Treblinka were working around the clock. So many were being 'processed' that the crematoria couldn't handle the piles of bodies. So shallow cuts were made into the earth, the victims were stripped and shot at the edges, then the squirming mass of the dead and wounded were bulldozed under. Scars from the slaughter still pock the earth.

"And of course, right behind the killing squads and just outside the crematoria were trucks and railway cars ready to haul off the gold. The watches, the rings, the fillings, the menorahs, the crosses and icons were all shuttled back to the Fatherland to be melted down or pawned. The Reichsbank weighed and measured every gram of gold, every carat of stone.

"But great artwork and other things with value beyond their melted down weight, like the religious artifacts, were culled from the booty and slipped through neutral countries then shipped again to galleries in New York, Paris, and London. From there the pieces went into the hands of collectors or through the back doors of museums like the Louvre and the Met."

He took a deep breath and coughed. I could tell he was getting tired.

"In New York, the spoils were piling up faster than Jeffrey could get rid of them.

"Your mother showed Laughlin the horde in a locked room at the basement of the shop. She said he actually sighed," Gershowitz said as I continued to pace, my back now to him.

"The room was lined with crude wooden shelves, groaning under the weight of objects of indescribable splendor, gold and silver, most covered in jewels.

"Laughlin almost killed her then. But your mother was clever. She took an ornate candelabra from the shelf and gave it to him, telling him to keep it, that there would be more. She was still worried about her family."

I stood still and faced him.

"But didn't Jeffrey miss it?" I asked.

"No. Jeffrey knew how the artifacts could be sold and to whom, but wouldn't know a pre-Christian chalice from a Byzantine candlestick. However, your mother, with her art education and experience from her father's business, did, and she spent hours identifying and cataloging the growing pile of booty. She kept the records."

I nodded that I understood.

"Your mother had read Laughlin like a book. By offering him the candlestick, and more to come, she'd tapped into his greed. But now she was wedged between two masters: Jeffrey and Laughlin.

If she betrayed Jeffrey, her family died. If Laughlin exposed the operation, the same thing would happen. She knew it and Laughlin knew it. Why would Laughlin kill the goose that laid the golden eggs? It was a perfect deal for a man like him and played to his vanity."

I stole a glance at my watch. It was almost an hour since my conversation with Laughlin. He might call any minute now, and if he did, I might never hear the rest of the story.

"Laughlin should be calling soon," I said quietly, urging him to hurry.

Gershowitz understood and nodded.

According to Gershowitz, Rosen had told him that whenever they could, my father, Laughlin, Deere, and Rosen would always manage a side trip to New York after one of their TDYs. I knew that was when my father's assassinations for the OSS were going on. But unbelievably, this fact, something that alone would once have shaken me to the core, was now a nonissue.

He explained how Laughlin, my father, and Deere let Rosen in on the story of what happened that night after he left, promising him he could keep on taking any of the Judaica and do with it what he pleased.

Gershowitz's voice became weaker then. I knew it was because this was when he could have done things differently but didn't.

"By this time, your mother and father were lovers, dreaming of a future. Your father didn't care about the money, just Olivia. So he told Laughlin he wanted nothing of the loot; he could split it all with Deere and Rosen. But he warned them that if anything happened to Olivia, they were dead men."

On one of the nights they were together, my mother shared her deepest fear to my father. She told him she suspected the letters from her family were fakes. Yes, the penmanship was the same as her mother's, but not the words; the language was bland and neutral, qualities she said her mother didn't possess.

"Your father thought of a way to find out. He asked Olivia if there was anything that no one but she and her mother would know. There was."

In the next letter to her family in Switzerland, Olivia wrote about their old miniature schnauzer Shatzi; how she missed playing with the cheerful little dog, cuddling with it on her bed at night. The family had indeed owned a miniature schnauzer named Shatzi, but it was a snappy and vicious little beast that either was put out in the garden or confined to the cellar.

The return letter from her mother in Switzerland said she too missed the adorable Shatzi, but that once the war was over and they were reunited they could buy another dog, just as sweet and lovable.

"So she knew her family was dead," Gershowitz said.

I felt a shiver.

"She wanted to run away that night. But your father was still in the army. So they couldn't run together. And if she left on her own, there'd be no one to protect her from Jeffrey or Laughlin."

The rabbi explained that by then, the tide of the war had finally turned. The Nazis were being hammered. The Soviets were pounding them from the East, the Americans and English from the West and South. Everyone knew it wouldn't be long before the once invincible German army would be crushed between the two.

Gershowitz leaned forward, resting his hand on his cane.

"That's when your mother came up with the plan," he said, shaking his head ruefully. "They would continue as before, with one difference: She wanted my father to start taking his share of the icons. She would select and skim the rarest, most holy objects she came across and could hide from Jeffrey and slip them to him or hide them herself. And when the war ended, they would return the priceless relics to the communities from which they'd been stripped.

"Your father thought it was too risky. But your mother wouldn't budge, and in the blush of their young love and the loss and death surrounding them, he finally agreed."

She started keeping a record of the trade in the artifacts: the where and who. Dates, Names. Addresses. Anything she came across that might help.

"It was bold. It was daring," Gershowitz said, his voice rougher and weaker. "But, like so many other brave and noble plans, it was destined to fail. It relied on the most elusive and delicate of concepts: justice and truth—things almost as rare as the artifacts. But the most important reason it could never work was that it failed to factor in the strongest of all human frailties: greed."

I knew he was talking not only about the star-crossed lovers but himself as well.

The rest of the story came out in chopped bursts, just as I imagined it must have seemed as events rushed past them all: Gershowitz, Rosen, my mother and father, Laughlin.

As Gershowitz told it, it was a frigid night in New York—January of '45. The end of the war was in sight. The OSS forays fewer. Another TDY in Manhattan. Laughlin said this might be the last of their missions and proposed making one last score at the gallery while they still had the chance.

Rosen called Gershowitz. The rabbi arranged a truck and space in Beth Israel's basement to hide the artifacts.

They pulled up to the gallery late that night. My father rushed to tell Olivia what was happening and helped her throw together her suitcase. She retrieved their small but priceless stash of artifacts from a small compartment in her closet and mixed them in with her clothes as she packed.

"As Rosen, Deere, and Laughlin looted the basement storeroom for a final time, your father took your mother to a hotel and told her to wait for him. It was only then she realized that in the rush, she'd forgotten the diary with all of the names and addresses. But it was too late, because by the time your father got back to the gallery, the truck was gone and flames leaped from the show window, licking the floor above—they'd torched the building."

The chirp of the cell phone pierced Gershowitz's voice.

I opened the cover slowly and without a hello.

"I'm here," Laughlin said with annoyance. "Where the hell are you?"

I waited a second or two before answering. "Remember Temple Beth Israel, Laughlin?"

"I'm running out of patience, Maguire."

"Just answer the question."

"Yeah. I know where it is."

"Be at the temple in ten minutes. Exactly. Come through the alley door, my father and Lita first. Then you. Meet us in the mikvah room."

"This is amateur hour . . ."

I hung up on him.

"He'll be here in ten minutes," I said, standing and pulling the pistol from my waistband.

I had forgotten the cold in my feet and legs; all I could think about was my mother and how little I'd really known her. How when he disappeared, my father had robbed me not only of his presence but of hers as well. I could see that they'd lied to protect me, but that didn't ease the pain. If there was any comfort, it was in the knowledge that my mother was as heroic and brave as my father was, maybe more. And her life had been twice as tragic; she'd lost not one family but two. Perhaps now I could lay to rest the guilt I still felt about her long silences and black moods, knowing they'd been born long before me.

And now I could also leave behind any doubts I might have had about my plan to kill Laughlin. He'd stolen them both from me, and for that there would be no mercy.

21

I WAS BEHIND a pillar about fifteen feet from the bottom of the stairs when I heard the steps. I raised my pistol, holding it in both hands, bracing my forearms against the post.

My father came into view. He was favoring his bad side slightly. He was pale and drawn, his face still covered with gray stubble.

"Over here, Dad," I called softly.

He saw me.

"Move to the side," I said, motioning with my head toward the mikvah. I wanted to make sure I had a clear shot when Laughlin came down.

"Danny—" my father said, holding up a hand. "There's something—"

"Later, Dad," I said, motioning this time with my gun hand for him to move.

My eyes caught movement on the stairs.

Lita appeared. She looked worn out and there was a new hardness to her eyes.

"Stand next to my father, Lita," I said firmly.

My hands were steady, my pulse slow. I was ice. I concentrated on the stair. I'd wait until I could see Laughlin's thighs. Then I'd knee-cap him and finish him off as he tumbled down the steps, before I had to listen to a word of explanation.

I counted to ten and still no Laughlin.

Then he called from the top of the stairway.

"I'm coming down," the by-now-familiar voice announced. "In case you're thinking of anything funny, I want you to see something first. Show him, Sean."

I looked at my father. He lifted his shirt. Taped around his waist was a small black box; it sat right over his bandage.

"I was trying to tell you, Danny," my father said quietly.

"It's a bomb," the voice from the stairwell said. "A small shaped charge just big enough to slice him in two. I have my hand on the transmitter. If my finger comes off the switch—kaboom!—and bye-bye, Papa. So you don't want me to sneeze or trip," he said, his voice strong and sure. "Do we understand each other?"

"Got it," I shouted.

And then he sauntered down the stairs, a small box in his left hand. His thumb holding down a little red button. A snub-nose revolver was in his right hand, held casually at his side. He was wearing a long black leather jacket. His silvery-white mane was windswept and his handsome face had the kind of even tan that only politicians and movie stars manage to maintain. A smile was on his face.

"Young Maguire," he said when he stopped, "why don't you step away from the column so we can meet properly?"

I'd been an idiot. I figured Laughlin would have someone behind him, but I'd never imagined this. The best I could expect was that after I shot him, my father would explode before my eyes.

"I think I'll stay where I am," I said, wondering what the hell to do next. Where was Tarkan? The "oh shit" chant started to echo through my brain.

"If that's the way you want it," he said with a laugh. "So. Here I am. How do you want to do it?"

I pulled another card from my increasingly meager hand.

"Rabbi," I called over my shoulder.

Gershowitz moved crablike from the shadows to the center of the room.

"Hello, Francis," the old rabbi said.

"Good evening, Isaac," Laughlin said, taking a long look at Gershowitz. "Long time no see. You haven't aged well, have you, Rabbi?"

"It's over," Gershowitz said, ignoring the jibe. "The time for the truth is here. Why don't you admit it?"

Laughlin laughed and waved his pistol in the air as if it were a cigarette in a long ivory holder.

"You always were a pessimist. An Old Testament worrywart. Even then . . . But," he said, his light tone turning ugly, "I say it isn't over. I say I'm on top of the world and you and Maguire and the rest of the bleeding-heart apologists are shit. What's done is done," he said. "Dredging up the past doesn't help anyone."

"Is that what you tell yourself?" I asked, my gun aimed at his chest. "What about the survivors? What do you tell them?"

"They survived!" he said. "That should be enough! Now all they talk about is money and gold."

He actually spit on the floor.

I thought of the grandparents and uncle I never knew, reduced to soot stains on a chimney somewhere in Poland. I was amazed that I could find even more of Laughlin to hate.

"The money and gold you have and they don't."

"It's been the same since time began: 'To the victor belong the spoils.' "

"But it's all coming out," I said. "Read the papers. Watch the news. If it's not us, it will be someone else."

"Don't count on it," Laughlin said. Then without another word, he fired once, the boom echoing against the basement walls. Gershowitz fell and lay still.

Lita started towards the fallen rabbi.

"Stop!" Laughlin shouted, pointing the gun at her.

"He's alive," Laughlin said to me. "I just winged him. Why don't you go save the precious rabbi? Be a hero. Do the right thing. He'll bleed to death if you don't."

A small pool of blood formed near Gershowitz's shoulder.

Where the hell was Tarkan? My sides ran with sweat. I made one last desperate play.

"There's a copy of Rosen's letter," I said. "It's in a safe place. If its keeper doesn't hear from me in two hours, the letter goes to *The New York Times*."

Laughlin threw his head back and howled with laughter.

"There is no letter," he said, wiping a tear from his eye with the back of the hand that held the detonator. "Did you think I ever bought that?"

It felt as if all the air had been sucked out of me; it took several seconds before I could breathe.

"Then why did you come?" I asked calmly, already guessing the answer.

"For this. The chance to get all of my troubles in one place and finally see the end of them."

He traced a small circle with the muzzle of his gun. "And as you can see, it worked. You can always count on familial love . . ."

"You're sick!" I shouted.

He stood in mock surrender and pouted. "So shoot me." He laughed, holding his pistol at his side. "You have a clear shot. You can't miss."

I wanted to kill him so badly I was trembling. But I held my fire.

"See?" he said. "Even now you can't bring yourself to do it. You're just like your mother—"

I came out from behind the column and moved my gun hand until his head filled my sight. My finger tightened around the trigger.

He held up the small black box in his hand and waved it with a smile. He knew I wouldn't shoot.

"I know it won't make a difference," he said. "But I think you should know. Even if there was a confessional letter from Rosen, and even if it had names and dates and finally did make it to an editor's desk, they'd have to call Langley to verify it. And you know what would happen?"

I didn't answer.

"It would be denied from top to bottom. 'OSS assassinations in New York during the war, you say? . . . Francis X. Laughlin was involved? Why, that's preposterous! Come see our records. We can account for every day of his life from the time he entered the army until he retired as director. . . . Stolen religious icons? . . . The CIA trading relics for Nazis' freedom? . . . Did Elvis tell you that? Were you abducted by aliens?' So you see, you'd need something more than a 'purported' letter from a dead man."

I thought about the angel's wing in my father's pack, Judas' dagger, the worn copies of my father's transport orders, the Essene bowl in Gershowitz's apartment.

"Someone would listen," I said, almost to myself.

"Yes. Someone might listen, and that's why we're here tonight. Even though no one would publish your outrageous claims, there would be questions. I don't need the grief. And neither does this fine country of ours. What's done is done. Why stir up the pot? No one," he said, "has the slightest intention of opening up old wounds."

Laughlin wasn't alone. He wasn't a pawn; he was more like a bishop or a knight.

"Who are you working with?" I asked.

"Let's just say there are other interested parties who need a little outside help."

"In the name of national security?" I asked suspiciously.

"More like national shame," my father broke in.

Laughlin shook his head.

"The Maguire clan!" he said, his voice thick with sarcasm. "Out to fight for Truth, Justice, and the American Way . . ."

There were noises from the top of the stairs. A scrape, then the slamming of the door, and finally a rumbling sound like weak thunder as something tumbled down the stairs and landed in a heap. It was Tarkan.

Laughlin's head cocked to one side.

A large man in a surplus store parka followed and, with a strong kick, pushed Tarkan to the middle of the room. The detective, blood dripping from the corner of his mouth, groaned.

"He was coming in the door," the big man said.

"Who is he?"

"A cop."

"Shit," Laughlin said, visibly losing a bit of his cool. Then he seemed to think things through and relaxed again.

"Forget him," Laughlin instructed his goon. I imagined that killing a cop or two was within his mission brief. He looked at me and smiled.

"Are you expecting anyone else?" he asked. He didn't wait for an answer. "Good. I didn't think so. Now all I have to do is find the rest of the Maguire spoor and I'm done."

He was talking about Tuesday and the kids.

"They don't know anything!" I became hysterical in spite of myself. "I swear! Leave them alone!"

He slapped his knee.

"You're a riot, kid," he said. "But I never make the same mistake twice; this time I'm doing it right. Cleaning up from A to Z. They'll be easy to find."

He looked at his watch and motioned to the big man in the parka. He took a step forward and leveled a nasty-looking assault gun at us. Laughlin took a step up the stair.

"I think that about wraps it up," he said, raising his pistol and pointing it at my father.

My eyes were drawn from the barrel of Laughlin's gun to movement on the floor.

Tarkan, now on all fours, kicked out his leg at the man with the rifle, catching him at the knee. The crack of the man's knee snapping was drowned out by his scream and the sound of his gun on full automatic. The giant toppled. The bullets from his gun stitched a line across the ceiling, sending down a shower of plaster dust.

At what seemed like the exact same instant, my father threw himself into the mikvah.

Laughlin smiled and lifted his thumb from the little transmitter. I held my breath waiting for the *whoosh* of an explosion and fountain of water. None came.

Laughlin cursed and threw the transmitter at me and started shooting at the same time. My father was right—he *was* fast. I ducked behind the column and returned fire, but he was already bounding up the steps, firing over his shoulder to cover his retreat.

The shooting stopped and I heard the door at the head of the stairs slam shut. I raced after him. At the top of the steps, I tried the door. It was locked.

When I came back down, Tarkan stood over the big man, fitting him with a pair of plastic thumb cuffs.

"Door's locked," I said, out of breath.

My father was standing waist deep in the frigid pool, painfully peeling tape from the waterlogged bomb. I walked over to him.

"You okay?" I asked, offering my hand.

He nodded.

"Good thinking, Pop," I said.

He was gritting his teeth in pain as he pulled the last of the tape from above his wound.

"Water and electronics usually don't mix," he said, dropping the bundle of tape and small black box into the pool. It sank into the dark water. "I got lucky," he said, reaching for my outstretched hand.

I helped him over the tiled edge of the pool. He started shivering. I took off my jacket and made him put it on.

"Who's the man with the kick?" he wanted to know.

"You can trust him. I'll explain later."

Lita was leaning over Gershowitz, taking his pulse.

"How is he?" I asked.

She shook her head slowly. "He's lost a lot of blood . . ."

"Let's get out of here," I said, kneeling and putting my hands beneath the rabbi's arms.

And then I smelled it.

"Gas!"

"Laughlin must have opened the valve upstairs," Tarkan said.

I thought about the eternal flame and wondered how long it would take for the gas to reach it.

"Shit! Even if we got that door open, Laughlin probably locked the alley door too," I said, remembering the hasp on the outside door, the gate at the front, and the meshed windows. Gershowitz's lips moved. I put my ear close.

"There's a coal chute . . ."

"What?"

He raised his good hand and pointed to a pair of small doors near the floor at the wall of the basement along the alley.

"Old coal scuttle," he said. "It leads to the alley. Then the backyard . . . Open fence there . . ."

I started to pull him to the door. He groaned. His good hand found my forearm and squeezed.

"Leave me," he whispered. "There's no time . . ."

I looked into his good eye. It was rock solid.

I laid his head gently on the floor. Tarkan stripped off his coat and gave it to me. I rolled it into a pillow and slipped it under the rabbi's head.

I reached into my pocket took out the Tree of Life. I took the pendant, its jewels vibrant even in the dim basement light, and placed it in his open palm.

He shook his head slowly and pushed the charm back at me softly.

"No," he said, every word a struggle. "Return it. And the other things too. . . ."

I closed my fingers around his bony hand. "I will, Rabbi. Somehow, I will."

He smiled weakly.

"Thank you . . . for . . . the . . . chance," he whispered.

"No, Rabbi," I said quietly. "Thank *you*. May you find peace."

He nodded, just once, then his eyes closed and his lips began moving in what I knew must be a prayer.

Tarkan's voice finally reached me.

"Come on, Danny," he said, making the sign of the cross over Gershowitz. "This place could blow any minute."

I threw one of my father's arms over my shoulder, and pulled him to the door. Tarkan and Lita followed. The odor of gas had become thick. It was getting hard to breathe.

I yanked open the doors Gershowitz had pointed to. Painted shut from years of disuse, they opened with a crack. Inside was a blackened concrete shaft. I stood and felt over my head in the pitch-black space. I felt rusted metal and could picture the two sidewalk doors above. I found the edge of a handle and twisted it. It resisted then finally gave way with a screech. I pushed on the doors. They wouldn't budge. I could feel the freshly healed burn on my hand tear open.

I tried again. No luck.

"I need some help!" I cried.

Tarkan squeezed into the narrow shaft.

"The doors are frozen shut. Help me push."

His beefy arms joined mine. The doors lifted but didn't open.

"Again!"

We pushed, eyes shut and screaming. The twin steel doors gave way with the ear-splitting groan of metal against metal.

Tarkan went first, scrambling up the narrow chute to the alley, then dropped his hand. I called to Lita, When she was next to me, I lifted her by the waist into Tarkan's waiting hands. She went up in a flash. Then I helped my father, still soaking wet and shivering, and he was lifted from the pit.

Finally Tarkan's hand found mine, and I too was pulled out.

I collapsed in the alley, hands on knees, gulping the fresh winter air.

"C'mon," Tarkan said.

My father was heavy against my side.

"I don't think I've got anything left," he said.

I threw him over my shoulder in a fireman's carry and followed Tarkan and Lita down the alley to the backyard.

The chain-link fence at the back of the narrow, litter-strewn yard behind the temple was rusted and topped with a triple strand of razor wire. It looked impenetrable. We were trapped.

"Over here!" Tarkan shouted.

He'd spotted a ragged opening leading to the neighboring backyard. He and Lita stooped and squeezed through.

Then the explosion came. The back windows of the temple blew out showering us in broken glass. The next thing I knew, my father and I were thrown against the fence like leaves in a storm. I scrambled for the hole, pushing my father ahead of me. Once he'd crawled through, I followed. As I pulled myself to the other side, there was a deafening roar as another explosion ripped through the building, seeming to lift it from its foundation and drop it again in a cloud of dust.

My ears were ringing and I was dizzy.

Tarkan helped me up.

"Let's move," he said, pulling me to my feet.

Blue flames shot out of the windows. My face felt as if it were on fire. With my father's arm slung over my shoulder, we scurried down the alley, away from the searing heat.

We ran until we were out of the alley and on the sidewalk.

"Where's your car?" I called, panting.

"End of the block."

As we stumbled onto the street, the first sirens could be heard.

22

I TURNED TO look into the backseat as Tarkan sped up the West Side Highway. Lita cradled my father's head in her lap. I was afraid to ask, but had to.

"How is he?"

"Weak. He was doing well until . . ." She paused with a shudder. "Until they took us. We were blindfolded and kept in a room. They wouldn't let me change his dressings or keep the IV going. . . ."

As her voice faded, I turned away, unwilling to hear more.

With Tarkan at the wheel, we were on the Henry Hudson and at the northernmost tip of Manhattan in minutes.

Careening through the night, I replayed those last moments in the temple basement. Maybe there was something to the "oh shit" chant.

Tarkan stopped in front of a pair of imposing wrought-iron gates set in a pair of tall stone columns and waited. A figure emerged from the darkness on the side, pushed a button on the stone pillar, and the gates swung soundlessly open.

Tarkan rolled down his window. The man moved a step closer but was still in the shadows. All I could make out was that he was a large man with a hooded coat.

"Bring them to the chapel when they arrive," Tarkan said. "They should be here soon."

The hood nodded then the man receded into the shadows.

Tarkan edged past to a small garage modeled to look like a cottage.

"Who's Igor?" I asked, hooking a thumb back toward the gate.

"He's a mute. And his name is Mark."

"Does he always lurk in the shadows?"

"No," Tarkan said, opening his door. "He's the caretaker. He's a friend of mine." Like most of Tarkan's answers, this one seemed to beg others.

We were at the Cloisters, a branch of the Metropolitan Museum that sits on a granite promontory in Fort Tryon Park with a commanding view of the Hudson River, much as a small French monastery from the twelfth century might have. The Cloisters has a Romanesque chapel, four reconstructed Cloisters, a chapter house, and a series of period outbuildings.

I'd been here just once, with a high school date I thought would be impressed by my sensitivity and worldliness. I never got far with the girl, a beauty named Katherine, but always remembered the meticulously crafted stone buildings. And the artwork within the walls was the kind that would make a Baptist blush: rich tapestries, paintings, and crucifixes filled with the power and mystique of the Catholic church at the height of its powers—the time of the Crusades. To be driven through its gates by Peter fit like a glove.

We stopped in front of a small structure just beyond the chapter house. Lita roused my father. He was pale and drawn and sat up with obvious effort. Once out of the car, he draped his arm over Lita's shoulder and walked slowly beside her.

Tarkan led us down a colonnaded flagstone path. At this time of night the Cloisters was dark and brooding, the light spilling from the wall sconces no brighter than candlelight. I felt as if we'd stepped a thousand years back in time. The only sound was our shoes as they tapped and scraped against the stone flagging.

Tarkan stopped at a heavy wooden door and took his key ring out, slipping an old-fashioned skeleton key into the lock.

"The caretaker's cottage," he said as we walked in.

It was a simple apartment with old furniture and worn rugs. But everything was thick and solid, built to last. And it was warm. The only decoration was a foot-tall porcelain Christ nailed to a wooden cross and hanging on the center of a wall.

Lita helped my father onto the couch, then lifted his shirt and started to examine his wound.

"Mark has a small apartment upstairs," Tarkan said. "You can use the ground floor. There are two bedrooms, a small kitchen, and a bath. There's a separate stair to the second floor on the outside, so no one will bother you."

"You sound like you're going somewhere."

"I am," he said.

"Where?"

"Things are getting out of control, Danny . . ."

"Who are you?" my father broke in, his voice weak.

Tarkan looked to me.

"His name is Sam Tarkan," I said. "Detective Sam Tarkan, NYPD. But you can call him Peter."

My father pushed himself to a sitting position and studied Tarkan carefully.

"The article?" my father asked me. "The one in the cigar tin?"

I nodded.

"I kept hoping you'd find it," my father told me. "If things hadn't happened the way they did, I would have called myself."

Then he turned to Peter. "I've followed your career closely. I had a feeling it might be you. Putting a man in the police department where he could watch the trade in artifacts was a good move. I knew your predecessor well. Did he know about your placement?"

"It was his idea," Tarkan said. "He was one of the advisors and recruited me while I was still at Fordham. Then he trained me and helped me develop the qualifications. He pulled the strings to get me into the department."

My father shook his head slowly from side to side. "He always was a great strategist. I respected him and counted him as a friend."

"He told me about you as well," Peter said. "He said you could be trusted. And he told me you weren't dead so I knew you had to be around. I felt it. Looked for you for years . . . But I couldn't find you."

"And now you see why. Laughlin has made things difficult."

"Yes," Tarkan answered solemnly. "I can see that."

My father sat a bit straighter. "So, Peter, now that you've met the devil face to face, do you still want to bargain with him?"

Tarkan ran a hand through his hair. "It's not my decision."

My father's gray eyes narrowed. "You mean you're just following orders . . ."

"Don't mock me, Mr. Maguire."

"Then don't hide from the truth. I've heard it before, Peter," my father said. "Even from myself. But it takes only one man to make it happen. It's always been the way. One man willing to stand up and do the right thing. And right now that man is you."

"I don't have that kind of power."

"Yes, you do. You just never used it before. Think," my father said. "Think of all you know. Who you know. You have everything you need. You have the full force of the police department behind you. The velvet-gloved iron fist of the Church."

"What do you propose?" Tarkan asked, his voice neutral.

"Laughlin's been blackmailing the church all these years. Threatening that if he was exposed, he would take the church down with him. Am I right?"

"Go on."

"And now that you've seen him, heard him talk, watched him in action, do you think he gives a rat's ass what happens to the church? Or that he cares about anyone or anything but himself? Is he a man you can trust?"

Tarkan didn't answer.

"And we know now that it's not just him we have to worry about, that it goes further up. He said as much."

It was as if Tarkan's mind left his body. I could see that wherever his thoughts were, they were very far away. My father saw it too.

"Do you have my knapsack?" he asked me.

"It's in the car."

"Get it, please."

Tarkan was deep in thought and missed the exchange. I had to ask him for the keys and explain why. He tossed them to me and I retrieved the worn canvas pack from the car, setting it on the couch next to my father.

"Anyone have a knife?" he asked.

Back among us, Tarkan pulled a folding knife from his pocket and handed it to my father.

My father flipped back the top of the pack, then, with the knife, split the seam attaching the cover to the pack and reached into a space between the two layers of olive-drab canvas.

His hand came out with a creased envelope. He tapped it against his thigh.

"I think this may help," he said.

"What is it?" I asked.

"Rosen's letter," he said bluntly.

"But you told me it didn't exist!" I said, the blood rushing to my head.

"It was all I had left," he said. "I never thought we'd really have to use it. If we could have taken care of Laughlin, I thought that would be enough. Now there's no choice."

"Why didn't you tell me!" I said. I was enraged.

"I thought it was best, Danny. I'm sorry."

I knew he was right. Before I knew what I did now, I might have traded the letter and still have lost. But we still had a problem.

"Laughlin said that even if there were a letter, it would be denied," I said. "That no one wants to open old wounds."

"That was before," my father said, his fingers tracing the edges of the still-sealed envelope containing Rosen's letter. "Before Peter agreed to back us up. To tell the truth about the church's role. Open the past to the light of day and finally be free of it."

"I haven't agreed to anything, Mr. Maguire."

"Call me Sean," my father said quietly. "And I think you already have."

"What makes you so sure?"

"Because you had your chance. In the temple. All you had to do was tell Laughlin who you were and you could have walked out with him."

"It crossed my mind . . ."

"But you didn't."

It took him awhile to answer.

"No," Tarkan said, his big smile returning. "I didn't. The rabbi was right. The time has come. There is someone . . ."

My father was about to answer when there was the sound of running feet outside. The door opened. Nick, Marie, and Tuesday stood at the threshold. A gust of wild river wind raced past them.

I rushed to hold them. Arms encircled me. I kissed Tuesday and stroked my children's hair, closing my eyes.

I edged them into the small apartment and looked outside before closing the door. The mute named Mark was standing to the side. He was smiling.

PETER LEFT SOON after my family arrived, telling us that he had to check into his office but would return in the morning. He assured us that Mark would stand watch until then.

Tuesday bathed the kids while Lita dressed my father's and my wounds as best she could, using torn bedsheets for bandages. Tuesday found some instant hot chocolate for Nick and Marie, and the kids soon fell into an exhausted sleep. Lita firmly led my father to the other room and closed the door behind them.

In the small hours of the morning, the spare little apartment was dark and still. The only light came from the winter's moon, framed in the arched window of the living room. Tuesday and I lay on a blanket spread in the middle of the floor, our heads resting on cushions we'd taken from the sofa.

And it was only then, with the river wind whistling through the night, her head resting on my chest, that I started to tell her what had happened since she'd gone to Connecticut.

She put a finger to my lips to silence me, then got to her knees and pulled off her simple nightdress. Her skin was smooth and coppery in the cold silver moonlight. Her eyes held mine as she straddled me and guided me into her. We made love, slowly and quietly. Then I pulled her to me, rolled until I was on her, and kissed her hard. We made love again, this time not as slowly, or as quietly.

Then, before I fell asleep, I stroked her hair and told her about the rabbi. About my mother. Laughlin. The pictures in Lita's apartment. The articles I'd read.

I didn't dream.

I OPENED MY eyes in slow motion, knowing even before I did that Marie was sandwiched between Tuesday and me. She must have come to us while we slept. She did that now and then, and I loved it. It gave me a chance to look at her without making her self-conscious. I used to do it with Nick too—before he stopped taking naps.

I wanted to engrave every square inch of them, every smell, each of their gentle inhalations in my memory.

In the first rays of the rising sun, I kissed my daughter's cheek. She rolled toward me, opened her eyes a fraction, looked at me and smiled, then went back to sleep.

I eased from the floor, my back stiff, my hand throbbing. I looked outside. A light dusting of snow covered the ground and tiny flakes swept past the window.

I came out of the shower to the smell of coffee coming from the kitchen at the rear of the cottage.

I found my father sitting at a solid little oak table.

He motioned with one of his massive hands to the stove.

"Instant," he said. "But it will have to do."

I stirred some boiling water into a spoonful of black powder and sat with him. He still looked worn, but he'd shaved and combed his hair. Some of the color had returned to his cheeks. Instead of favoring his side, he now sat ramrod straight as he sipped his coffee.

"You did well, son."

"I got lucky."

"You make your luck. You know that."

"Still . . ."

"Still nothing. We'd all be dead if you hadn't done what you did."

In the quiet apartment, we both heard the front door's lock click and the door open and close.

I held a finger to my lips. He understood. I picked the pot full of scalding water up and stood with my back to the door.

Tarkan walked past me and put two sacks of groceries on the counter. A box of cereal poked from the top of one.

"It's just me," he said, pulling a copy of The New York Times from the other bag and setting it on the table.

"Why didn't you knock?" I asked.

"Mark said just you and your father were up. I didn't want to wake the rest of them."

"How the hell does Mark know who's awake?"

"He's mute. Not deaf," Tarkan noted, moving past me and fixing his own cup of coffee. "Many people lose one sense only to have another become that much more acute. Mark's hearing has become supersensitive. He heard people moving downstairs and knew by their footsteps it was you and your father and not the women or children."

I pictured Tuesday and me on the living-room floor last night and wondered what else Mark had heard through the floorboards.

When we were all sitting down, Tarkan opened the paper to the Metro section. In the middle was a photo of Beth Israel surrounded by fire trucks, flames leaping from its windows. The story read:

New York: Explosion and fire gutted a small synagogue named Temple Beth Israel on the Upper West Side. The blast occurred sometime just after eight last evening. It is not yet known if anyone was inside the building at the time, though witnesses report seeing several people enter just minutes before. A gas leak is suspected, but the Fire Department is withholding a determination until their investigation is complete. Chief Logan reports that due to the extensive damage, the structure is unsafe and may have to be demolished before a detailed analysis can be performed. The police hate crime unit is also investigating.

I remembered Gershowitz, his final gesture to refuse the Tree of Life, his temple now his tomb. I could still hear Laughlin's hyena-like laugh and my hatred for the man glowed anew.

And then I felt a sudden thrill. Even if Laughlin had waited out front to wait for the explosion, we'd gone through the backyard. It would be only logical for him to conclude that all of us—Gershowitz, my father, Lita and me, as well as his own man and Tarkan—lay torn and charred in the temple basement.

"Why are you smiling?" Tarkan asked.

"Right now Laughlin's probably feeling like he's almost home free. I mean he's got to assume we're toast," I said pointing to the newspaper photograph.

My father stroked his chin.

"You're right," he said. "It gives us a few hours' head start—at least."

"We're going to need every advantage we can get," Tarkan said, his face impenetrable.

"Why's that?" I asked.

"When I got back to my apartment, there was a message from the Commissioner. He told me to come downtown, some people from the CIA want to talk to me about Lindquist. I told him I had the flu."

"I thought Lindquist was in custody," my father said.

In a few words, I told him how Lindquist had been taken, ostensibly by the CIA, to the Federal Building only to end up doing a swan dive from one of its windows.

"Osborne," my father said quietly.

"Probably," I said.

"Maybe that can help," he said.

"How do you figure?" I asked.

"Let's assume you're right," my father said. "Laughlin's still a tough man to get to, and now that he thinks we're dead, we need something to get him close to us again. Maybe we can use Osborne as bait."

"I'm not sure," I said. "Do we really want to get the CIA involved?"

"I didn't say the whole agency," my father said. "Just Osborne. Laughlin has enough on Osborne to make him do whatever he wants, and Osborne is the only guy I can think of who probably knows Laughlin's home phone number. I wouldn't doubt if Laughlin has Osborne by the short hairs too; probably shared some of the profits with him from the trading after the war."

I sipped my coffee, thinking it through. It made sense.

"There's another problem," Tarkan added quietly, pulling a folded piece of paper from his pocket and passing it to me.

I unfolded it. It was thick expensive stationery with the raised gold and red seal of the cardinal of New York. It was dated today:

Peter:

Your presence is requested in Rome. Enclosed is a first-
class ticket for this afternoon's Alitalia flight.

Peace be with you.

I passed the letter to my father. He read it and handed it back to Peter, who refolded it and tapped it on the tabletop.

"It was delivered at five this morning by a priest from St. Patrick's."

"Looks like Laughlin got to someone in Rome," my father said.

Tarkan leaned back in his chair until it balanced on two legs. If we lost him now, we were as good as finished. He knew it too.

"I want to tell you a little story," the detective said. "It goes like this. After a visit to one of the death camps, a general asks Hitler how he expected to carry out the 'Final Solution' without world outcry. Hitler's answer was a question: 'Do you remember what the Turks did to the Armenians?' The aide answers no. 'And neither does anyone else,' Hitler responded, and the discussion was closed."

Tarkan let his chair return to all four feet.

"Hitler was right. In 1918 the Turks massacred almost a million Armenians, and by 1930 the world had forgotten. Out of three generations consisting of almost ninety people, my grandfather was the only one of my family who survived.

"The conversation may or may not have occurred," the detective said. "But it doesn't matter. The fact remains that aside from the original crime of the bloodletting, the next worst crime is forgetting. And," he said, pushing the letter from the cardinal back in his pocket, "to deny it ever happened is the worst crime of all."

23

WHEN I SAID good-bye to my family this time, it was, if possible, even more difficult than before. Not because they cried or carried on, but because they didn't. The kids seemed to have gotten used to it, and that is what made it unbearable.

As my father, Tarkan, and I pulled away in his car, I noticed the man named Mark pointing out something to Nick and motioning with his hands. Nick seemed to nod in understanding. I was jealous; it should have been me explaining the intricacies of architecture and stonework to my son.

"Where are we going?" I asked as Tarkan flipped down his NYPD visor and hit the gas.

"Washington."

"It's a long drive," I said.

"O ye of little faith," he said, pulling the dome light from under his seat and hitting the siren.

We raced down the off ramp and pulled up to the chain-link fence of the helicopter pier on the West Side. Using a slick, practiced move, Tarkan flashed his badge to the rent-a-cop at the gate, mumbling something about official police business. The gate swung wide.

As he parked, Tarkan clipped his gold detective's shield to his coat.

"Just hang back and let me do the talking," he warned us.

We walked into the little office. Tarkan strode up to the counter and asked the young woman manning the desk to see the manager. She took one look at the badge and hustled to a small back office.

A few seconds later, a tall and rangy guy in a navy-blue turtleneck approached us. He gave Tarkan the once-over, stopping to study the badge.

"Can I help you?"

Tarkan turned his accent up to a fever pitch.

"I need a helicopter to take me and my associates to Washington, D.C.," he said, flipping open his NYPD ID.

The manager looked us over.

"This is highly unusual," he said. "You guys usually call us the night before . . ."

Tarkan leaned in close, his fierce grin appearing. "There wasn't time, Mr. . . . ?"

"Alston. Jim Alston."

Tarkan looked in both directions to make sure no one was listening. Still, when he spoke, he lowered his voice.

"Mr. Alston," he said. "This is important. A joint effort of the FBI and the NYPD."

Alston's eyes narrowed. "I'll have to call—"

"We're in a rush."

"But—"

Tarkan motioned Alston closer with his finger.

"Listen, Alston," he said when they were just a foot apart. "You look like the kinda guy I can talk to and wants do the right thing. So I'll give it to you straight. But if a word of this gets out, I'll know it was you that talked and I'll come back for you. Guaranteed. Understand?"

Alston nodded.

"You ever heard of the Bronx Militia?"

Alston shook his head.

"Yeah. Not too many people have. But I'm gonna tell you. They're a bunch of loonies up around Yankee Stadium. They called this morning to say they've put a bomb somewhere in the subway and we have until six P.M. to meet their demands."

Tarkan let it sink in. I could tell by the look in Alston's eyes that Tarkan had him, hook, line, and sinker.

"These guys," he said, glancing over his shoulder at my father and I, "have been undercover, I mean right in the middle of those nuts, for six months. And I've got to get them to the Task Force in D.C. Pronto."

Tarkan stood and held the manager's eyes with his own.

Alston looked at my father and me, then nodded and turned to Tarkan.

"See the green chopper out there?" he said.

Tarkan nodded.

"Go get in and belt up. I'll fly you there myself."

ALSTON GOT CLEARANCE to take off. The turbine started to whine and the big rotor blade became a blur. The flurries had stopped, but the river was a mess of short jangled whitecaps, and the wind rocked the helicopter as Alston flipped switches and read dials and did what I knew was the short form of the preflight.

Alston's voice came through the headphones.

"Tighten those belts," he said. "It's a little rough out there."

And with that he executed a full-throttle dipping take-off that I was sure was going to drop us in the river.

I shook my head. I knew the type: a hotshot. I hadn't been in a helicopter since Vietnam. I hadn't liked them then, and didn't like them now, especially when they were flown by guys who liked doing things with them I just knew helicopters weren't meant to do—things like the tight ascending turn Alston put us into that dropped my stomach to my knees.

If Tarkan hadn't ordered us to keep quiet, I'd have asked

whether it was the army or marines that had trained Alston, then challenged him to a duel when we landed.

I looked over at my father. He gave me the thumbs-up, as if to say "Isn't this a kick?" I smiled thinly then did what I used to do in Vietnam; I shut my eyes and found a happy thought—the days before helicopters and young helicopter pilots.

The next thing I knew, my father was shaking my shoulder. My mouth was dry and it took me a minute to realize we'd landed and the hatch was open. Tarkan and Alston were already on the ground, busy talking.

My father and I hopped out and joined them. When he saw us, Alston stopped talking and came over and offered his hand to us.

"Detective Tarkan told me all about it," he said without a smile. "Good luck; and thanks. We need more guys like you."

I had to ask. "Army or Marines?"

Alston smiled and pulled up his turtleneck sleeve, revealing a bulldog tattoo with the USMC initials above it.

"Semper Fi!"

"I knew it."

"You?"

"Army."

"Good luck, dog puke," he said with a smile.

"Thanks, frog piss," I answered, returning the grin.

"I'm glad you two are becoming such good friends," Tarkan said. "But we've gotta move."

A black stretch Lincoln limo was idling just outside the fence. Tarkan led us to it.

"Where the hell did this come from?" I asked him.

"I called ahead."

"Have you ever thought of being an actor?" I said as we settled into the rich soft leather. "Your routine with Alston could have gotten you an Oscar."

"You forget, Danny. It's what I do."

The limo eased forward.

"Where are we going?"

"Georgetown University," Tarkan said.

"Why?"

"To see someone I know."

"Do you trust him?" my father asked.

"With my very life," Tarkan answered as he looked out the window, "and soul."

THE LIMO SLIPPED silently through the rows of neat houses in Georgetown. The area was so tidy, it felt more like a theme park than a living, breathing neighborhood.

We stopped in front of a magnificent little house with brilliant white siding and jet-black shutters that shimmered in the bright winter sun.

Tarkan told the driver to wait. People were moving with that curious pre-Christmas bustle. Laden with shopping bags, they wore one of two expressions: the "visions of sugar plums" smile or the Scrooge scowl.

Tarkan rapped the brass knocker twice. The paneled door with the simple wreath was answered by a man with a tightly trimmed salt-and-pepper beard, short-cropped matching hair, and the palest blue eyes I'd ever seen. I guessed him to be around sixty, but he was the type that could have been either a young-looking seventy or a very worn fifty.

I don't know what I was expecting, but the man's expression was hard and anything but friendly.

"You didn't tell me you were bringing guests, Sam," he said to the detective, completely ignoring my father and me.

"I'll explain inside," Tarkan answered.

After a moment's hesitation, the gray-haired man stepped aside.

"Hang your coats there," he ordered, pointing to a row of pegs on the wall. "We'll talk in the living room."

As I took off my father's pack, which now never left my side, I took a quick look around. Everything was diminutive; doorways were short and squat, the ceilings low. But though the polished oak floors slanted this way and that, and the small double-hung windows drooped like tired eyes, I knew the old house had been lovingly cared for. The little house, like our host, was chilly, about five degrees below the comfort zone.

I felt like Gulliver in the land of the Lilliputians as the man led us to a living room smaller than the closet I was building for Mrs. Safter's shoes. It was lined with shelves neatly packed with leather-bound books and meticulous scale models of old sailing ships.

Our host sat in a leather armchair then tapped out a nonfil-tered cigarette and lit it.

"May I?" my father asked, pointing to the smokes.

"Help yourself," he said, offering my father a smoke but not a light. My father's hand went to his pocket and out came his worn Zippo.

The two men each took a couple of drags and studied each other. The blue haze of tobacco smoke filled the small room.

"Who are they?" the man with the Husky eyes asked Tarkan without a glance our way.

I'd had it.

"Listen, Peter," I taunted, just barely under control, "you brought us here because you said you trusted this guy, but so far your friend here is acting like we've got the plague."

The bearded man's eyes were fixed on mine. He stubbed out his cigarette and looked over at Tarkan, something silent and heavy passing between them.

"Peter?" the man said, immediately lighting another cigarette.

I looked quickly to Tarkan, trying to judge how badly I'd slipped. Instead of a scowl, I got a smile.

"They know, Frederick," Tarkan told our host. "And well they should, as you will learn."

The detective's recommendation broke the ice.

"My name is Frederick Hansen," our host finally said. "And since you call him Peter, you may call me John. And you are . . . ?"

"Danny Maguire," I said. "And this is my father, Sean."

He nodded.

"So," he said, looking at my father. "We finally meet."

My father's head tilted to one side.

"Do I know you?" he asked.

"No," the man named Hansen said, standing and adjusting the sails on one of the small ships. "But I know of you. When Peter called me last night at four in the morning, whispering like a fugitive, I knew something was amiss. And if you are here, with Peter, then I think it safe to say that I was right."

He sat again. "Please accept my apologies for the way I welcomed you to my home. But these are dangerous times and trust is in short supply."

Hansen lit another cigarette and passed the pack to my father. Tarkan reached in his pocket, pulled out the letter from the cardinal, and handed it to Hansen.

He tucked the cigarette in the corner of his mouth and squinted away the smoke while he read. When he was finished, Hansen folded it slowly and looked at Tarkan.

"You should be en route to Rome," he said, stubbing out the cigarette. "Not here."

"I know that," Tarkan said. "And if after I've told you why we've come, you still think I belong on that plane, then we'll leave and you can do what you wish."

Hansen looked out of the window to the street beyond. "I'm listening."

HANSEN DIDN'T HAVE to listen long. I imagined that Tarkan had given many complicated briefings and he was damned good at it, focused and very dry. It also was obvious that Hansen knew the history of the artifacts as well as Gershowitz's Committee because he hurried Tarkan over past history to what had happened these last few days. Starting with his arrest of Lindquist, the detective jumped to my call, the kidnapping of my father and our meeting with Gershowitz. He wrapped up with a blow-by-blow of the confrontation with Laughlin and the fiery explosion at the temple.

Hansen stood and walked to another one of his model ships and wiped away an imaginary speck of dust, then moved it a fraction of an inch, all—I could tell—as a way of buying a little time.

When he looked at Tarkan, his eyes were the color of arctic ice. "You should have called me earlier, Peter."

"There wasn't time."

"What is it you want from me?" he asked, his tone accusatory.

"Something only you can do," Tarkan said.

"And that is?"

"I want you to take us to talk with the President."

Just two days ago I would have thought the whole idea so ridiculous that I'd have laughed out loud. Not anymore. I still wasn't sure how or why Hansen had access to the President, but I knew from his answer that he did.

"And if I refuse?" Hansen said, his tone as cold as his eyes.

"Then I've misjudged you," Tarkan said, his own tone dropping to a little above freezing. "And we'll find another way."

"Do you know what this means, Peter?" Hansen asked as if it were just the two of them in the tiny room. "Everything we've worked so hard to protect these many years will be made public. The church will be pilloried. Heads will roll from Rome to Reno. Think of the headlines. And why would the President want all of it to come out, especially now?"

"It all depends," Tarkan said.

"On what?"

"On whether the story is dragged in pieces from us and the government against our will, as it will surely be. Whether we hide and duck and lie when it is. Or whether we come forward and say what we know, admit our role, take credit for what we did right and blame for what we did wrong. Whether we beat our chests and say *mea culpa* loud and clear for the world to hear."

"That is not our way, Peter. You of all of us should know this. You've spent your life making sure that this never happened, that we'd stay quiet and behind the scenes."

Tarkan stood and faced Hansen. "And it worked. Until now. But it won't work any longer. The gates are opening and we won't escape the flood, whatever we do. There is no longer any reason to keep dark secrets. They grow worse by the day. Here is a chance for our church and the government to come clean," he said. " 'Magna est veritas et praevalet.' "

"Great is the truth, and it will prevail," Hansen translated, nodding his head.

"You taught me those words," Tarkan said, "right here. In this room. You said that once uttered, the echo would last for all eternity."

I could almost see the synapses firing in Hansen's brain as he tested then discarded options and alternatives. All he had to do was say yes or no, but I got the feeling it was the toughest decision of his life.

"What will you ask from him?" Hansen wanted to know.

"The same thing I've asked of you," Tarkan said quietly. "To hear us out."

Hansen found a handle and pulled.

"On one condition," he said, his eyes glued to Tarkan.

"What?"

"That if he refuses, you come with me to Rome."

Instead of answering, Tarkan looked at my father, then me. If he agreed and the President didn't want, or couldn't find a way, to help, then my father and I as well as Lita and my wife and children were as good as dead. If Tarkan left with us now, the same thing would happen, but it would just take a little longer. As usual, it was really no choice at all.

I nodded once that the deal was okay.

"You have my word," Tarkan said.

Hansen studied us a moment longer, then picked up an old black phone and dialed.

"Steve? This is Fritz. Yeah . . . Same here . . ." His voice turned serious. "I have to see you—privately. How about half an hour . . .

Yeah. The usual place. There'll be three men with me . . . Who? . . .
Just tell the Secret Service guys they're friends. I'll explain later.
Right. See you in a few."

Steve? Fritz?

He hung up the phone and stood.

"Let's go," Hansen said, already on the way to the door, Tarkan
close behind. My father and I had to hurry to catch up.

24

Hansen gave the driver an address on Massachusetts Avenue and sat back with another cigarette.

"Just one question," I said in the otherwise silent limousine.

"Shoot," Hansen said.

"How is it that you can call the President of the United States by his first name and set up an appointment with him like that?" I said, snapping my fingers.

"I'm his spiritual advisor," Hansen said, blowing smoke out of his nose like a dragon.

"Even so . . ." I said.

Hansen and Tarkan looked at each other. Tarkan nodded okay.

"You know the President is an orphan, right?" Hansen asked me.

"Even my kids know that," I said. It was one of the things that made him so appealing. The man who was to become President Stephen Hammer was left on the doorstep of St. Anthony's Home for Boys on a frigid January evening fifty-eight years ago when he was just a toddler. He stayed there until he was eighteen. Then it was the U.S. Navy, college, local politics, and finally the White House.

"Well, so was I," Hansen said. "An orphan at St. Anthony's, I mean. I was six when Stephen arrived. He was shy and sensitive. I felt sorry for him, so I took him under my wing. As the years passed we became as close as real brothers. Maybe closer."

I could see why any hint of the church being involved in the trade or hoarding of religious artifacts stolen by the Nazis would be very bad news for Hammer. As only the second Catholic president in the country's history—the first having been John F. Kennedy—Stephen Hammer was always under scrutiny. Even today whispers and innuendo could be heard that any President who was also a Catholic would have his loyalties divided between the Union and the Vatican.

And if Hansen was a man named John and seemed to be Peter's superior, a member of what appeared to be a bunch of undercover Jesuits or some other secret order that could give 007 a run for his money, the ramifications were globe-rattling.

It also explained why both Peter and Hansen had been so reluctant to help; there was the very real possibility that problems with the CIA and the Vatican could quickly reach the White House. It didn't take much knowledge about American public opinion to know that if it happened, it would be a cold day in hell before John Doe ever voted for another Catholic.

"It's hard to understand how close two kids can become unless you've been raised in an orphanage," Hansen said as he looked out of the window. "From the time I could understand, it was drummed into me that I had no family other than the church. To think differently would be a sin of ingratitude that would damn me to a life of pain and eternal suffering. But I always hoped that someday I'd find out I wasn't really alone and unwanted. In spite of the threats, it was my secret daily prayer. And my prayers were answered when Stephen was dropped on the doorstep."

"But I've never heard of you," I said.

Hansen stubbed out his cigarette and smiled. "Amazing, isn't it? Only a few people know how close we are. It started back at St. Anthony's. Like I told you, getting too attached to another orphan was discouraged. I know it sounds cruel, but it was actually well intended. Because if two kids got too close, it might make the children resist being separated and therefore hinder any hopes for adoption. So after the first time Stephen and I were punished for spending too much time together, we swore an oath to keep our friendship a secret."

He looked at me intently. "And that's the way we've kept it all these years."

"When people ask," I wanted to know, brushing aside the threat, "how do you explain your relationship?"

"I'm a full professor of theology at Georgetown. If anyone asks, he tells them I'm his spiritual advisor."

I thought that would fly. But, I asked myself, if the secret was so important to him, why would he tell us? I could only think of one reason.

"Laughlin discovered your true relationship with Hammer, didn't he?" I asked. "He found out and he's let you know. Right?"

Hansen nodded once.

I sat back feeling drained and defeated. Laughlin seemed to be everywhere.

I looked at my father. Of all the expressions I might have expected, the one he was wearing wasn't one of them. He was smiling.

"It's serendipity," he said, motioning to Hansen that he wanted another cigarette.

I thought he'd finally snapped.

"Are you all right, Dad?"

"Never better," he said from behind a cloud of smoke. "I couldn't have done better myself, even if I'd have been able to dream it up, which of course I never could have. It's too Machiavellian even for me . . . Hats off to you boys," he said, tipping an imaginary cap at Tarkan and Hansen.

Tarkan and Hansen remained strangely silent. They seemed to understand my father's obtuse compliment. I still didn't.

My temples started to throb. I was about to ask him to please explain what the hell he was talking about, when the car stopped in front of a stately building and Hansen got out without looking back.

As we followed Tarkan and Hansen, my father's hand found my elbow and pulled me to a stop.

"Watch me closely and follow my cues," he whispered to me, no longer sounding at all abstract. "Okay?"

"Sure, Pop. Whatever you say."

THE DOOR WAS answered by two men with slits for mouths and coals for eyes. They closed the door as soon as we were inside.

Two other men, each holding a lethal-looking weapon, came at us from either side.

"Mr. Hansen," one said.

"Hello, Marty," Hansen said, and raised his arms. The man named Marty frisked him and passed a hand-held metal detector over him, then motioned him into the foyer, just beyond his armed partners.

Tarkan raised his arms.

"I'm a New York City Detective. My ID's in my coat pocket. There's a nine-millimeter pistol in a holster at my back."

Marty expertly relieved Tarkan of his gun and gave him the same expert frisk Hansen had received.

Then they did the same thing to my father and let him through.

I was next. Thankfully, I'd thought ahead and put the silenced automatic in the pack while we were in the limo.

Marty patted me down.

"What's in the backpack?" he asked.

"Artwork. Some papers."

He wasn't buying.

"Put the pack on the floor," he said, unholstering his own gun. "Slowly."

I moved as slowly as I could. The man next to him, who hadn't said a word, passed a strange-looking device over the pack. Two green lights glowed and flickered, then one of them turned red. He

gingerly opened the top of the pack and started emptying the contents and searching through them. He didn't pause at the angel's
wing, or icons and papers. Judas' dagger slowed him down a little.
The box of ammunition didn't thrill him either. But it was the automatic and silencer that stopped him cold.

"Who the hell are you?" Marty asked.

I was starting to sweat.

Hansen dove in, trying to slow things down.

"It's all right Marty," he said. They're with me. Keep the
weapons out here."

"I'm not sure I can do that," the Secret Service man said.

"Ask Steve," Hansen said calmly.

Marty wasn't happy, but he disappeared down the hall. His
partners stood mute and kept their guns on me.

Marty came back in less than a minute. He was scowling. "All
right. The boss says okay. But I don't like it."

He kept the dagger, the cartridges, and my gun, then put the
rest back in the pack and handed it to me.

He holstered his weapon but kept a wary eye on me.

"You'll get it all back," Marty said to me when he was finished.
"If I'm told to give it to you. Otherwise I have a few questions."

We moved in formation through the hall, Marty in front, then
Hansen, Tarkan, my father and me, followed by the pair with the
guns, a half dozen steps back. The other guy stayed at the entry.

Marty stopped at a door and knocked.

"C'mon in," a deep voice from the other side said.

President Stephen Hammer sat in the middle of a dark-blue
sofa wearing light-gray suit pants and a white shirt with loosened
tie. His feet were on the coffee table and a pair of reading glasses
sat at the end of his nose. A thick bound report was on his lap.

"Thanks, Marty," Hammer said, giving us the once-over. "I'll
call you if I need you."

"With your permission, Mr. President," Marty said, giving me
the evil eye, "I'd like to stay."

"That won't be necessary," Hammer said as he stood.

"But . . ."

Hammer held up a hand. "That's an order, Marty."

"We'll be posted at the door," the Secret Service man said look-ing straight at me. "If I hear anything funny, I'm coming in."

"Sure, Marty," Hammer said easily. "You got it. Now please . . ."

Marty's stare held me a moment longer, then he left, closing the door behind him.

Hansen walked over and gave the President a bear hug, then in-troduced us, starting with Tarkan. The President's grip was firm. Amazingly, his eyes were even lighter than Hansen's, a haunting pale blue. But otherwise they were physical opposites: the Presi-dent, fit and almost regal-looking with a Roman nose and cleft chin; Hansen shorter and rougher with a pug's face and the pallor of a chain smoker.

I was uncomfortable. The highest-ranking official I'd ever met, aside from a colonel in Virginia back in 1970, was the mayor of my town in Port Washington. Being with the President of the United States had me a little off balance. Hammer invited us to sit, re-suming his position on the couch.

Hansen pulled out a cigarette and lit it. Without a word, Ham-mer opened his hand and Hansen dropped the rumpled pack and book of matches into it. They'd obviously done it a thousand times before.

The President lit up. Then my father held out his hand, and the President tossed the pack to him. I watched as it sailed through the air and my father caught it with one hand, grinning.

I got the same feeling I used to get in the boys' room in high school when I'd join my friends and do same thing: the unique thrill of the illicit, the feeling of being cool and accepted as part of the gang. I wasn't even a smoker, but back then I'd light up with the rest of them. It was an act of rebellion and solidarity. If one of us got busted, the rest went down with him. And that was the whole point. In those days it didn't have a name. Today I guessed they called it adolescent bonding. But watching three guys, one of them the President of the United States, and the others, all of whom should have known better, do it now gave me a glimmer of hope.

"Damn that's good," Hammer said, taking a deep drag and smiling. "This is the only place I can grab a smoke. No. I take that back. Here and my friggin' bathroom at the White House . . . Heaven forbid someone caught me. It'd make the cover of *Time*. Says something, huh?"

He kicked back and put his feet back on the table.

"Okay, Fritz," he said. "What's so damned important you had to interrupt my meeting with the Secretary of Commerce? Which, by the way, I thank you for from the bottom of my heart."

Hansen too knew the fine art of condensing things to their essence. It also seemed that Hammer knew most of the story already, so all John had to do was hit the high points.

"This is Sean Maguire. The Maguire that was part of Laughlin's OSS team. The one who disappeared. And this is his son, Danny. And that's Detective Sam Tarkan, NYPD. Our Peter."

Hammer absorbed it all without blinking.

"Yesterday Laughlin tried to kill them all. These men got away by the skin of their teeth. Rabbi Gershowitz didn't."

The President's face hardened a bit and his eyes narrowed. "Who else knows about this?"

The sound of my own voice surprised me. "No one—except my wife."

"Where is she?" Hammer said, reaching once again for the pack of cigarettes.

"With friends," Peter said, giving me a look that let me know to keep my mouth shut.

Hammer sat forward and put his elbows on his knees.

"What else?" he asked Hansen.

"Last week Peter, that is, Tarkan, arrested a man in New York named Lindquist for trading in antiquities. Someone from the CIA took him from NYPD custody to the Federal Building. He was dead two hours later."

"How?" Hammer asked Tarkan.

"The report is that he broke a window and jumped."

"Bullshit," the President said, smoke billowing from his mouth.

"It had to be Osborne," my father said.

Hammer locked eyes with my father. "Probably . . ." He motioned Hansen to continue.

"About the same time, Laughlin decides to take out Maguire, the elder. He misses, and the Maguire clan gets reunited and hits the road."

My father cleared his throat.

"So," he said, shaking one of Hansen's smokes loose from the quickly emptying pack, "as you can see we're all in the same boat." He lit up and blew a smoke ring before continuing. "The only difference is that neither you, Mr. President, nor your friends John and Peter can do anything.

"You could drop the H-bomb on Iraq easier than snuff Laughlin. As soon as Frankie X. got a whiff that you were after him, he'd make it all public," my father continued. "You need us as much as we need you. You can't take Laughlin on, but you can help us try to. If we lose, the worst case is you're no better off than you are now; Laughlin and Osborne have you by the short hairs . . ."

The other men were quiet. My father's earlier roundabout allusions to things being "perfect" began to make sense.

"But," my father concluded, "if we succeed, your problems are over."

Hansen's and Hammer's eyes were flat. The only face that seemed pained was Tarkan's. I wondered if it was another of his bravura performances or the real thing. There was only one way to find out.

"When did you set us up for this, Peter?" I asked him. "Last night? This morning?"

"It's not like that, Danny," he said.

I wanted to believe him. Really did. Then I remembered his routine with Alston when he conned the helicopter trip. The man was a professional liar. My voice stayed low but inside I was fuming.

"What about the rest of it, Peter? Was it all garbage? Did you ever intend to help the church come clean, or was that just a line? Did you and John over there rehearse this thing or just ad-lib it? C'mon, man," I said, my voice starting to rise, "I want to hear."

It was only the sound of my father's voice that stopped me.

"Easy, Danny," he said, no longer smiling. "It's all right. At least we all know where we stand," he said, flicking an ash into the half-full ashtray. "I do hereby declare the preliminaries over and motion we stop screwing around and get down to business."

The President spoke. "I'll second that. Motion noted and carried. Can I offer you men a drink?"

25

HAMMER POURED FOUR tumblers half full of a clear pale-yellow liquid from an unlabeled bottle.

"From the Brothers at St. Anthony's. Seems they have a little still . . ."

He raised his glass and proposed a toast to "Victory."

My father countered with "Here's mud in your eye."

I took a sip. It took my breath away.

Hammer laughed and said, "Praise the Lord."

"And pass the peas," Hansen answered, breaking up.

They were a regular laugh riot. If it weren't for the fact that my family was sitting in a Vatican safe house and we were all being hunted by a nut with the CIA on his side, I might have laughed.

"Yo ho ho," I said, no longer in awe of a President and his buddy who acted like high school sophomores. Hansen put his glass down with a slap. I'd ruined the fun.

"Let's hear it," I said, slipping on my best Maguire grin.

"Hear what?" Hansen answered.

"The plan, damn it." I said too loudly. The door cracked open and Marty peeked in, gun drawn. Hammer waved him away with an annoyed swat of his hand.

The door closed. I wanted to get their undivided attention, so I kept it simple.

"As in how you plan to have us kill Laughlin and get away with it?"

My father winked at me to let me know I was doing just fine, and reached for another cigarette.

"We never—" Hammer started.

"Is this place bugged?" I asked, my voice surprisingly normal.

"No."

"Then let's cut the crap," I said. I couldn't believe I was speaking to the President like this, and yet I couldn't stop myself.

"The deal is we take care of Laughlin," I said, "and you take care of Osborne. Have I missed anything?"

Enough time went by for Hansen to take a deep drag.

"No," he said, leaning forward and crushing out the smoke. "That about sums it up."

"Well, then," I said, relaxing enough to take another sip of the white lightning. "Let's get on with it."

THE PLAN REMINDED me of my CO's take on the Vietnam war. In a less-than-sober moment, he'd thrown his arm around my shoulder and given me some words of wisdom, his heavy southern drawl thick with whiskey. "Listen, Maguire," he'd said. "What the army's policy here in Vietnam lacks in finesse is more than made up for by its sheer unpredictability." In the back streets of Saigon it made sense. Not only was the whole thing absurd, but its utter absurdity had a logic of its own and, if you looked at it a certain way, made perfect sense.

As the setting winter sun turned the room of the Massachusetts Avenue town house a pale orange, I felt the same way I did in Vietnam with my CO's arm slung around me. The war in Vietnam relied on a slew of iffy assumptions and a lot of maybes. My current war was the same: If any one assumption proved false or didn't come down the way we figured, Hammer would still be president, but my father, myself, and my family would be dead.

To start our planning session, my father, with a move worthy of a prestidigitator, withdrew Rosen's letter from the pack.

All eyes fell to the envelope, yellowed with age. Ignoring the stares, my father stood and walked to the President's desk, picking up a letter opener.

He sat down again and looked at Hammer.

"I've kept this letter sealed for what seems like an eternity," he said simply, his voice suddenly weary. "It's like Pandora's box. Once opened, what lies inside can never be put back. Do you understand?"

No one spoke.

My father slipped the polished blade under the flap and drew it through the paper in a single strong stroke. The paper hissed in response as if it were a living thing. Then he blew softly into the opening and gently withdrew Rosen's letter, handing it to me first.

It was in longhand on old-fashioned legal paper and covered a dozen pages. It was dated November 12, 1967, two weeks before my father disappeared and just two days before Rosen's supposed suicide.

The letter was just as my father had promised, and more. It told everything about the illegal and still classified OSS war on U.S. soil. As I read, I guessed that Rosen too had maintained a hidden journal, but with a difference. Where my father kept everything vague and coded, Rosen's appeared to have been infinitely more detailed. Either that, or he had a photographic memory that allowed him to recall the name of every man they'd killed, as well as when and where. I had no doubt that if anyone bothered to look under "unsolved homicides" in Boston, Taunton, Fall River, and New York for the dates listed, bodies and times would start to match up. It might not pass legal muster, but it would sure get past the editor's desk and onto the front page.

In August '43 the first references to the artifacts and icons appeared, followed by information about Gershowitz, the Committee, and Peter. At the bottom was Rosen's signature. Next to it, my father had signed and listed himself as witness.

When I was finished reading, I passed it silently to Hammer, who took a bit longer than me to get through it. When he was done, he handed it to Hansen, who then gave it to Tarkan. No one said a word during all of this.

Finally Tarkan passed the letter back to my father, who carefully refolded it and put it back in the envelope.

"Do we get a copy?" Hansen asked.

"It depends," my father said, slipping the letter back in the pack.

"On what?"

"On how things go."

"But we'll need it if—"

My father held up his hand. It looked as big as a first baseman's mitt. "No ifs. No buts," he said, putting the issue to rest.

So there was part one of the plan: the letter. It was our bait and our insurance. Now we were down to the hard part. The President took the lead.

When we left, Hammer would call Osborne to the town house and tell him about the letter. Even though it didn't mention Osborne specifically, Hammer felt confident that the CIA man would recognize that if it was made public, no matter how well he'd covered his tracks, his connection with Laughlin would be clear. With enough digging the truth would come out. He'd not only lose his job but probably end up in federal prison for the rest of his days.

Once hooked, Hammer would offer Osborne two choices: resign immediately, as in before he left the townhouse, or the letter went anonymously to *The Washington Post* by fax. If Osborne countered that he'd make public what he knew about Hammer's link to Hansen and the church, Hammer would call his bluff.

"Osborne's a coward," the President said with his hands behind his neck. "He'll fold in a New York minute." That was Assumption Number One.

Once Hammer had gotten Osborne's resignation, he would instruct him to call Laughlin and tell him something big was up and they had to meet. Possible ruses included him saying that the

NYPD was nosing around Lindquist's odd departure or, alternately, news from the Hill was that Aronstein's committee was gearing up to move forward with the investigation.

"Osborne may be slippery, but he's no dummy," the President said. "He'll know that Laughlin is being set up. I'll make sure he understands he doesn't have to go down with Laughlin, that he can still save his skin. If and only if he plays ball. Don't worry," the President assured us. "Osborne will go for it. Guaranteed." This was Assumption Number Two.

Assumption Number Three and Four were that Laughlin believed my father and I were already dead and he wouldn't sense the trap that we were setting for him.

And if Assumptions One through Four came off as we figured, Hansen and Hammer would avert their eyes and we'd take care of Francis 'X. Marks the Spot' Laughlin once and for all. They didn't have to say that if Osborne got hurt in the process, well, that's how these things went . . . The how and where we took care of things was up to us.

Peter would have the job of being our "facilitator"—so help me, Hammer used the word—and cut-out. He was given a cellular phone that would ring Hammer directly if he pushed 1 and "send." He told us the phone was fully scrambled, untappable, untraceable, and invisible. And when we were finished, all Tarkan had to do was to push the "send" and "power" buttons at the same time. This would erase all memories and render it dead. Then he could drop it into the garbage. What he was really saying was that after Laughlin was out of the picture, there would be no further communications between us and Hansen or Hammer. Everything would go through Peter, and of course, "This meeting never happened."

"In other words," my father said, "if everything turns to shit, we're on our own."

Hansen just smiled.

As I said, it was as meticulously planned as a military operation, and it gave me the same warm and fuzzy feeling I used to get behind the sandbags of the fire bases in Southeast Asia as I repeated the "oh shit" chant.

The meeting was over. Hammer stood and shook our hands, his politician's smile returning. Hansen wished us well as he lit the last cigarette and crushed the package, the cellophane crinkling.

It was only at Hammer's command that Marty reluctantly gave Tarkan back his gun, me my bullets, silenced automatic, and the dagger, and my father his coat. We were then escorted into the chilly Washington night. It was full dark and a light rain was falling.

The limo was gone, probably shooed away by Marty or one of his clones.

My father stretched widely without wincing and said, "Let's find a place for me to buy some cigars, then get a bite. I'm starved."

We walked in silence. We'd just put together the most cockeyed plan for an assassination with the cooperation of the President of the United States. I was wondering if I'd lost my mind. My father, by contrast, was hungry. I looked at him with a perverse feeling of pride. My old man was really back, I told myself. He was a tough old coot, he never gave up, and he never, ever quit. He still had a lot to teach me, and I was even more determined than ever to make sure we'd both live long enough for him to have the chance.

26

WE HAILED A cab. Not surprisingly, it seemed my father knew a bit about D.C. too. He told the cabbie to drop us off back in Georgetown. First stop was the Georgetown Tobacco Store, where he loaded up on cigars. Then he took us to a small pub. There were two dinner options on the menu: fish and chips or steak and kidney pie. We had the pie. We were halfway through a dessert of bread pudding when Hammer's little cellular chirped.

I motioned to Tarkan that I wanted to take the call.

"Hello?"

"Who is this?"

"Danny."

"Let me speak with Peter." It was Hansen.

I looked at Tarkan. "You'll be speaking with me from now on."

There was a rustle as he covered the mouthpiece. I knew he was running it by Hammer. The rustling stopped.

"If that's the way you want it . . ."

"It is."

"All right," he said. I heard a match strike as he lit another cigarette.

"Osborne's in the next room writing his resignation." Assumption Number One was in the bag. "Where do you want the . . ."

He struggled to find a good euphemism for Laughlin's murder, ". . . conference," he finally said, "to happen?"

During dinner we'd run through possible sites for our "conference" with Laughlin. D.C. was handy now that we were here, but neither Peter nor my father—even though he knew where a decent pub and tobacconist were—knew it that well. Not to mention the fact that it wasn't really our turf. New York sounded right but had the disadvantage of being Laughlin's home field also.

Peter suggested the Cloisters. He said it was the perfect spot for an ambush. Isolated and with limited access. And after closing, deserted. And, Tarkan had said with a wry smile, if things got messy, he could take care of it. All we had to do was get Lita, Tuesday, and the kids out before the "conference." I looked at my father. He nodded okay. I agreed. It was unanimous.

"Have Osborne be in New York tomorrow morning," I told Hansen without revealing the rest of our preparations or the final destination. "Give him the number of this cell phone," I instructed him, "and have him call it at noon. Sharp."

"Fine. Then—"

"Oh. There's one other thing," I said. "We need a plane to take us to LaGuardia . . ."

"Mr. Maguire," he said, sounding exactly like a pissed-off professor, "you should know we—"

"A plane," I repeated, interrupting him yet again.

More rustling, a few raised voices. "Where are you?"

I told him.

"A car will pick you up in half an hour," he said. "Be outside."

The line went dead.

My father gave me an exaggerated wink.

"Half an hour," I said, waving down the waitress for another coffee.

THE CAR WAS standard government issue. I knew it was for us when we got in and the driver didn't bother to ask us who we were or where we were going. He took off as soon as the door closed.

In just a few minutes, the car pulled up to a waiting Gulf Stream at National Airport. Before we buckled our seatbelts, the steps were pulled up and the cockpit door locked. We were in the air five minutes later.

At LaGuardia we got the same treatment, in reverse. The steps went down and a car was waiting. Tarkan gave the driver the address of the West Side Heliport so he could pick up his car, and the driver took off without a backward glance.

We were now officially on our own.

BACK AT TARKAN'S apartment, we took turns showering and shaving. Then Tarkan helped my father and me change the dressings on our wounds. My hand was a mess but not infected. Still, it was going to leave a hell of a scar. The entry and exit wounds on my father's waist were bright red and a little puckered, but there was no swelling and he seemed to be back to normal.

Tarkan let us rummage through his closet for fresh clothes. Not a perfect fit for either my father or myself but the jeans and sweatshirts would have to do.

I wanted to make sure that things were all right with Tuesday and the kids. I got the number from Tarkan and went through our little code.

"Tuesday?" I asked hopefully when it was answered.

"No. This is Lita. Tuesday is reading the kids to sleep."

"Is everything okay?"

"It's hard on the kids to hide all day while the place is full of visitors. But otherwise yes. Mark keeps them entertained."

"Good," I said. "Tell them to just hang on. We're almost at the end of things now . . ."

"Does that mean—"

"We'll be there tomorrow," I interrupted, "and if everything works out, that will be the last of it."

"Can I speak to Sean?"

"Hold on."

I passed him the phone. My father turned away and spoke quietly to Lita for a few minutes before hanging up.

"What did you tell her?"

He lit a little cigar and held my eyes. "That if for whatever reason she didn't hear from us by tomorrow, to take your wife and kids and disappear for a while. Italy . . . Spain. Somewhere out of the way."

He let it sink in.

"You can get out now, Danny," he said. "Go to them. Hit the road. Peter and I can finish this up."

Peter nodded.

They were giving me a chance to cut and run. My very last chance. But I couldn't let Peter, a man who seemed to be a chameleon, and my father, a seventy-five-year-old warrior with a bullet wound, face Laughlin and whatever he would throw at them.

I shook my head.

"Out of the question," I just managed to say, suddenly very very tired. Then I stretched out on the couch and rolled over. "See you in the morning," I said, and closed my eyes.

I WOKE UP at a little after six. I was stiff from the night on the couch but otherwise rested and alert with anticipation.

My father and Tarkan were in the small kitchen, a pot of coffee between them. My father was in the same chair where Gershowitz had sat just a couple of days ago. I chased away a feeling of foreboding along with my last image of the rabbi on the cold basement floor of Temple Beth Israel.

I poured some of the coffee and sipped it, looking out the window. Dawn was breaking overcast and still. The apartment was silent except for the purring cat in Tarkan's lap and an occasional clang from the radiator.

Tarkan broke the silence.

"I know you both think I set you up," he said as he stroked the cat. "And I did. I delivered you to Hansen and Hammer knowing they would use you as pawns. But only because if I didn't, you would both be dead by now.

"Sometimes there is no right choice," he continued. "Just a choice. I agree with the rabbi."

"What are you saying?" I asked quietly.

"I'm saying I want to help."

He was such a damned good actor I had no way of knowing if this was another performance or the truth. I wanted to hear him say it out loud.

"How?"

"It's like I said at Hansen's: '*Magna est veritas et praevalet.*'"

" 'Great is the truth, and it will prevail'?"

"Yes."

"But your bosses don't think so."

"No," he said, gently pushing the cat from his lap and laying his elbows on the table. "They don't. And I understand them. But I think they're wrong."

A smoke ring blew past my nose.

"What did you have in mind?" my father asked.

"I have some friends who share my opinions."

"In the church?"

His dangerous smile reappeared. "Yes. And others."

Others?

"Cops?"

"In a way."

"C'mon, Peter. This is getting old," I said, looking at my watch, nervous.

"I can't tell you more. That's why I'm asking for your trust."

"What did Hansen say?" I said, stroking my chin. "Oh yeah. Something like 'Trust is in short supply these days' or something like that."

"I know. And I wouldn't blame you if you ignored me. But I wouldn't count Laughlin or Osborne out just yet, and you're a lit-tle short-handed."

He was right. But if I was reading him correctly, what he was talking about was akin to mutiny or conspiracy, and I got the feeling this was not something he was prone to.

"Does Hansen know whoever it is you're talking about?"

"No. No one does but me . . . and now you."

"What do they get out of it?" I wanted to know.

"The same thing we all would: an accounting."

"Does this mean you're cutting your ties with the church?" my father asked.

"No. I'll stay as I've always done. And remain Peter and Tarkan."

"So you're not a double agent," I said, "you're actually a triple . . ."

"Something like that."

"Then who are you really, and who do you really serve?" I wanted to know.

He stood. "I am who you see, nothing more, nothing less. I serve what I think is the truth."

I studied Tarkan's profile. I guess you could say he'd betrayed us, but that wouldn't really be accurate. He'd acted more like a matchmaker, by putting us together with Hansen, and through him the President. He'd given us the lever to move the world. Without him, we'd be nowhere. And there had been other times, easier times, when he could have gotten us out of the picture. He could have snapped me up that morning in the library, or told Laughlin who he was in the temple, or at any time since. But it occurred to me that he might just be waiting until he had us all together: my father, myself, Laughlin, and Osborne. If he took care of all of us, then Hansen, Hammer, and his church would be safe.

"And if we agree?" my father asked. "What happens next?"

"First of all, you, Danny and his family as well as Dr. Ward will keep the story to yourselves: forever. You have to swear to me that it will die with you. And you must also promise never to look further into things, never seek to find out anything more about it."

"And in return?"

"Peace," he said, the word sounding like music. "Freedom. The chance to finish your years without worry or fear."

"Can you do that for us?"

"Yes," he said looking at me. "I can. But not alone."

I tried to imagine life before my father reappeared, before I'd been engulfed. The sameness of the days, the creeping fear of middle age, watching the kids grow, making love to Tuesday.

I stood.

"You have my word," I said, extending my hand.

"And mine," said my father.

"Then you'll excuse me while I make some calls . . ."

27

OSBORNE CALLED AT twelve on the dot and started complaining. I shut him up and gave him the drill. This was going to be the fun part. For the next several hours, he'd be our puppet. We'd tell him, for example, to go to Grand Central and call from track 19, then give him another address and have him run there and call in another hour. The schedule wasn't so grueling he couldn't keep up, but it would keep him moving, stop him from planning ahead. I admit it was my idea and totally unoriginal, but I liked the thought of putting Mr. Osborne of the CIA through his paces.

It was meant to make him think we'd be watching his every move to be sure he was alone. He didn't have to know that while he was running around the city we would be in Tarkan's apartment cleaning our guns and drinking coffee.

At six he called in from Barney's. He sounded done in. He'd been from the Staten Island Ferry terminal to Macy's, Bloomies to the World Trade Center, the Guggenheim and points in between. We'd played him long enough. It was time to bring him onto the boat.

We told him to be at the corner of West Broadway and Houston Street in forty minutes. He was instructed to have a paper under his left arm and a grocery bag in his right.

"Are we done yet?" he asked wearily.

"Almost," I said, hanging up.

I WAS SITTING behind the wheel of Tarkan's Suburban. My father was next to me, the snub-nose .38 looking like a child's toy in his hand. I felt in my pocket for the freshly loaded automatic, patting it twice just to make sure. We weren't expecting anything funny from Osborne, but it didn't hurt to be prepared. Tarkan was out on the street somewhere, invisible to us—our point man.

"There he is," my father said awhile later.

A man stopped at the corner. He was wearing a rumpled trench-coat. The newspaper was folded sloppily under his left arm, a plastic sack hung from his right hand. He was slight with horn-rimmed glasses and the shiny head of the long bald. James Bond he wasn't. He looked like any other harried executive on his last leg home. And with the accessories I'd demanded, he'd have a hard time making any fancy moves.

He looked at his watch; his patience about gone. Tarkan approached him from behind, his right hand in his pocket, wrapped, I knew, around his 9 mm. He took Osborne by the elbow and led him across the street, away from us, then to the other corner, giving my father and me a chance to see if anyone else was watching. The coast looked clear, so I flashed the headlights twice.

Osborne got in the car first, Tarkan right behind him. I pulled away and drove aimlessly for a few blocks as Tarkan checked our tail and my father our front.

"We're clean," Tarkan said.

"Of course we are," Osborne said in nasal voice. "You could have stopped this shit at three when I was at Bloomingdale's! I'm on your side. Remember?"

My father turned in his seat so Osborne could see him clearly.

"Are you really now?" he said with a smile.

The color started to drain from the top of Osborne's polished dome. Even his chin became pale. "Maguire . . ."

"None other."

"But . . ."

"Back from the dead." My father laughed.

Osborne looked in the rearview mirror. I smiled back at him and waved.

He visibly slumped.

"Frankie told you we were dead, didn't he?" my father said with a smile.

Osborne's chin reached for his chest.

My father's smile disappeared.

"You wouldn't be here if you didn't know the score, Ozzie," my father said. "Hammer has your resignation—right?"

Osborne nodded slowly.

"Good. And you know your end of the deal from here on in, right?"

Another nod.

"Now," he said, reaching over and handing Osborne Hammer's cell phone with one hand and showing him the barrel of the re-volver with the other. "You're going to call up our dear mutual friend and tell him you want to meet him at ten."

"Where?"

"Tell him you're working on it. You'll call him again around eight and let him know."

It was Osborne's turn to smile. "He'll smell a rat, Maguire. You guys don't know who you're dealing with."

He was right. It did sound a little fishy.

"Oh, yes we do," I said, as much to Osborne as Tarkan and my father. "But you're right. Call him and tell him you're on your way from D.C. and won't be in town until eight. That you're working on a place to meet and will let him know as soon as you can."

"And if he asks where?"

"Just tell him it'll be somewhere in Manhattan."

He shrugged.

"It's your funeral," he said, opening the phone.

"And yours too," I reminded him. "Unless you convince him."

That took a little wind from his sails.

He made the call. His eyes focused on my father's hand and the black gun almost buried in his palm.

"Francis? This is Perry . . . Yes. I'm leaving now. I'll be in New York by eight tonight. We have to meet . . . Yes. Remember the guys from Buenos Aires . . . ?"

Buenos Aires? This wasn't in the script.

My father pulled back the hammer of the revolver. It made a loud *click* in the quiet car. Osborne's eyes were now glued to my father's finger, the one he had wrapped around the trigger.

Osborne held up his hand, as if to beg our momentary trust.

"Right. The ones who traded the Russian Cross? Well, it seems they have something else they want to show us . . . Yeah. They said the water is getting hot down there and they think we can cool it off . . . Yes . . ." He listened for a while, then said, "Listen, if you're too busy, I can take care of it myself . . . No? Then I'll call you when I know."

He shut off the phone and handed it to Tarkan.

My father let the hammer down, ever so slowly. "Next time tell us what you have in mind. Got it?"

Osborne smiled. His upper lip was coated with perspiration.

"You told me to make up a story to get him here without raising his suspicions," he said, wiping his lip with the back of his hand. "There's only three things I know of that will work every time with him: money, dames, or the chance to make someone squirm. My story has two out of three. There's no way he'd miss an opportunity like this."

BY THE TIME we were on the West Side Highway, snow had started to fall. The kind of snow that slid past the windshield and was so fine it made swirling rivers on the pavement as it was blown by the wind.

When we were a few minutes away from the Cloisters, Tarkan called ahead. Mark was at the gate to meet us. Like that first night, he stayed in the shadows. But tonight the snow stuck to the hood of his coat and he cradled a nasty-looking automatic under one arm.

Tarkan rolled down his window.

"All set?"

Mark nodded and pointed in three directions. I followed his finger and thought I saw movement from behind one of the bushes but wasn't sure because of the snow.

"Your friends?" I asked.

Tarkan smiled.

My father and I dropped Tarkan and Osborne off at the chapel then we went back to the caretaker's cottage to pack up my family and Lita and get them out of the way. The snow started to fall in earnest, the flakes getting larger and heavier.

We were walking down the slated path when I heard what sounded like a branch breaking, followed by a growl that made my hair stand on end. Wild dogs, I thought.

Nick answered my knock and opened the door, his coat already on. My father followed and I was holding Nick in my arms when we heard what sounded like paper being ripped and a man's high warbling howl. I knew the sound. I'd heard it before. It was gunfire.

I pushed Nick backward into the little apartment and slammed the door behind us.

"Get down!" I yelled, as the small window near the door shattered. I hit the light switch and pulled out my automatic at the same time.

"Kill the lights!" I screamed as another burst of gunfire peppered the thick wooden door behind me, followed quickly by the sound of another gun and another scream. Then silence.

"Everyone in the bathroom!" I said, remembering the windowless room. The outside wall was solid stone, the interior walls thick plaster. I grabbed Nick's hand.

My eyes started to adjust to the dark. I heard Marie's cry and made my way to her in the dark. Tuesday was with her, Lita right beside them.

I led them to the bathroom.

"Listen," I said as calmly as I could. "Stay here. Don't move. Don't make a sound. When we leave, lock that door and don't open it unless it's my father or me."

"Daddy!" It was Marie.

"Quiet, sugar," I said. "Please."

She hushed. Her eyes were wide and frightened. Nick put his arm around her shoulder.

"Remember," I said. "Lock the door."

I backed out of the bathroom and closed the door. I heard the old-fashioned lock snap into place.

My father pulled me by the elbow until we were back near the front door.

"Fucking Osborne double-crossed us," he said.

"Must have a transmitter on him," I added. "They were right behind us."

"Next time we'll pat the bastard down."

"Next time?"

"Just kidding."

All was quiet.

"Maybe Peter's men took care of them," I said.

"Or maybe it's the other way round."

"Only one way to tell."

He started to move to the door.

"Forget it, Dad," I said gently, my hand on his shoulder. "Stay here. Just one thing," I said, my whole being focused. "Don't let anyone get to my family. Anyone."

He nodded.

I put my hand on the knob.

"Danny . . ." he said.

I looked into his eyes and saw his strength. "What?"

"Leave Laughlin for me."

I TOOK A few deep breaths, every nerve and muscle alive. I twisted the knob, pulled open the door, and rolled to shelter behind a column, the automatic in both hands. I waited for a bullet. It didn't come. I heard the door to the little apartment close and lock and the sound of a chair being pushed behind it.

"Way to go, Dad," I said to myself.

I looked both ways on the narrow colonnade. Nothing. I peeked from behind the column. A man lay faceup on the grass ten yards away, arms outstretched, his gun a few feet away, as if he were about to make a snow angel. But of course he wasn't. He was dead.

I was safe behind three feet of chiseled stone. So safe that I was on the verge of being frozen in place by my own fear. It was only when another burst of fire from the direction of the chapel erupted that I stood and sprinted to the next column in a crouch. No one fired at me. Then I did it again. And again.

I kept sprinting from column to column until I could see the chapel. It looked like a postcard, beams of colored light spilling from stained glass windows and falling softly onto the sparkling fresh-fallen snow. I'd just pushed off from the last column to make the dash across the open space when I slipped on the wet snow and fell flat on my stomach, the gun flying from my hand.

As soon as my face hit the snow a hail of bullets tore over where I lay. I covered my head and started to roll away down into a little drainage swale, chanting my "oh shit" mantra.

The shooter adjusted his aim and bullets started to spit up clods of frozen dirt and snow that showered me as I tumbled. Just when I thought the next shots would find their mark, there was the sound of another gun and a man's scream. The firing stopped. Still, I pushed my body into the shallow gully I'd rolled into, wishing myself as thin as a dime.

I'm not sure how long I stayed there with my hands over my head but the next thing I knew, the still-hot barrel of a gun was on my neck and a hand was tapping my shoulder.

And it was at that moment I almost found the words for a prayer.

The tapping on my shoulder continued.

I opened my eyes slowly and looked up at my executioner.

Standing silently above me was Mark.

He pulled me to my feet and we half ran, half crawled to the side of the chapel, a rainbow of light falling from one of its stained glass windows. He held a gloved finger to his lips, motioning me to be quiet, then reached into his pocket and handed me a short-barreled revolver.

I was about to get up when his hand found my shoulder again and pushed. He cupped his hand to his ear, motioning for me to listen. All I heard was the wind. I wished to have his extraordinary hearing. I closed my eyes and tried again. This time I heard it.

Voices came from a small crack of one of the windows: Osborne's, then Tarkan's. And then I heard something I'd never forget: Laughlin's laugh.

28

I PUT MY mouth near Mark's ear and whispered softly. "How many of your men are left?"

He pointed to himself. Then me.

"How many of theirs?"

He shrugged his shoulders. He didn't know.

Great.

"Let's split up," I said. "I'll go into the chapel. You stay near the cottage, make sure my wife and children are safe."

He nodded and was about ready to move out.

I put my hand on his shoulder. "Thanks, Mark."

He smiled. Then he was gone.

The doors to the chapel were less than twenty yards away. I crawled on my belly the way I'd learned to a hundred years ago in the mud of Southeast Asia. I was a snake. The new snow looked soft and inviting, but it was only half an inch deep and beneath was jagged snow and ice from the storm earlier in the week. I wasn't halfway to the doors before my jeans ripped at the knee, and I felt the skin there open up.

The door to the chapel was slightly ajar. Just enough for me to see Laughlin and Osborne sitting on the steps to the altar. Laughlin looked rested, almost relaxed. Tarkan sat between them. The same little gun he'd had in the temple was held casually in Laughlin's hand, the barrel pointed somewhere at Tarkan's midsection. Osborne was examining his fingernails. He was bored.

I pushed open the door.

"Ah, the prodigal son," Laughlin said with a smile. "We were waiting for you. Do come in."

I stepped inside.

"In the good old days we used to call this a stalemate," Osborne said, folding his hands in his lap. "I think it's time to renegotiate."

I needed time. Time for Mark to check the grounds, time for Peter's reinforcements—if there were any. Time.

"What do you propose?" I said, doing my damnedest to keep my voice level, playing every second of the clock.

"Simple. A return to the status quo," Laughlin said. "You and your family go about with your lives, I go on with mine. The past stays buried. The future remains an open book."

"It's a little late for that," I said, studying the pews in front of me and wondering if the oak backs were thick enough to stop a bullet. "That deal already fell through."

Laughlin shrugged. "That's business. Sometimes you win, sometimes you don't."

"And if I just shoot you?"

"We have more men on the way," Osborne said.

He said it quickly. Too quickly.

"Bullshit," I said, taking a few steps closer, my gun hand coming level with Laughlin.

Laughlin didn't flinch. But Osborne did. And that's when I knew he was lying. They had no more of their men coming. This was it.

It was my choice. Again. The same choice I'd had in the temple basement. At this range I could probably shoot Laughlin and Osborne, but not before Laughlin pulled the trigger on Tarkan. I looked at Tarkan. He was wearing his let's-rumble grin that seemed to say "I'm ready."

Laughlin was smiling too. But it was a different smile, a sick, twisted grimace. He was counting on my weakness, my terminal empathy.

I fired once. The explosion filled the space. Laughlin's gun went off, but by the time it did, it was pointed at the floor, not at Tarkan.

Still he sat there. Still he smiled. I felt a chill from my feet to my scalp.

Then his gun fell to the floor, he folded at the waist and fell forward. His head hit the stone floor with a *thud*.

I turned the gun on Osborne. His lips moved but no sound came out. A stain started to spread on his pants leg, and next there was the sound of his urine dripping on the flagging.

Peter stepped in front of me, blocking my line of fire.

"It's over, Danny," he said.

"He betrayed us," I said, still looking at the shaking Osborne, blood lust filling my senses.

"We can use him," Peter said, gently pushing my gun hand down. "Killing him won't do anything."

I walked over to Laughlin and turned him over, my gun pointed at his head, ready to kill him again if I had to. But there was no need. He was stone cold dead. His eyes were still open and he was still smiling, but a tiny red dot on his starched white shirt told the story. My bullet must have torn his heart to shreds, stopping it instantly. A lucky shot.

Tarkan took a small syringe and bottle from his pocket. Osborne took one look at it and fainted. Still, Tarkan filled a few ccs of the clear liquid, lifted Osborne's sopped pants leg, and injected it into his calf.

"That'll keep him out for a while. Until we get him where we want him."

"And where is that?" I asked.

He turned to me and shook his head. "Remember. This is it for you. The end."

I heard the doors behind us close and turned to see two men in parkas and woolen face masks covering everything but their eyes.

They carried silenced automatics and stood at the rear of the chapel.

I ducked and was about to fire when Tarkan yelled out. "No! They're ours!"

I lowered my gun and the two men approached.

Tarkan spoke to them in a language I couldn't understand but knew by its sound: Hebrew.

The men nodded. The larger one handed his weapon to his partner and threw Osborne over his shoulder as if he were a sack of potatoes. Then they left.

"Israelis?" I asked.

Tarkan nodded.

"Yes. But that's all I'll say." He paused. "And, Danny? Don't ask any more questions I can't answer."

We stepped over Laughlin's corpse and out into the night.

THE SNOW WAS still falling, the bare branches of the trees outlined in white. The ground sparkled, millions of tiny diamonds reflecting the slightest light.

There were bodies just outside the door to the caretaker's apartment. The two men were locked in what could have been mistaken for a lovers' embrace, except they were both as still as the surrounding trees and a thin layer of snow already covered them.

The body on the bottom had one leg bent awkwardly at the knee and his face was swollen, his tongue hanging out. Strangled. The one on top, his hands still clutching the lifeless neck of the man below him, his face twisted in a grimace of pain, I recognized as Mark.

My knees grew weak. I ran to the bullet-pocked door. It was still locked. I knocked frantically. Nothing. I was about to kick it in when my wits returned and I used the coded knock: two short raps, a pause, then another.

The lock clicked and my father opened the door, his gun still at the ready.

When he saw me his eyes asked the silent question.

"It's done," I said slowly. "Over."

He ran his hand across my cheek. His eyes grew moist and he turned away.

I knocked on the bathroom door. It opened slowly.

"You can put on the lights now," I told Nick.

Marie took one look at my scratched face and bloody knees, gave a little cry, ran to me, and wrapped her arms around my thighs. Nicky stood next to me. I put my arm around him and pulled him close.

I held out my hand for Tuesday. Her grip was firm and dry, her eyes clear. She knew it was over. She was waiting for me to say something—anything. But I was spent. The words would have to wait.

Lita's eyes were an open question.

"He's fine," I said, and she brushed past me into the apartment.

MARK AND THE man he killed were gone, and there were now more men in street clothes moving around in the snow. The cleanup squad.

The lights in the chapel were out again, the doors locked. A glazier worked on the broken window of the cottage. A man in overalls scooped mortar onto a trowel and was patching the bullet chipped stone. One of the men was shoveling bloodstained snow and bits of things I didn't want to look at too closely into a large plastic bag.

A small caravan of cars and vans filled the drive.

Two leather-coated men lugged a sagging body bag up the ramp of a large panel truck, the sides of which announced it was from The Sisters of Mercy.

The man at the top slipped and the bag fell. He cursed. Once again I didn't understand the words, but recognized the same sloppy precision and inflection that Peter had used and I knew from the streets of New York: Israeli Hebrew. The two men jumped from the truck, quickly retrieved the bag, and this time, instead of trying to negotiate the ramp, rocked it back and forth three times, then heaved it into the back of the truck. It landed with a *thump*.

Tuesday came to my side. She stroked Marie's silken hair, then put her hand on my elbow and guided me gently to the parked cars.

Peter stood at the driver's door of his car, key in hand.

"What's next?" I asked.

"We give Osborne the chance to tell us what he knows, help us. I think he's ready now. And we keep working: in the shadows. Recovering as much as possible. Returning what we can to the living, guarding the rest in memory of the dead, for the children, their children's children."

"And us? Is it really over now?"

He nodded and handed me the keys.

"Will we see you again?"

"I don't think so, Danny. It will be better that way."

My father came around the side of the car, the worn knapsack dangling from one hand. He handed it to Peter.

"This is the last of it," he said, studying him. "You did well. Peter would have been proud."

He lit up a cigar and looked at me. "Ready, son?"

"Almost," I said, looking around me. I saw Gershowitz's face, heard his whispered prayers. I saw my mother sitting at a table somewhere in Berlin, a thousand years ago, laughing with her parents and brother. I thought of angel's wings and assassin's daggers, crosses and bowls—the articles of faith that had brought so much pain and death. I wondered if this was really the end of it. And I wondered where reason ended and faith began; wondered why I slipped in the snow just in time for the bullets to miss me, or how my own bullet was sent straight through Laughlin's heart as perfectly as a ray of light reflecting from a child's eye. And I knew I'd never find out and that it didn't really matter.

A snowflake landed on the end of my nose and melted.

There was just one more thing.

I reached in my pocket and took out the Tree of Life, feeling its smoothness, remembering how Gershowitz gently pushed it back to me when I offered it to him as he lay dying.

I tossed the pendant to Peter, giving it a flip so it spun through the air in a blur of light.

He caught it in one hand.

"Make sure this gets to where it belongs," I said. "And tell them it's a gift from Rabbi Isaac Gershowitz."

I was the last one in the car.

"Everybody get comfortable," I said when my family was settled. "It's a long way home."

29

W E GOT LUCKY. One of our neighbors had noted the papers and mail piling up and the sudden absence of activity. Surprisingly, she didn't call the police or otherwise blow a gasket. She had assumed that we'd taken a last-minute vacation, a notion I agreed to with head-bobbing alacrity when she forwarded it.

I took the train out to the sad little Cape in Southold and retrieved our crappy old van. I looked at it in a new light and vowed to love and adore until it needed a new transmission or other major assembly.

I also wasn't surprised when a young clean-cut man knocked on our front door and asked for Tarkan's keys. I didn't ask for ID and he didn't offer any. He could have been a rookie cop or a young priest; it didn't matter.

The kids, being kids, settled back into their lives with hardly a hiccup. I'd told Nick to stick to the short vacation lie with his pals, and being the good soldier that he was, he held the party line. I guess that whatever Marie told her friends didn't make much sense but worried little about whatever might slip out.

I made profuse and abject apologies to both Mr. and Mrs. Safter. It seemed to work—particularly when my crew and subs and I worked seventy-two hours straight and handed them the keys to their apartment along with a dozen long-stemmed roses and a chilled bottle of Veuve Cliquot in a silver bucket.

Tuesday had the hardest time explaining her absence. All she could do was apologize to her students and double up on the rehearsals for her performance. My father and I worked side by side, night after night, putting the finishing touches on the set design. We didn't talk much. Lita helped Tuesday sew costumes.

We did have our family Christmas, albeit a third of a century late and without my mother, but it was the real deal: turkey, eggnog, the works. My father and Lita even took the kids to midnight Mass. Tuesday and I stayed home and made love on the living-room floor under the twinkling lights of the tree.

The first sign that Tarkan and everyone else were swinging into action on the cover-up came Christmas day.

A small story in the Metro section reported a thwarted robbery attempt at the Cloisters. I was sad to see there was no mention of Mark or his sacrifice. It seems he was silent not only in life but in death as well.

Not surprisingly, there was no news about Osborne.

New Year's came with champagne in front of a roaring fireplace at Lita's brownstone. And just like the carefully timed Christmas stories, it was New Year's day when news of Laughlin's death was finally announced. It was, surprise surprise, a heart attack that brought down the last of the cold warriors. The CNN news bite showed Hammer giving a stirring eulogy as Laughlin was laid to rest with full honors in Arlington. The President actually swiped an imaginary tear from one of his ice-blue eyes as the twenty-one guns went off and the missing-V formation of jets roared past overhead. My father and I howled with laughter.

Tuesday's performance came off without a hitch—almost. One of the girls lost her tutu during a pirouette causing a short, unanticipated intermission. But aside from that, the kids and the parents were thrilled and the local paper gave the dance a rave review.

Tuesday paid a visit to the Buddhist shrine the next day and burned joss sticks around the house for two more days. One day I'll understand.

We finally made that trip to Hawaii too. Lita begged off, telling us she had work to do. She was giving me a gift. She needed my father as much as I did, but we both knew he was tired and that every day with him was a bonus.

My father showed us the Hawaii he knew but we'd never seen. We explored the Big Island, Kauai, Maui, went to luaus, did the hula, the whole nine yards. The kids ate it up. Tuesday and I snorkeled and made love while my father baby-sat. It was the first real vacation we'd ever taken.

We were staying in a condo in Wailea, Maui, when Peter called. Some sixth sense told me the call would come, I just didn't know when. I didn't ask him how he found us or why he'd waited this long. I knew he wouldn't tell me. And that was okay with me.

"Hello, Danny," he said, the connection so clear I wondered if he wasn't in the next room.

"Peter."

"How's Hawaii?"

He wasn't calling to talk about the weather, but I indulged him. "Just like New York. Except greener and warmer and nobody has an accent like yours."

"Tonight's forecast is the same as yesterday's," he said with a laugh. "Sleet and freezing rain. Don't gloat."

"Why shouldn't I?"

He laughed again and I could envision his bone-breaking smile five thousand miles away. I almost missed the guy. If things had been different, I think we might have been friends.

"It's happening," he said quietly.

"What's happening?"

"You'll see. It may be slow but the truth will come out."

" 'Magna est veritas et praevalet'?"

"You remembered," he said. I could tell he was impressed. So was I.

"Yes. We're working with our friends."

"The ones from the Old Book?" I asked. He knew I meant the Israelis.

"Yes. The people I represent," he said, keeping it vague, though I know he meant the church, "have agreed it's time to come clean."

"Finally," I said, looking out at the deep blue of the Pacific.

"Yes. Finally. Keep your eye on the papers."

"I will."

He'd done it.

"Thanks for calling."

"You deserved to know. Tell your father."

He was about to say good-bye. I just had one more thing to say.

"Peter?"

"Yes, Danny."

"Next time you speak to the guy upstairs, tell him to take good care of Mark for me."

"You can do it yourself, Danny," he said.

"Trust me," I said, thinking of my "oh shit" chant, "it will be better if you do it."

He laughed again. "Sure. Consider it done."

This was it then.

"Thanks, Peter."

"Thank you, Danny. Maybe one day we can talk again."

"I'd like that," I said, knowing it would never happen. "Take care."

"You too."

The connection was broken.

I stood at the sliding glass doors facing the ocean and saw my father and Nick sitting on a low stone wall idly tossing stones into the surf and talking. I could also see Tuesday and Marie hopping over the small waves, hand in hand.

It was really over.

Except for the dreams.

Usually it's the woman in the snow in Brooklyn. But sometimes it's Gershowitz in the basement. Or both of them. Once I dreamed that the body in the reeds was discovered and the police knocked on my door in the middle of the night. But the one I hate the most and the only one that repeats itself is the one where Laughlin, my bullet in his heart, gets up off the chapel floor and starts laughing and shooting. But the dreams are getting less frequent now and someday I hope they'll stop.

I put on my flip-flops and headed to the beach. All was well with the world. My father was back. We'd slain dragons together, spit in the devil's eye—and lived to tell the tale. My family was alive and there was a tomorrow. It would be a sin to ask for more.

AUTHOR'S AFTERWORD

THE TRUE EXTENT of Nazi loot is just now coming to the surface. Most of the focus is rightfully on the billions taken by the Germans during their rape of Europe. The looting of the central banks of the vanquished by the victor can be seen as traditional spoils of war—almost. It's the other wealth, the melted gold fillings and wedding bands of the victims of the Holocaust, that cannot. By commingling spoils with gold soaked in blood, we are forced to face the past in all its horror and demand an accounting.

In the same vein, the role of the so-called neutral countries such as Switzerland, Sweden, and Portugal in the trade of this tainted bullion is something that also must be confronted head on and looks as if it finally is.

But as I wrote this story, what filled my mind was the barely mentioned and seemingly invisible plunder, the everyday things that pale in comparison to bars of shiny gold: the farms, the villages, the shops, the businesses, the furniture, and the clothes. The list is endless. And I realized how wide the blanket of guilt can be spread.

I tried to imagine turning ten million Americans to ash then incorporating their possessions into the remaining nation: the homes, the cars, the factories, the farms, the shoes, the hats, the plates, the suitcases—all of it. Would there be an American left who somehow didn't profit from the extermination? Even if they didn't directly participate in the "Final Solution"? I don't think so.

So yes, of course it's the gold bullion and numbered accounts still contested in Swiss banks. But it's more. Whose living room did that oil painting hanging in the Louvre come from? Whose land is that hotel in Paris built on? Is the grain that makes your Polish vodka being reaped from land that once belonged to a Jew now nothing but soot in an abandoned chimney? The questions are endless, the answers disturbing.

Was there trading of religious icons and artifacts looted by the Nazis during and after World War II, as I've created in this book? We now know that fine art was traded. Why not fine furniture and other objects with a value greater than their melted-down weight? Perhaps we'll never know, but like the rest of it, I wouldn't be surprised.

As for the other part of my story, the part about the clandestine war of assassination and terror fought by the OSS on U.S. soil, of that there is no doubt. How do I know? Because my father told me about it, in his own words. People in Boston and New York did die. And he was part of it.

He was a dutiful son, a loving father, a hard worker, and a devoted, if difficult, husband. He was also a very complex man with a barely concealed rage, someone to be reckoned with. And sadly, I never really understood him until near the end of his life, when I found out about his war.

Did the people he killed deserve to die? Doubts about what he did plagued him until he died. In trying to help me understand, he explained that he was a young man at the time and believed we were fighting a great evil. That the lives he took might mean that others, loved ones and his fellow soldiers on cramped convoys heading across the North Atlantic, might be saved.

During the confusing years of the 1960s, I never understood his unflagging patriotism, even in the face of the emerging mess of the Vietnam war. It was hard to see how a man with his fierce and independent intelligence could be so blind.

And he might never have told me his story if one of his old army and OSS friends hadn't written a book that included names and dates. This was in the late 1970s. The publisher submitted the book to the CIA for review. My father (and probably others as well) was summoned to Langley. There his service records were altered and all trace of his involvement in the OSS erased. That done, the CIA denied the information in the submitted manuscript in its entirety. The book was never published.

And it was then that he told me and I began to understand. He had done things for his country that he thought were right but that still haunted him.

Perhaps one day the real story will come out and the truth will finally be known. For now, my humble tale will have to do.